Work, eat, pray, Cosmos thinks. That's all I'm going to be able to do here.

He wraps his arms across his chest and thinks of the coyote who escaped being hit by Uncle Henry's car. He gets up and takes out the raven totem that his father gave him. Raven, the Trickster. There aren't any ravens around here. But there are coyotes, at least a few of them. And the ones who have made it seem to know how to dodge big cars and cyanide traps. Every religious ear around here is going to be my cyanide trap, he thinks. The only way I can survive here is by being as quick and wary as that coyote. I'll have to be two people: one to show on the outside, the other one to keep alive on the inside. Coyote: now you see me, now you don't. Cosmos Coyote. That's the real one. The phony one will be the nice one he shows on the outside: William the Nice.

He gets up and walks to the mirror. "William the Nice," he says to himself, "you are the only person people are going to see. Understand? Yes, sir," he answers himself.

COSMOS COYOTE
COYOTE
and
WILLIAM
the NICE

Jim Heynen

HarperTempest
An Imprint of HarperCollins Publishers

To my longtime friends at the Northwest
Writing Institute at Lewis and Clark College:
Kim Stafford, Diane McDevitt,
and Joanne Mulcahy

Library of Congress Cataloging-in-Publication Data
Heynen, Jim, 1940–
    Cosmos Coyote and William the Nice / Jim Heynen.
        p.   cm.
Originally published : New York : Henry Holt, 2000.
    Summary: When sent to live on a farm in Iowa as an
alternative to juvenile detention, seventeen-year-old
Cosmos falls in love with a religious girl and reconsiders
his values and beliefs.
    ISBN 0-06-447256-6 (pbk.)
    [1. Interpersonal relations—Fiction.   2. Farm life—
Iowa—Fiction.   3. Iowa—Fiction.]   I. Title.
PZ7.H484 Co   2002   2002020730
[Fic]—dc21

Typography by Larissa Lawrynenko
❖
First HarperTempest edition, 2002
Visit us on the World Wide Web!
www.harperteen.com

Acknowledgments

My hearty thanks to the many people who helped along the way, especially Anne Williams for the seclusive perch at Lake Fredenberg, Bill and Nancy Booth for their wonderful accommodations at Cry of the Loon Lodge, to Bob Richardson, Dr. Jim McCarron, Dr. Nancy Pranger, to the informative crew at the University of Iowa summer writing program, especially Peggy Houston and Amy Margolis, to Craig Lihs, John Margolis, Dan Connolly, Emily and Geoffrey Heynen, Bill Holm, Jim Schaap, Steve Sanfield, Edna Kovacs, Josip Novakovitch, Bill Ransom, Eric Nelson, Jon Davis, Becky Teagarden, Christian Friesen, H. A. Wicks, Cy Field, Colin Wells, the Reverend Daniel Pearson, and, as always, to Sally Williams.

Contents

Remember that word—you're
going to need it

HANS PUTS TWO PLATES DOWN on the table and says, "Cosmos, you're in worse trouble than you thought. We've got to talk."

"Sure, Dad." As usual his father has saved the most serious conversation until dinner. Cosmos sits down at the oak kitchen table and pushes his hair back away from his face. Hans slides the salad bowl mounded with fresh greens toward Cosmos, then digs into a platter of Dungeness crab. He pressures a crab leg to split between his large thumb and forefinger and shakes jagged chunks of crabmeat onto his salad.

"They're talking Juvie," says Hans. "They're talking six months."

"What? Says who?"

"Says Noreen. You couldn't have a better PO, but she says the jig is up. The prosecutor wants to nail you good. Make an example. Noreen says the Commissioner is going to go along with it. Six months. Maybe longer."

"What's going on with this stupid system? It's not as if I stabbed somebody."

"Shut up," says Hans. "I know it's not fair. Never said it was. They say it's the accumulation thing. You know how many times you've been in trouble since you were four-teen? Would you believe thirteen? Thirteen. Want to count them?"

"Most of it was all that little shit. The cops were just bored. Rambo muthers."

"Shut up and listen," says Hans. "Commissioner Levy is calling it the 'hole syndrome.' He's talking a pattern of noncompliance. He's talking 'habitual offender.' Son, if we don't do something, you *will* go to Juvie."

Since the divorce three years ago, Cosmos and his father have been living in a small Victorian house, two city blocks from the Strait of Juan de Fuca. Little blank spots of silence are pretty common over dinner, and Cosmos enters one of those blank spots now. He stares at his plate. He stares at the large salad bowl his father shoves toward him. His father made that salad bowl. His father made almost everything wooden that Cosmos can see from the table. His father made the table.

The sharp sound of another splintering crab leg brings Cosmos to attention. "All right," he says. "I'm listening."

Hans takes a bite of what has become his crabmeat salad, chews and swallows, then puts his fork down. "I'm not going to have you locked up with a bunch of violent weirdos," says Hans. "No De Haag goes to jail."

Cosmos does not change his grim expression. "Thanks," he says.

"So here's what we do," Hans goes on. "We've filed a petition for a youth-at-risk hearing with Commissioner Levy on Friday. We're going to admit all the old stuff and, sure, your second-time graffiti offense in Seattle, and the little matter of the water gun you pointed at that psycho on the ferry. Yes! Yes! It's bad, you know. Don't deny it's bad. We plead guilty guilty guilty!"

"'Guilty guilty guilty' doesn't sound like my kind of song," says Cosmos.

Hans chomps hard on another mouthful of crab and lettuce. Cosmos can tell by the way his dad's eyebrows are coming together in a wrinkle over his nose that he's getting madder and madder. And not at Cosmos.

"The cops are going nuts these days," says Hans. "When I was a kid on the farm in Iowa, we stole watermelons out of farmers' fields, tipped outhouses on Halloween, stuck corncobs in people's mufflers, hid behind trees and threw tomatoes at cars when we went into town on Saturday nights, drank sloe gin mixed in with our Cokes right in front of the cops, went tearing through farmers' fields at night with spotlights hunting jackrabbits, spray-painted our names on every rock and overpass in Iowa, drove eighty miles an hour down gravel roads. And that's just for starters. Jeez! When I think about it. And I never got a ticket for anything! Never got in trouble with the law. Not once!"

"Yeah, and today they'll cuff a kid for cutting across somebody's lawn at night. Spruce got cited for jump-starting his dad's car—had one foot out of the door trying to get the car to roll forward, and they ticketed him! Can you believe it!?"

"I know, I know," says Hans. "Today everything's turned on its head. The country is trying to criminalize its youth! That's what's happening!" Hans guzzles his mineral water and slams it down on the table.

Cosmos loves to hear his dad go on one of his diatribes. "Amen," he says.

"Remember that word," says Hans. "You're going to need it."

"What word? Amen?"

"Amen. You see, I've got this idea for an alternative sentence for you. It's the only thing I can think of to get around this stupid system that would want to put you in Juvie."

"Amen," Cosmos says again. "You mean like community service? Amen! Last time I did community service it was for the women's shelter. That was cool. I learned a lot."

"No, I mean as in 'For Jesus' sake, amen.'"

"What do you mean, 'For Jesus' sake, amen'?"

Hans gets up and walks to the sliding glass doors that open from the kitchen onto a large wooden deck. Hans is a big guy, a good six foot three when he unslouches his shoulders. He has wild curly blond hair and a Santa Claus beard that's more red than blond. He's wearing what he usually wears: a red plaid shirt and baggy jeans, caulk boots, and a red kerchief around his forehead. His hands are huge and his long arms angle up to narrow shoulders. He's pear-shaped but strong as a forklift, and he's Port Swan's finest woodworker. Standing in front of the glass doors, he looks like a scruffy king with brilliantly red rhododendron bushes as his crown. Even with his lighter build and much smaller stature, Cosmos knows he still looks like a chip off the old block, right now a shriveled chip off the old block.

Hans turns back to Cosmos. "I'm going to propose to the Commissioner that you spend your senior year in high school living with your uncle and aunt on the farm in Iowa and going to the Dutch Center Christian Academy. You remember your uncle Henry and aunt Minnie from our summer visits, right? My big brother, you know. They're De Haags and they're in their fifties, no kids left in the house, nice people. Real nice."

Like a cartoon character who does not yet know he's just run over a cliff, Cosmos hovers for a few seconds, his face expressionless, then plunges. "What?!" he yells. "Are you nuts, Dad?"

"Think about it," says Hans quickly. "Nine months of wide-open spaces in Iowa would beat six months locked up with a bunch of bad-ass delinquents in Washington."

Cosmos holds out his palms toward his father's face and shakes them the way he might if someone were coming at him with a gun. "No no no, Dad, you're not thinking," he says. "You wouldn't send me to those religious freaks in Iowa! All they do is pray and eat!"

"And work and live a decent country life. That's the old De Haag country, Coz. It will put you in touch with your roots. Our roots."

All the rhododendrons outside the kitchen could turn to ash just then and not register on Cosmos's mind. He lifts up his arms and whacks them down on the table. "That's crazy! No way in hell!" He jumps up from the table and bolts out the door. He steps up on the bench on the edge of the deck and looks over the rhododendron bushes, past the neighboring houses, to the Strait of Juan de Fuca, where a large Japanese freighter eases through the water toward Seattle.

This is home. This is Port Swan. This is the place where people like his father fled to get away from uptight worlds like the one in Iowa where he grew up. The rebels, the seekers, the dropouts, all perched out here in their own world on a little finger of a peninsula hooked into the Strait of Juan de Fuca. That's what his father wanted. That's what he wants too, to be a chip off the old block.

Cosmos holds out his arms. "Dad!" he yells. "This is home! I'd rather be in jail here than free in some Bible-thumping cow barn in Iowa!"

Cosmos leaps off the deck and runs across the yard, past Hans's woodworking shop, down the sidewalk, and straight for Main Street, Port Swan. Hans does not try to stop him. After one block at top speed, Cosmos stops to whack the fender of a car that has driven in front of him at the intersection. "Hey, jerk, ever seen a crosswalk? *Crosswalk?*" he yells and points at the white crossing lines, then, seeing the car has a Minnesota license plate, gives the bald-headed driver and his wife the finger. The wife gasps. "Yeah!" Cosmos sneers at them, and continues at a full run down the long slope toward the business district and the waterfront.

It's a warm August day, and the downtown sidewalks are like a scurrying ant colony of visitors, everything from yuppie sailors in snow-white deck shoes to the nicey-nice families with their groomed kids to a whole assortment of the hiking-and-camping set who look like they just fell out of an Eddie Bauer catalogue.

"Pollution! Pollution!" Cosmos shouts as he works his way through the tourists. A few turn to look at him in his baggy clothes and shoes taped together with duct tape, his matted hair flapping against his face like a dishrag. Cosmos has no use for their stares right now. He knows where he's going: straight to the apartment of his girl-friend, Salal.

A few of his friends are on a street corner forcing tourists to take a little detour around their game of hacky-sack.

Cosmos ignores them too and presses on toward the street-entrance stairway to Salal's apartment above Wendy's Wine Cellar.

"Hey, Coz!" comes a voice over the heads of two little kids with big ice-cream cones. It's his friends Rhody and Spruce—the other two members of his band, the OughtaBs. They're at their usual spot, hanging out on the bench in front of CC's Ice Cream. Spruce has dyed his hair orange. Rhody has on his crossbones T-shirt, and they both wear wrap-around sunglasses. They don't look like they're breaking any laws, but they are preserving their reputation as part of what the local merchants call "The Bad for Business Kids."

Cosmos holds up his hands the way he did to his father: "Not now, not now," he says, and keeps going.

"Don't forget we're jamming Saturday night at eight," says Spruce.

Cosmos keeps pushing his way along, and finally up the stairs to his refuge, Salal. He smells incense as he approaches the door but doesn't smell any marijuana smoke. He raps gently, then whispers earnestly, "Salal, Salal, I've got to see you."

When she opens the door, Cosmos beholds the person who to him is the most beautiful woman on earth. She is six feet tall and weighs 105 pounds. When she moves, she moves like a graceful twig. To Cosmos, she is elegance, sheer and magical elegance. He loves it when she clicks her tongue stud against her teeth. He loves to watch her use her tongue stud to carve a little furrow through an ice-cream cone when she licks it.

"What's up?" she says in her dark, liquid voice. "I've got company."

Cosmos looks across the room toward the windows that face Main Street. Soft teardroppy music is playing, and on the couch sits a brick of a woman in jeans and a man's workshirt. It's Bridgette. Cosmos hardly knows her, and wouldn't want to.

"Sorry," he says, "but I've got to see you. They're going to send me to Juvie unless we do something."

"Look," says Salal, and as her face hardens she looks even more beautiful, "can't it wait?" She furrows her brow in a way that doesn't tell whether she's impatient with him or sympathetic.

"No," he pleads. "My dad wants me to go to Iowa instead of Juvie. It's all too crazy."

"Let's step outside," she whispers. She closes the door behind her. "That's terrible, but didn't you sort of expect something heavy would come down after your last two citations?"

"No," he says. "I've never done anything violent. I didn't think they could do this to you unless you're a violent creep."

"I'm really sorry," says Salal, "but there's no way I can help you."

She has never sounded so cruel before, though her warm voice is still soothing even as the words sound distant and cold. Salal is Cosmos's dark angel who came down from alternative-rock heaven over a year ago and volunteered to be the manager of the OughtaBs. Spruce and Rhody think she's a great manager but Cosmos thinks she is more than that. She's five years older than Cosmos and his first and only lover.

"Salal, I need you now. I need your love now. I don't want to go to Juvie. I don't want to go to Iowa. Just hold me." He looks into her eyes, a few inches higher than his own. She shows no sign of anything. Not one of her three sets of earrings so much as quivers. "Please?"

"Cosmos," she says, "I can't save you. I can't be your mommy." She rubs her long fingers across her long forehead. "I know we have to talk, because I think it's time that things should be different between us."

"You're quitting the OughtaBs? Just dumping us?"

"No," she says. "I want to be your manager. It's just that things between you and me need to be different."

Salal's words make him feel like a person lost at sea who has just grabbed for a life raft that deflates at his touch. But this is not the first time in his life he has had to take a deep breath and continue on the strength he has left. He stares at her. Her expression does not change. "All right," he says softly. "All right, I hear you." He starts down the stairs. He stops and looks back. "Will you be at the practice session Saturday night?"

"Of course," she says.

"All right," he says. He forces his eyes to look away from her long, elegant beauty at the top of the stairs, and leaves.

On his way home, he moves even more slowly than the gawking and cumbersome tourists. Passing the show window of the Wood House, he stops to watch a middle-aged man dressed in a white cap, white shirt, and white pants admiring a miniature wooden sailboat. Cosmos knows that boat, watched it rise up from the sea of sawdust in his father's workshop. He knows the price tag too—$650, and if it sells, his father will make $325. It could be the only good news of the day.

When he gets home, he finds someone sitting in the chair he vacated at the kitchen table, none other than his probation officer, Noreen. Hans sits across from her. They have the look of adults who have been talking serious business about young people.

Noreen is a frizzy-haired redhead who always looks as if she just stuck her finger in an electrical socket, and she can live up to the reputation of the fiery redhead. But not now. She doesn't look like she's about to scold him. She seems defeated, as if she has lost a battle for a client.

Cosmos pulls up a third chair and sits down at the table with them. "I'm ready to hear more about your crazy Iowa idea," he says.

"We've been talking about that," says Noreen.

"There is precedent for alternative sentences for juveniles in Washington," says Hans. "Remember those Indian boys who got an alternative sentence to go live on their native island for a year? They were just going home to the origins of their Native American souls. We're going to propose to the Commissioner that you go back to the land of my people, your people, and live a year with your relatives in Iowa. And I think it will be good for you to spend one year as a De Haag, among De Haags, in the land where the De Haag soul has been nurtured for over a century. I think it will not be all bad. I think it will help you find yourself spiritually."

"I'm not going to find myself *spiritually* in the stupid cornfields of Iowa," says Cosmos. "Hey, if I could go live in the fir trees on a San Juan Island like those Indian kids, that would be cool. Catch my own fish. Camp out for a year. Yeah, that's spiritual. But Iowa? Iowa? Did you really say *Iowa*?"

"Look at your alternatives, Coz. Close your eyes and imagine two scenes. In one you get up at six in the morning and stand at attention outside your door—after cleaning your room and getting it ready for inspection. You go outside after breakfast. You can see the fence that you're not allowed to go past. A couple of tough big-city kids come up to you and say, 'You're going to be our dog.'"

"All right, all right, cut it out," says Cosmos. "Give me the other picture."

"In the other picture," says Hans, "there's a beautiful country house with trees around it and with beautiful white buildings and cows and pigs in the farmyards. You can look out forever across a rolling green world of alfalfa and bean and cornfields. You have a quiet room of your own upstairs in the house. You go out and work with pigs and cattle in the morning, take a bus to school, make decent friends, come home, have a wholesome dinner. Have a normal life in a new place. Consider it a vacation!"

"Yeah, right. If it's so nice, why would the court let me go? Tell me that one."

"It's the land of our people, the heritage of our people. And it's the most religious community left on the face of the earth."

"The most religious community since those cult crazies in Waco," says Cosmos.

"Coz, this is our only chance to keep you out of Juvie. And the parallel to those Indian kids, you know, I think it's real. I can make a case for it."

"So when did you get a law degree?"

"Listen to your father for a change," says Noreen.

"You've been there," says Hans. "I don't have to tell you. Everyone goes to church. Nobody swears in public.

Stores are closed on Sundays. No theaters in town. Only one bar and twelve churches. Christian high school that's bigger than the public school. It's as strange and rooted in tradition as any Indian culture. I already talked to your uncle Henry about it. I told him everything. He says they would love to have you stay with them. Henry's been worried about us. Not just because of the divorce, but because your mother has gone off the deep end and moved to Mexico to study with some strange guru. Your uncle Henry thinks that God told me to call him for your sake. He thinks this was meant to be. He thinks it is God's will."

"You make him sound even kookier than I remember him, Dad. And you're the one who always tells me how bad it was growing up around there. You moved all the way across the country to get away from that scene. Roots. Sounds more like a cemetery for the brain-dead."

"It's our tradition, Cosmos, it's our tradition. It's our people. Just settle down and listen. I'll make some tea. Chamomile. Calm our nerves."

They silently wait for the water to boil. Hans stands over the stove thinking. He puts three cups on the table and pours. "Having a tradition is not all bad," he says. "Even if you reject it. Having a tradition and rejecting it is better than having no tradition at all. Having a tradition gives you a core, gives you something to build around. Gives you character."

"Gives you a brain that won't think and gives you right-wing politics," says Cosmos. "Isn't that what you told me? They're all religious-freak right-wingers, right? Hypocritical, right-wing, money-grubbing—let's see, I think you had a few more words for 'our people.' Oh yeah, self-righteous and judgmental. Weren't those your words?"

"Knock it off. I don't expect you to go back there and buy into the whole package," says Hans, "but nobody can know where he's going if he doesn't know where he's from. Go back there and get in touch with the De Haag name and the Dutch community in Iowa. Those are your roots."

"My roots are with fir trees, not cornstalks," says Cosmos.

"What you're doing now demonstrates why you always get in trouble," says Noreen. "It's your mouth."

"When you come back from Iowa, you'll know who you are," says Hans. "And you'll know what you want to do with your life. Maybe college. Maybe music. Who knows? But you'll know, I guarantee it."

Cosmos puts his head in his hands, and his brain shoots him a meteor shower of laughing, scorning faces—cops, court officials, ugly women, and farmers in big blue gas-guzzling cars looking out their windows and pointing at him as if he were some kind of freak left behind by the circus.

"It's not fair," says Cosmos. "It's just not fair."

"Sounds to me like everybody is trying to give you a fair shake," says Noreen. "When are you ever going to learn to appreciate it?"

"Coz?" says Hans.

"Yeah?"

"Your uncle Henry is flying out so he can be at the hearing on Friday and help us make the case for an alternative sentence."

"He what?!"

"Shut up," says Hans. "We're going to beat this thing."

COSMOS LOOKS OVER HIS dad's shoulder at the proposal for an alternative sentence.

"Port Swan we can handle, even if Commissioner Levy here doesn't like us alternative types," says Hans. "But it's those jerks in Seattle who want to nail you to the cross and set you on fire. Bastards. Seattle is full of bastards. Full of bastards who are nothing but wannabe-thises and wannabe-thats."

Hans grabs his beard and pulls on it. "Wannabe realtors and wannabe artists," he says, growling out the words. "Wannabe computer programmers and wannabe Boeing execs. Wannabe architects, wannabe tourist agents, wannabe journalists, wannabe musicians. Most of them young and hungry easy-street wannabes. Every morning they get on the freeways in their leased BMWs and honk at each other. It might as well be called L.A. North. Seattle is going to hell in a yuppie handbasket."

"I think the Commissioner will take our proposal seriously," says Noreen, "but everything, including what happened in Seattle, is going to be on his 'green sheet.' Even the water gun on the ferry will be there."

"If everybody on that damned ferry didn't have cell phones, everybody could have ridden off and forgotten about everything!" Hans goes on. "Cell phones! They're evil! They tempt people to blabbermouth when they should be thinking. Hell. You can't even sit in a restaurant without some jackass at the next table ruining the atmosphere by trying to close some real-estate deal on a damn cell phone. Just like computers. Just like e-mail. E-mail has people throwing words around—blip blip—like they don't have to be processed by the brain!"

"Dad, I just want to stay out of jail, all right?" says Cosmos. "Why don't we just talk about keeping me out of Juvie."

"No way are we going to let Seattle get its hands on you," says Hans. "That Commissioner they got up there, that Nazi! You wouldn't believe how he talks about young people. He's trying to make a name for himself with how tough he can be on kids. He's a wannabe if I've ever seen one, and the Seattle wannabes think they own the place. It's a situation where the wannabes have it in for the being-hads."

"Totally," says Cosmos.

* * *

When Hans returns from SeaTac with Uncle Henry, the first thing Cosmos notices about him is that Jesus smile, that I'm-going-to-save-you glow. But the suit Uncle Henry wears blinds out his smile. It's a shiny green thing in a Western-style cut with little arrows on the stitches around the pockets. With a polka-dot green-and-white tie? And a big shiny silver belt buckle? And cowboy boots? Uncle Henry looks like he belongs here about as much as a Jell-O salad in a fancy French restaurant.

In the hearing room, Uncle Henry struts a little too confidently. He doesn't seem to have the foggiest idea of how he looks. Cosmos watches Commissioner Levy size his uncle up. Noreen is there too, wearing an avocado-colored blouse that looks left over from the seventies. Hans still has his work clothes on, with his sleeves rolled up as if he's ready to cold-cock somebody. With his own blond hair cut shorter and neatly combed, his ear studs taken out, and with his plain button-down tan shirt and matching corduroy pants and Good Will Rockports, Cosmos realizes it is that rare occasion when he is the most normal-looking person in sight. Even the Commissioner looks strange and out-of-place. His dark suit and little bald head and little glasses make him look like something from a movie set in the nineteenth century.

As things begin, Cosmos gets a strange feeling about the old courtroom where the hearing takes place. A charcoal-like grit is sifting in and onto the windowsills and floor, as if the old building is taking itself apart and scattering its brick mortar over everything as a warning that it's about to collapse on them. The room smells as if someone vomited in here a hundred years ago and the odor still has not quite worn off. That smell mixes with the smell of all the old dark and oily wood that has probably drunk up the sweat of a thousand accused people who have sat here before, waiting for their fate. The room is a combination of all the worst places Cosmos has ever been—dirty, tight, and stifling. And if this feeling is what being in a bad place is all about, Juvie will be hell on earth.

Cosmos tries to smile, but he knows it must look about as natural as the grin on the mouth of a dead salmon laid out at the fish market in Seattle.

Commissioner Levy listens to the prosecutor present the long list of accumulated infractions, then a bedraggled but young court-appointed attorney reads the proposal for the alternative sentence. Cosmos knows that what the attorney reads is nothing more than what Hans and Noreen prepared for him.

Cosmos's mind drifts. Being the unfortunate center of attention as the accused makes the room seem even more oppressive. Being here is like a dry run for Juvie. Everything about the room and the situation feels like everything that freedom isn't. Freedom. Wide-open spaces. Iowa seems more and more like heaven, even if the angels in that heaven look like Uncle Henry.

It's Uncle Henry's turn. He struts to the front and whips out a copy of Iowa's *Interstate Compact on Juveniles* and points to the chapter that outlines the Iowa code for transferring juveniles on probation. "And I have this," he says. It's a letter from the probation officer who would be handling Cosmos's case in Iowa. The Iowa probation officer's name is Michael Jonsma. It has a familiar ring to it. It is one of Cosmos's older Iowa cousins, his uncle Hilco's son.

"When I was a boy," Uncle Henry begins, and his voice rises in pitch and volume, "we didn't ever have to deal with your police or your courts, because the whole God-fearing community was the police and the courts. That's a fact. We had our problems—of course, of course, of course—sure we did, like every community, but everybody's business was everybody else's business. You see. We didn't have secrets. You see. We looked out for each other. Still do. We are our brother's keeper. And when somebody starts straying—and straying is human nature, let's remember that—human nature!—when somebody starts straying, I say, we don't let them fall in the pit. Everybody is there to make sure that doesn't happen. Maybe first a friend talks to the brother who is straying. Then maybe some relatives. Then maybe an elder in the church."

Cosmos sees Noreen look nervously at Hans. Cosmos has no idea how Uncle Henry is going over with the Commissioner. The Commissioner sits still as a stuffed mouse. His eyes don't even blink.

Uncle Henry is ready to go on. What next? Cosmos's only fear right now is that this crackerjack, this Uncle

Henry, is going to blow the whole alternative-sentence idea. The first part of Uncle Henry's speech must just have been a warmup, because now his voice gets even bigger. Cosmos can tell he's practiced this part. He knows when to pause. He knows when to look earnestly and directly into the eyes of the Commissioner. In a solemn voice that suggests he is about to make a big point, he goes back to the bit about how everybody keeps an eye on everybody: "Light for each other's paths," he says. "May it befit the wisdom of the court, Your Honor," he says, "that you release my fine nephew, William, into the arms of a loving community. The 'William' is after his grandfather 'Wilim,' you know," Uncle Henry adds. "You see. A fine Christian gentleman who is still alive and will provide his own guidance to the young William."

With that, Uncle Henry holds out his own arms as if he were all the arms of the whole community. But didn't he just say "William"? Cosmos realizes his uncle has turned his middle name into his first name.

Uncle Henry isn't quite finished. He steps directly in front of the Commissioner and ends his speech in a voice that is warm and smooth as mashed potatoes and gravy: "I have known my nephew since he was a tiny child. He has been to the farm very often. Right from the start I told Minnie, that's my wife, this hearty young lad would do very well on the farm. He has the spirit of a farm boy, that good strong farm-boy spirit. I can still see it in him. And I have work for him on the farm. You see. We will put him to good use, I'll tell you that. And in a few weeks he will go to the church academy. In our community, everyone goes to church. This will be part of his life too. He will have a warm protective atmosphere, just what a young man like him needs, with plenty to do. We are more than happy to take full responsibility for him, and, if it please the court, we will report as often as seems necessary."

When Uncle Henry finally finishes, Commissioner Levy watches him strut back to his seat. Cosmos sees suspicion in the Commissioner's eyes. He's probably never been on a farm, but he probably still knows bullshit when a load of it has just been dumped on him.

But it's not Uncle Henry that the Commissioner is suspicious of. "William," he says, "I have a few questions for you about your record." He picks up a stack of papers that is topped with the infamous "green sheet" that lists all of his infractions: date, time, place, nature of the crime, action taken. Cosmos knows it reads like a report card for a young outlaw. Under the "green sheet" sits a stack of papers thicker than a Seattle phone book. The Commissioner starts shuffling through it. Papers slide around on his desk, some on the floor, making Cosmos's record look like a spilled platter of spaghetti. Then he pulls out the paper he is looking for. "You know I've got all the paperwork from

Seattle here. Looks like it wasn't enough for you to get in trouble here in Port Swan. You had to spread your mischief to the big city."

"Yes, sir. I mean, I'm sorry, sir," Cosmos says politely.

"So what is this little matter about painting a swastika on the bronze pig at the entrance to the Pike Place Market in Seattle? Want to tell me about that?"

"No, no, that wasn't me, sir. I didn't paint any swastikas on anything. I painted a peace sign on Rachel where some skinheads spray-painted the swastika. The cops had it sandblasted off but you could still see a little bit of red paint."

"So you painted a peace sign where they had just removed some other graffiti?"

"It wasn't paint, sir, it was fingerpaint. Just fingerpaint. I was trying to make a point."

"Make a point?" says the Commissioner. "Make a point? What point might that have been—that it's all right to deface public property? I shouldn't even be hearing this, you know. You should be facing the people in Seattle. See what they'd say about making a point. And wasn't this your second-time graffiti offense in Seattle?"

"Yes, sir."

"And they have a second-time graffiti law there, you know that. They put people in jail in Seattle for second-time graffiti, you know that."

"Yes, sir."

"If I'm going to make a ruling here and report to the Seattle people what I have decided, I'm going to have to have a pretty good explanation. So why don't you tell me exactly what happened in Seattle."

The Commissioner shuffles through his stack of papers again. Cosmos glances at Noreen and Hans. They look tense.

"All right," says Cosmos. "You see, me and my band, the OughtaBs, and our manager, Salal, we were in Seattle to give this concert at the Rampage on Capitol Hill. It was our first gig in Seattle."

"Your first what?"

"Our first gig. A concert. So we stayed over, and the next morning I got up early to take a walk and I went down to Pike Place Market and it was a Sunday morning so no one was there so I was waiting for Rhody and Spruce and Salal to meet me at the pig. That's Rachel, the bronze pig at the Pike Place Market."

"I've been there," says the Commissioner.

"So I had this fingerpaint in my pocket from when we were making posters for the concert and I just sort of put a peace sign on Rachel's . . . on Rachel's . . . on Rachel's hind leg."

"And you got caught."

"Yep. Bike cop."

The Commissioner shuffles through more papers on his desk. "I seem to recall that wasn't the end of the day for you in Seattle. A little matter of a gun on the ferry back to Port Swan, I recall."

"Water gun," says Cosmos. "These two navy jerks, these two navy guys, they were drunk and they didn't like the way we looked so they picked a fight with us."

"Didn't like the way you looked? What was wrong with the way you looked?"

"We had on these long coats and we had our hair dyed green for the concert the night before. So this one guy takes a swing at me, and our manager, Salal, she reaches in her purse for a water gun and puts it in my hand. Scared the . . . scared the . . . scared the daylights out of these navy guys, and when we got off the ferry the cops arrested me."

"For assault," the Commissioner says.

"That was dropped," says Cosmos. "It was a water gun, and I didn't even know Salal had put the gun in my hand."

"Mitigating circumstances," says the Commissioner.

"That's it," says Cosmos.

"That's enough," says the Commissioner. He folds his hands. He takes off his glasses. "So here we are," he says. "You've made a mess of your life. You've made a mess in a lot of other people's lives too. And now you want to get away from it all. How can I be sure you won't make a mess in your uncle Henry's life?"

"I would never do that," says Cosmos.

The room is silent. Sweat is forming on Cosmos's forehead.

The Commissioner stares at the assembled group. "I am going to grant the transfer," he says, "but you're going to have to pay some restitution for damages."

"No problem," Uncle Henry volunteers. "He'll work hard on the farm and I'll send you his paycheck every week."

The Commissioner studies Uncle Henry. "I believe you will," he says. Then he turns back to Cosmos: "We're going to treat you like a minor in meting out your punishment, but we're going to expect you to behave like an adult in getting your life back together. I should warn you, Mr. De Haag, this is all going to happen very fast. You'd better go home and start packing your bags. Good luck to all of you."

"We won!" Hans shouts when they get outside.

At first Cosmos's smile doesn't want to come, but then it does. He is not going into detention. Whatever Iowa brings, it has to bring some kind of freedom. After all, his dad spent the first eighteen years of his life in Iowa, and look at him now! He's free. "Yeah!" says Cosmos, and gives his dad a high-five. "Yeah!" And now he is almost yelling. "This is great!"

Outside the courtroom, Uncle Henry keeps talking about how wonderful everything has turned out, how the Lord will help all of them through this hour of trial, blah blah blah. Hans continues in his cheerful Santa Claus way too. Noreen is the most bubbly one of all, giving Cosmos a full-body hippie-hug. But then she says, "Greyhound therapy!"

"What?" says Hans.

"Greyhound therapy—that's when one state gets rid of its problem by shipping it off to another state. The only reason the State of Washington made it so easy is that they were glad to get rid of you."

Cosmos knows she is only teasing him, but it's as if his own little bubble of happiness has been pricked. It's not just about leaving Port Swan. It's about leaving his dad. And it's about leaving his friends, Rhody, Spruce, and especially beautiful Salal, even if she is cooling off on him. Wherever he goes and no matter what happens, there can never be another Salal.

You've got so much soul, baby

"WE'RE GONNA MISS YOU, Coz," says Rhody. "You're the E-flat in our C-minor chord."

"Tapes," says Spruce. "Let's just keep sending each other tapes. We'll all get better, and when you get back we'll be hot hot hot."

"Just send us some cool corn-fed Iowa lyrics," says Rhody.

"Yeah," says Cosmos. "I won't have anything else to do there. You know, what can you do in Iowa but play music, you know?"

The final few days before departure have been a blur of music, and the OughtaBs are in their usual practice spot in the garage behind Rhody's house. Salal is there too, as she has been for every practice session since the hearing, but she slips away afterward instead of joining Cosmos for one of their walks to Fort Wheeler State Park and lovemaking under the stars on top of one of the old gun emplacements overlooking the Strait.

Rhody on bass and Spruce on drums act as if nothing is going to change, as if it hasn't really dawned on them that without Cosmos's guitar and Cosmos's voice the OughtaBs will be the Hasbeens before they've ever had the chance to find out just how good they might be. Rhody is the best musician among them. He can come up with music for anything Cosmos writes. Spruce is the most wired member of the band, always bouncing, always jittering around. He's drumming even when he sits still.

Salal thinks that a nine-month separation shouldn't hurt the band. "I'm invested in you guys," she says. "If you keep practicing while you're apart, you'll be better when you get back together."

Salal really does act as if she's committed to the OughtaBs. As their manager, she has been sending demo tapes around. She's the one who got them their first gig in Seattle. Salal has connections. But until the sudden change, she was connected to Cosmos in a way Cosmos had never before been connected to a woman.

At the final practice the night before Cosmos is to leave, she is a combination of groupie and coach, sometimes sighing or dancing when she likes what she hears, sometimes scolding them when they start to get sloppy. At one point, Cosmos thinks he sees signs of the old sexy warmth in her smile, but mostly he sees a manager, a woman who is more interested in business than loving. When the romance between her and Cosmos started, she said she was fond of him because he was sincere, fearless, and funny. He told her she was a magic wand of beauty and inspiration. "I look at you and my whole body wants to sing," he said. "My dark angel, let me shine in the dark light of your shadow." Something about Salal made it easy to talk like that.

"Anything is better than Juvie," Rhody says. "What I hear, Juvie is hell with the heat turned up."

Cosmos responds with a minor-key run on his guitar.

> *"Oh, wouldn't it be groovy*
> *just to spend some time in Juvie,"*

he sings in a hollow, flat voice. Spruce jitters into place and does a rat-a-tat and thunk-thunk on the drums.

Rhody laughs and finds the key on bass. He picks out a tune that might work as a melody line. Cosmos repeats it and adds a touch of his own.

> *"There ain't no bail*
> *'cause this ain't jail,*
> *here in Juvie.*
> *Can't rent a movie,*
> *not in Juvie,"*

he sings. Salal applauds and sways. Everybody's laughing, but Cosmos keeps working toward a tune, with Rhody following and then improving on it. Cosmos plays back to him. They watch each other, as if their instruments have feelings and are sending messages through the players' eyes. In a minute, they're together. They're on a roll.

"Let's try that again," says Cosmos. "This could be cool." He repeats the lyrics and Rhody and Spruce are with him.

Salal gets up, wearing black jeans that are loose everywhere except on her buttocks. On top she wears a short-sleeved black V-neck that almost shows enough cleavage to reveal the little red heart she has tattooed on her left breast. She has her snake bracelet on, the one that starts above her left elbow and winds around her upper arm. She starts swaying. Chain necklaces dance across her chest. The snake's green eyes glint. Cosmos stares at her. She is so long, so elegant, so awesome. "This sounds good, this sounds good," she says in her mellow voice.

She opens a beer and starts drinking fast as she sways. "I'm a seasonal eater," she once said. "If I eat a big dinner at Christmas, I'm not hungry until Easter." But she's always ready for a beer. She can take on a beer like a sea lion a young salmon any time of the day.

> *"Who'll make my bed,*
> *who'll rub my head?"*

sings Cosmos, looking at Salal swaying to the beat.

> *"Here in Juvie,"*

they all sing.

> *"The food is bad*
> *and we're all sad.*
> *So sad,"*

sings Cosmos.

> *"Here in Juvie,"*

they all sing.

> *"We've done no wrong,*
> *They took our bong,*
> *So sing along.*
> *Can't buy no booze,*
> *nothing to lose,"*

sings Cosmos.

> *"Here in Juvie,"*

they all sing.

Cosmos can't think of another line, and things start to fall apart. "I'll work on that," he says.

Everybody settles down, but Cosmos can't take his eyes off Salal. She is more beautiful than ever. Her long dyed hair glows in the afternoon light, and the snake slithers around her arm as her arm moves. She has three dangling silver earrings in one ear and two in the other. Her skin gleams ivory around her purple lipstick. Her face is long and her lips are large. She has a safety pin in her left eyebrow and a ring in her left nostril. Her eyes are dark, large, and sad, and when she directs them at Cosmos it's as if a creamy wave comes at him, draws him into its undertow, and pulls him helplessly down and under her power.

"Hey, guys," says Cosmos. "I want to do the Salal song, all right?"

"Let Coz call it," says Spruce.

The Salal song is the first song Cosmos ever wrote, back when the band was still trying to be a jazz band and Rhody was leading them on the saxophone. The jazz band lasted long enough for Cosmos to write the song, and it was inspired by Salal shortly after she listened to and then smiled on them and exactly when Cosmos fell in love with her.

"That would be so sweet," says Salal. "I'll dance for you."

Salal came to the first performance of this song at a Port Swan teen dance and danced in front of the stage as Cosmos ground out the lyrics and Rhody embellished them with saxophone riffs. As always, Rhody has his sax at the ready. He lays down his bass and warms up the sax. Remembering that first performance, Cosmos sings:

> *"You've got so much soul, baby,*
> *don't know where your body's gone.*

Oh, you've got so much soul, baby,
can't tell where your body's gone."

At this point, Salal gets up to do a tall, slithery dance, and Rhody does a sexy riff. Then Cosmos's lyrics go on:

"You've got so much soul, baby,
it's spreading all around.
You've got so much soul, baby,
you're floating off the ground."

Salal lifts her arms and waves them slowly like a large bird while the band plays and plays to make the song longer. Cosmos finishes with the final stanza:

"You've got so much soul, baby,
can't tell where your pretty body's gone.
You've got so much soul, baby,
can't tell where your pretty body's gone.
Oh, come come come on, baby,
I say, Come come come on, baby,
put your body back on.
I say, Oh, come come come on, baby,
put your pretty body back on."

With that, Salal freezes in profile and thrusts her breasts upward. A real crowd-pleaser.

When the band breaks up, Salal lingers. "Could we meet at the gate at Fort Wheeler in an hour?" she says to Cosmos. "I really want to see you alone before you leave for Iowa."

"I'd like that," says Cosmos, and resists the urge to fall to his knees and kiss her toes. The look she gives him is enough to make his throat tighten.

Cosmos is at the gate to Fort Wheeler fifteen minutes early. He walks in circles around one of the gate pillars, trying to calm himself down. Right now he feels as if he would spend nine months in Juvie, let alone nine months in Iowa, for a one-night love feast with Salal.

When Salal arrives ten minutes late, she has changed clothes, and the way she is dressed now is the first signal that all may not go as he hopes. She has on her high-laced boots, tight leather jeans, and a tight, neck-fitting sweater. She looks great, but the clothes are a fortress around her slim body, a bunker of an outfit. She doesn't reach out to take his hand. Instead, she leads the way at a quick pace, up the path, under the madrone and Douglas-fir trees, past salmonberries, Oregon grape, blackberry vines, Scotch broom, and salal bushes thick as an Iowa cornfield.

She is not heading toward their love nest on top of the old bunkers. She is walking fast to the best vista on the Fort: a cliff that stands two hundred feet over the beach and from which they can see all the way to Victoria, B.C. A great view, but hardly a place to get naked. The sun has set and is spreading its orange light across the water, lighting up a few white sails and setting a large cargo ship off in a majestic silhouette. They walk off the path, around a few salal bushes. Cosmos picks off a leaf and tucks it inside one of her earrings. "Salal for Salal," he says, and leans to kiss her cheek.

"So sweet," she says but moves away from him toward the edge of the sandstone cliff. No matter what she says, her voice is beautiful to Cosmos. It sounds as if it's coming up through a lion's chest and out through the mouth of a canary. Sweet and deep. Her voice sounds the way he imagines the hands of a really good masseuse would feel.

Salal leans against the wooden safety fence, then steps over it and walks dangerously close to the dropoff. She stands there looking out toward the west, where the Strait of Juan de Fuca stretches out toward the Pacific. With the light fading, she looks like an elongated bronze statue. Her earrings sparkle like slashes of light on water, and then her long hair unfurls like a flag, and the wind holds it in midair. Cosmos knows one of these trances can last a half-hour or longer. He waits. When she finally turns to Cosmos, her large eyes look distant and sad.

"It's Bridgette," she says. "We're lovers." She steps back over the fence. "I'm sorry, Coz."

Bridgette is the waitress who was in Salal's apartment the day he went running to her for comfort.

"My God," says Cosmos.

"Why do you say that? And why do you say that like that?" Her voice is harsher than he expected, sharp against the softness of her eyes.

"She's such a loser," he says, then clutches. This is one of those moments when his own sharp tongue could cut through the last feeble strand of their relationship.

"It's because she's a woman, isn't it? Isn't it? You don't care that I've been with other men, but a woman, that's different, right?"

Now Cosmos's voice rises to meet Salal's. "Sure, it's different, but, hey, why am I the one who's defending himself? You're the one who's dumping me."

"I'm not dumping you. Things just need to be different."

"Because of Bridgette."

"Yes, because of Bridgette. We're in love and don't want to hide it any longer."

She stops and her manner softens. "Oh, Coz, I don't want to hurt you."

"I'm too blown away by all this to hurt," he says. "This is too crazy."

"But you always say you care about me because I'm not ordinary. Well, you're right, I'm not ordinary. I don't look ordinary, I don't think ordinary, and I don't behave ordinary." Salal reaches into her purse and takes out two cans of beer. She pops them and hands one to Cosmos. He takes three quick swallows.

"No, you're not ordinary," he says. "That's what I love

about you. You're beautiful, and I don't want things to change between us, that's all."

"You've always known I hate barriers. I hate age barriers. I hate gender barriers too. I need to be free to find the true me without some stupid barrier that society has built up."

"I don't like barriers either," says Cosmos. "But right now I feel you've built one between us. How can feelings change the way yours have, *psst,* just like that?"

"If I'm going to grow, if I'm going to find out all the world has to offer, I have to be free from barriers, Cosmos. Free."

"I can't believe that's you talking," says Cosmos. "It's not even your real voice. You sound like one of those people who join a cult and come back brainwashed. I've never heard you talk like this before," he says. "Where's the old Salal?" He walks closer and leans toward her. "Hello? Where are you?"

"I am on a journey, Cosmos. You're part of it, but you're not all of it. Please understand. Right now I need to be with Bridgette. Don't be my barrier."

Instead of sweet ocean smells, Cosmos catches the stench of rotting seaweed and dead fish. He finishes his beer and throws the can over the embankment.

Salal watches silently. "That wasn't like you," she says, still not raising her voice. "Don't get violent."

"Violent. Hell," he says, and starts walking down the path toward the gate.

"Don't be bitter," she says, trailing behind him a few steps.

"'Bitter' isn't the word. I just feel like a fool. I thought I knew you."

As badly as the night ends, Salal leaves him a present the next morning before he leaves with his dad for the airport—a thick leather-bound journal and a note that says, "Know that I will always care about you. I want you in my life. Please understand. Love always, Salal."

Cosmos throws the note away but keeps the fine journal. He opens it. This is as good a place to start as any, a blank page.

Be my black widow and bite me tonight

THIS ISN'T SUCH A BAD alternative: window seat 15A on the Boeing 747 from Seattle soaring along at thirty-five thousand feet toward Minneapolis. If not away from trouble, at least above it. Minneapolis and then the short hop to Sioux Falls, South Dakota, before the forty-minute drive in Uncle Henry and Aunt Minnie's cruise-mobile across the Big Sioux River into northwest Iowa and straight-and-narrow Dutchville, U.S.A.

He reaches into his backpack and pulls out the journal Salal gave him. Already he can feel the first impulses to let Salal go. Just let her go. Poof. Like a little cloud over the Rockies. Poof. Oh, but it isn't this easy. He picks up his new journal and kisses it. Then he reaches into his backpack and takes out the little wrapped box that his father gave him as he got on the plane. Inside is a beautifully carved and polished wooden totem of a raven. It is made of old red cedar, fine-grained, and light. It's not much bigger than a golf ball and fits into his palm. Cosmos turns it over. On the bottom of the base Hans has carved, in very fine print, the words "Raven—the Trickster—De Haag, 2000." With his dad's name carved on the bottom, this little raven would be a hundred-dollar item at the Wood House.

The flight attendants come around with drinks. Cosmos sips a ginger ale and tries to cheer himself up by looking down on the wheat fields below. Iowa will not be this kind of big-sky country, but it will still be wide-open spaces where he'll be able to walk blindfolded for an hour without running into anything or having to climb a hill. And if he did open his eyes, what would he have? Sky. A big blue sky with puffy white Iowa clouds in it. And on the ground, not ground really when the corn is tall, but miles and miles of green stalks waving in the wind like the waters of Puget Sound. And the animals: all those warm-bodied cows just chewing their cud and spacing out, and all those pigs with their big ears and curly tails chilling in mud holes. What could be so bad about all this, really? Ah, the pigs. "Pigs outnumber people four to one in Iowa," Hans told him with a big laugh last week. "If you can't beat 'em, join 'em."

Of course, there will be people too. The people, those blond-haired, nice people who go to church when they're not working or listening to country-Western music. Country-Western music and gospel. Too much of the wrong music could drive me out of my mind, Cosmos thinks. He stirs in his seat. To sweeten the bad fantasy of a world full of country-Western and gospel, he pictures himself alone in his room, looking out over an Iowa landscape of corn, alfalfa, and beans into a broad rosy sunset. In this fantasy, he has his headphones on, he's listening to a Seattle band, and he's thinking of new lyrics that he'll set to music and send to the OughtaBs to rehearse and have ready when he gets back home.

Starting to feel at peace with the sky, at peace with the world, at peace with this, the first great adventure of his life, Cosmos puts his seat back and closes his eyes.

He wakes up to a voice on the plane's intercom announcing the descent over the blue lakes of Minnesota and into Minneapolis. He has an hour in the airport before his flight to Sioux Falls. Strolling around, he sees the Starbucks coffee stand. It's like being back in the Northwest, a little bit of home away from home. He drinks two double-lattes and gets on the Boeing 727 to Sioux Falls wired. This plane is only half full. A few of the Seattle passengers are still with him, and look like the healthiest people on board, the only people with any kind of sparkle to them at all, that lean and healthy look of people who eat fish and vegetables and don't get too much sun. When the plane makes its final approach for Sioux Falls, passengers start looking down at the cornfields and feedlots glowing a pale gold in the light of the setting sun. As the small city appears below them, one of the Seattle passengers nudges her husband, grins, and says, "Look, honey, affordable housing."

Somewhere down there a big car waits for him, one that glistens with Simoniz on the outside and smells like hog manure on the inside. He thinks again about the Indian boys who got sentenced to their year living alone on a Northwest island. Something inside him says they just might have gotten a lot better deal.

"Fasten your seat belts and return your seats and tray tables to their full upright positions," comes the voice over the speakers. Cosmos puts the tiny raven away, then sits upright and pushes his hair back. He feels his earlobes and the empty puncture spots where he has removed his earrings.

Cosmos does what he usually does when he feels panic setting in: he reaches for his pencil and something to write on. He makes his first entry in his new journal:

> *Good-bye, seagulls singing through the fog!*
> *Hello, cow manure and mangy farm dog!*
> *Good-bye, noble sea lions lulling in the bay.*
> *Hello, field mice screwing in the hay.*

But he can't have words like that in his new journal. If his uncle Henry and aunt Minnie see questionable words, he'll have their religious breath on his neck before he feels the hot Midwestern sun. As the plane vibrates through the air currents, it passes its shudder through Cosmos. He flips over his pencil and erases half of what he has put down. He rewrites:

Good-bye, ugly seagulls screeching through the fog!
Hello, pretty cows and happy farm dog!
Good-bye, dorky sea lions belching in the bay.
Hello, pretty field mice a-playing in the hay.

That should do it, he figures. He tucks the journal in the seat-back in front of him.

As the plane touches down, it is as if the curtain on his old life has fallen. He retrieves his journal and writes: "Good-bye, Port Swan. Good-bye, green friend; good-bye, morning fogs rolling over the hills; good-bye, foghorns; good-bye, Fort Wheeler; good-bye, ferries and ferry horns; good-bye, rain; good-bye, tide pools and anemones; good-bye, warm sun and cool breeze; and good-bye, Seattle, sweet smells of Pike Place Market, sweet smells of head shops filled with incense. Good-bye, street bums and your bags of wine. Good-bye, music, oh, sweet Port Swan, sweet Seattle music, crazy Seattle music scene, good-bye. Good-bye, Rhody. Good-bye, Dad. Good-bye, Spruce. Good-bye, Salal. Damn you, Salal, good-bye." Before he can erase the "Damn," a flight attendant announces, "Remain in your seats until we have come to a complete stop and the captain has turned off the seat-belt sign. Thank you for choosing Northwest."

* * *

As odd as his uncle Henry had looked to him in the Port Swan hearing room, now, in the Sioux Falls terminal, Cosmos can't pick out his uncle's face from the crowd. Everybody looks alike, a whole waiting area of white-faced stocky people. Then Uncle Henry emerges, strutting along in his confident way, and Aunt Minnie follows right behind him like a jittery shadow.

Uncle Henry gives Cosmos a firm handshake, steps aside to let Aunt Minnie do the same thing. "You won't need a baggage-claim ticket here, the way you do in Seattle," he says. "We can just pick up your luggage and go."

"We don't have much stealing around here," says Aunt Minnie with an eager smile.

Uncle Henry is a take-care-of-business sort of guy, and in a few minutes they have Cosmos's music equipment and clothes loaded into the trunk of his big car. The inside of the car does not smell like hog manure the way Cosmos thought it would, it smells like a sugar-sweet car-deodorizer. Rose. Or is it cherry? Whatever it is, it smells like the color of the Jell-O salads he'll probably be eating for the next nine months.

To Uncle Henry and Aunt Minnie, riding in the car means listening to the radio. For the first ten minutes the radio blares country-Western—"Checkerboard square on the table, your move, I just can't believe that you're gone," wails through the rear speakers as the huge blue car guzzles along through the dark-green corn and tidy bean fields. "The only easy street's the one that dead-ends at my heart."

When Uncle Henry turns the air conditioner off and rolls down his window, Cosmos is reminded that Iowa is more than open spaces and cornfields. It is the smell of farm animals, waves and waves of stench as they pass different farms with different kinds of feedlots. The way a cat box can smell a little bit like cat food, cattle manure hints of the smell of the grain that went into the animal's mouth before it was processed back into the world. Cosmos hasn't forgotten these smells from his visits to Iowa. The smells are like primary colors, and it is as easy for him to remember the difference between the smells of the hog lots and the cattle lots as it is to remember the difference between red and green.

"Aren't people amazing?" Cosmos says from the back seat, where he has been sitting, quiet but nervous as a puppy on the way to the vet.

"Yes, they are," says Aunt Minnie. "All of God's children have a little different kind of God's light left in them."

It's my big mouth that is going to get me in trouble, Cosmos reminds himself, and crawls back inside his silence.

Uncle Henry turns the radio down. "What did you mean, William?" he says.

Cosmos leans forward in the back seat. "As we were going past that one farm," he says, "I was just thinking. That's hog manure, right?"

"Right," says Uncle Henry. "That's the Ver Sloet place. Big operation."

"I was just thinking, aren't people amazing, that they can smell something like that and still eat pork chops?"

The question seemed safe before he asked it, but now the front seat is as quiet as an elevator where somebody has just passed gas. Uh-oh, thinks Cosmos. If that insulted them, wait till we start talking about the real stuff, like: What's more important, preserving the earth or talking all day about God?

In a minute, Aunt Minnie answers his question about the smell of pork chops before they're pork chops. "Yes," she says. "You're right about that. It does take some getting used to. But to people around here, pig manure smells like money." With that, she turns the music back up. Aunt Minnie, she may have her head in the religious ozone, but her heart is on earth: Cosmos can sense it right from the start. She's going to look out for him.

The countryside outside the car window is not exactly a dome of darkness. Big lights illuminate the farmyards, making them look more like the suburbs than the country. Then, as if in a strange dream, as the cruise-mobile lunges along down the two-lane blacktop toward Uncle Henry and Aunt Minnie's house, out of the darkness arises a huge ferry boat, moving along with its double-layered lights over the undulant bean fields of Iowa. It looks like the *Tacoma* approaching the dock with its lights on. The long stream of two-layered lights move steadily forward over the calm fields, edging up toward the dock on Bainbridge Island. The ferry boat disappears behind a hill for a moment as the car swoops down into a valley, then appears over the waves of bean fields as the car comes back up and crests the hill. Cosmos feels stoned, as if he is living inside the weirdest *déjà-vu* of his life. It's too surreal. "What's that?" he says.

"That's a new turkey operation," says Uncle Henry. "Six thousand turkeys. They did really well last year, yessirree."

Cosmos sees now that it is a stationary and long, very long, metal building with two rows of well-lit windows. The smells that come into the car are not those of seaweed and beach grass. "The building looks just like a ferry boat," he says.

The front seat is back to being a clam. The comparison felt pretty safe to Cosmos, but the silence from the front seat suggests that they think it is dumb. Then Uncle Henry says, "You won't be seeing any ferry boats out here, I'm afraid. I hope there are some things you can look at without thinking of something else."

Cosmos stares out the window. The buildings and feedlots look like they're under stage lights, enough light to let his eyes confirm what his nose is smelling. Enough light to expose everyone and everything at all times. Can the farmers even look up and see stars anymore? he wonders.

"Don't all those lights burn up a lot of electricity?" asks Cosmos.

"You've got your trade-offs," says Uncle Henry. "The lights make it possible for the livestock to eat at night, gain weight faster, you see. Farmers nowadays need all the help they can get if we're going to make enough money to stay in business."

"With God's grace," adds Aunt Minnie.

Cosmos tries to follow the logic of all this: hog manure smells like money, lights stay on so animals can eat more so they'll get fat faster, which would mean that they defecate more, which would mean more manure, which would mean more bad smells, which would mean more money. God's grace must be frosting on the cake.

"Oh, I get it," says Cosmos in a voice like that of a kid who finally understands that two plus two equals four.

Aunt Minnie turns down the country-Western music. "You probably don't like country-Western," she says.

"It's fine," he says. "My friends and I sometimes listen to country-Western and then try to come up with our own country-Western lines, you know?"

"Really?" says Uncle Henry. "Your dad told me you were good at music."

"What were some of the words you wrote, William?" asks Aunt Minnie.

"Oh, I don't know," says Cosmos, though his confidence button has been pushed by the possibility that they just might be impressed by something he does. "You know, like, 'Would you roll over for a roll of quarters, my casino baby?' Country-Western is full of puns and paradox, you know."

"That sounded pretty nasty."

"Oh, that one wasn't mine," Cosmos says quickly. "One of my friends back home came up with that one."

"You actually make up words for a song?" asks Aunt Minnie. "What were some of yours?"

"Let's see. I think I wrote, 'I'm a fat potato, I got eyes for you.'"

"That's cute. Any more?"

"Let's see. 'If it's a sin to tell a lie, why not lie with me and sin?' Or I think there was one that went a little something like, 'I can get over being under the weather under the covers with you.'"

"What?" says Uncle Henry. "That's pretty off-color for around here."

All of the warnings that Cosmos's father gave him about the religious folks in Iowa come chilling down on him. But Hans only warned him about not making fun of religion. He never said anything about getting a little bit "off-color," as Uncle Henry puts it. "Sorry," says Cosmos. "We never sang that anywhere. We were just joking around."

"They're just jokes," Aunt Minnie says to Uncle Henry.

Then she turns around and smiles at Cosmos where he shrivels in the corner of the back seat. "Maybe you better keep those in the family," she says.

Aunt Minnie changes the channel to a religious station where every song is a little sermon or the story of some heart-wrenching acceptance of the right answer: "Fill my heart with light divine, in the world's darkness, let my life shine."

"We have quite a bit of variety here," says Aunt Minnie. She starts cruising the channels: religious talk, country-Western, country-Western, religious music, news, golden oldies, country-Western, country-Western, religious talk, baseball, country-Western, market report, country-Western.

"They're almost all country-Western!" says Cosmos in a voice that doesn't hide his astonishment. "We can barely get one country-Western station in Port Swan."

"You're in the country now, William," says Uncle Henry.

Aunt Minnie stops on a country-Western station that comes through loud and clear. Some gravelly-voiced cowboy sings, "Be my black widow and bite me tonight."

"My goodness," says Aunt Minnie, and changes the station back to a religious channel.

"Smut," says Uncle Henry. "Nothing but smut. No wonder young people talk the way they do. No reverence. No respect. There was this boy in the public school used some off-color language, and when the teacher scolded him, he went and hit her. Hit a teacher! And the little reprobate was expelled for only a week. They should have horsewhipped him and run him out of town."

"Totally," says Cosmos.

"What?" says Uncle Henry.

"What stations do you have back home?" Aunt Minnie interrupts.

"Oh, a little bit of everything, you know," says Cosmos. "Jazz, rock, classical, not much country."

"What do you like?"

"I like young-people music," says Cosmos.

"Probably no worse than what we just heard," says Uncle Henry.

"Any kind of music is better than no music," says Cosmos. "Your music is fine with me."

Uncle Henry turns the radio off. Cosmos stares at the back of his gray-blond head and wonders what's going on inside it. Uncle Henry doesn't make him wait very long. "We're almost home," he says. "After you unpack, Minnie and I would like to have a little talk with you, if that's all right with you?"

"That's fine," says Cosmos.

"My goodness, that was a deep breath you just let out," Aunt Minnie says to Cosmos and turns to look back at him.

"Just relaxing," says Cosmos. He closes his eyes and tries to imagine a sunset over Puget Sound.

Instead of seeing a Puget Sound sunset, he hears the

sound of squealing tires and feels the sudden tug of his seat belt. Aunt Minnie screams. The car makes a sharp swerve to the left, then veers back into the proper lane.

"That was close," says Uncle Henry. "Real close. I should have hit it. I thought it was a dog."

"Oh, Henry! That scared me so much!"

"What was it?" says Cosmos. He can feel his heart pounding in his neck.

"Was it a fox, Henry?" says Aunt Minnie. Her voice is trembling.

"Coyote," says Uncle Henry. "Didn't use to have to worry about those critters."

"I see it! I see it!" says Cosmos. "There it is, out there in that pasture. Look, it's looking back at us."

Uncle Henry accelerates and the animal disappears from view.

"Thought we got rid of those varmints when we got rid of rats in these parts. The d-Con got rid of the rats. Everybody figured cyanide traps got rid of the coyotes. Now they're coming back. Time for more cyanide traps."

Cosmos looks out the back window, trying to catch one last glimpse of the coyote. A dozen questions go through his mind about the survival of wildlife, but he does not let even one of them pass his lips.

Uncle Henry turns off the highway down a gravel road. They are almost to the farm. Cosmos watches the head-lights catch the big white square thing with a large lean-to porch on its front that will be his home.

The porch is filled by a deep-freeze, a sewing machine, and a long row of hooks for coats and hats. Eye-catching wall plaques with cute sayings hang on the porch walls: "The Faster I Go, the Behinder I Get," says one; "We get too soon old, and too late smart," says another. In the kitchen the plaques get religious. Cosmos remembers what Hans told him about the Trinity, and here the idea of things coming in threes follows through: "Jesus is the Way, the Truth, and the Light," and "Without food we have hunger, without drink we have thirst, without Jesus we have nothing." The living room arranges itself in threes too: three windows, three easy chairs, three family portraits on top of the piano. Even the bookshelf carries the Trinity idea. It has a mere three books: one biography of Lawrence Welk, one book by Pat Robertson, and one by Garrison Keillor. All three books are hardbacks, and none of them shows any signs of having been read.

Cosmos has seen the farm before—some years ago, when Hans was still married to his mother, Melba. He remembers tobogganing behind a tractor through the fields and ditches in winter and playing in the hay field in summer. But this is the first time he has been here alone, without the buffer of his father who knows the strange ways of his religious relatives. His father probably could have saved him from all the mistakes he made on the ride home.

* * *

"Now it's time for our little talk," says Uncle Henry. "Let's go sit in the front room."

Uncle Henry walks across the room in a way that reminds Cosmos of how he walked up to Commissioner Levy in the hearing room. No hesitation in this man: he knows what he's going to say. He sits down in the green easy chair. Cosmos sits on the matching sofa.

"We want to provide a warm, safe home for you here, William," he begins.

Cosmos clasps his hands and leans back. "I appreciate that," he says.

"And a warm, safe home means safe and warm for the body, it means safe and warm for the mind, and it means safe and warm for the spirit. You see."

"I just want everybody to be happy," says Aunt Minnie, who sits down beside Cosmos on the sofa.

"Yes," says Uncle Henry. "And happiness here will mean that you are going to have to make some changes from the way things were for you back in Washington. That's a fact. You understand that?"

"Totally," says Cosmos.

"Would you like some tea?" asks Aunt Minnie.

"Yes," says Cosmos. "Some chamomile would be great."

"Some what?"

"Any kind would be fine."

Uncle Henry continues as Aunt Minnie goes for tea.

"Let me tell you a story that should help."

Uncle Henry's story is about a young couple who moved to Dutch Center about ten years ago, when the sock factory opened. They both got jobs at the factory. They were not Dutch. They were not church people. On Sundays, instead of going to church, they set a boom box outside their house playing loud Godless music while they worked in their garden. Then they would lay blankets out in their back yard, lie down in bathing suits, sunbathe, and drink beer. "On Sunday," Uncle Henry kept emphasizing. "On the Lord's Day." Then the wife was suspected of stealing socks from the factory. The husband got into a fight with a co-worker who told him his wife was a thief. The wife bumped her car into someone else in a parking lot and shouted obscenities at the other driver. Pretty soon the husband was drinking too much and getting to work late. They got speeding tickets. They didn't know how to handle money and got in trouble for bad checks. They left town in disgrace, and some people are just waiting for them to show their faces in town so they can settle a score or two with this irresponsible couple.

Aunt Minnie comes with the tea just as Uncle Henry is giving the moral to the story. "What I'm trying to show you, William, is that one thing leads to another. If Satan gets his foot in the door, he keeps pushing until the whole house falls down. You see what I'm saying?"

"Would you like some milk in your tea?" asks Aunt Minnie.

"A lot," says Cosmos. "Please." He turns back to Uncle Henry. "I understand."

"You can have a new life here, without the kinds of problems you faced in Washington. You see. But you've got to get started on the right foot. Watch how you talk. Watch how you act. What it really boils down to is being right with the Lord. If you're right with the Lord, everything else will fall into place."

"We've been praying for you," says Aunt Minnie.

"And we've been praying that you will pray to the Lord for guidance in your life," adds Uncle Henry. "One thing leads to another, and if you start with the Lord, then one good thing will lead to another good thing, that's what I'm saying. You see."

Cosmos holds it together through the moral of the story. Alone in his room, he lies on his back in bed. He knows how tired he is, and yet his whole body feels tight as a fist. Fear? Panic? He doesn't feel like writing in his journal. He doesn't even dare to put on one of his CDs until he makes sure his headset keeps the sound in his ears only. He listens to the corn-drying blowers in the silos outside droning like the engines of a jet.

Work, eat, pray, he thinks. That's all I'm going to be able to do here. He looks out his bedroom window to see the light-studded countryside. If there aren't any secrets during the day, there probably aren't any at night either. Nowhere to hide.

He wraps his arms across his chest and thinks of the coyote who escaped being hit by Uncle Henry's car. He gets up and takes out the raven totem that his father gave him. Raven, the Trickster. There aren't any ravens around here. But there are coyotes, at least a few of them. And the ones who have made it seem to know how to dodge big cars and cyanide traps. Every religious ear around here is going to be my cyanide trap, he thinks. The only way I can survive here is by being as quick and wary as that coyote. I'll have to be two people: one to show on the outside, the other one to keep alive on the inside. Coyote: now you see me, now you don't. Cosmos Coyote. That's the real one. The phony one will be the nice one he shows on the outside: William the Nice.

He gets up and walks to the mirror. "William the Nice," he says to himself, "you are the only person people are going to see. Understand? Yes, sir," he answers himself.

"William, is that you? Are you all right?" comes Aunt Minnie's voice from downstairs.

You get right with the Lord

DAYS START ON THE FARM at six-thirty for morning chores—
cleaning hog pens and feeding cracked corn and silage
to the cattle. Every work period is followed by food and
devotions—grace before each meal, reading of the Bible
and closing prayer after each meal. Day after day of work
and meat and potatoes and prayer and pork chops and
eggs and devotions and work and steak and canned tomatoes and Jell-O salad and prayer. *"Ora et labora"* says the
caption on *The Daily Light*, a devotional pamphlet. That
about does it: "Pray and work." That's life.

Cosmos finds a few moments of escape inside his head
when he walks the bean fields for milkweeds and even a
few moments of excitement when he learns to drive the
enormous John Deere tractor, easing it like a cumbersome
elephant through the cattle yards, where the Hereford
steers mildly ease aside at the sight of his awesome,
growling approach. But mostly he learns that farm work
is dusty and sweaty and tedious and boring, the daily
schedule coming at him like a metronome with a wide,
sweeping arm.

At least the schedule makes living the straight life of "William" easier. Impulses have nowhere to go when he knows that in a half-hour the pigs need to be fed or the cattle need to be checked and counted. Sometimes he feels as if life in less than a week has gotten as programmed and predictable as the cattle that walk like robots toward the feed troughs at the sound of the electric feed-auger.

Through it all, even as his mind grows numb with the routine, Cosmos knows he has to keep some part of his brain alert so that he doesn't fall out of character: Am I William the nice boy right now, or Cosmos-the-true, Cosmos-the-free, Cosmos-the-wily-Coyote? Uncle Henry and Aunt Minnie introduce him as "William" to people he doesn't know, and this helps him remember to behave like a William while the sound and meaning of the name hang over him like a guillotine that will drop if he accidentally switches to Cosmos-the-rebel, the juvenile delinquent on probation. To be William is to be the good boy whose past is as mysterious as the sea gulls that come out of nowhere to peck worms from freshly cultivated Iowa dirt. Where do they come from? Where have they been? No one seems to know or care. That's the way he hopes it will be with him.

In the few minutes in bed before going to sleep, instead of following Uncle Henry's request that he pray, Cosmos asks himself the only question that makes sense: What's phony? What's real? He finds he has to be phony most of the time if he wants to be real any of the time. Alone in his room at night, he can escape into a world that sounds safe, and he can turn up the nastiest lyrics in his collection: "In your face! In your face! Look at me! I'm your disgrace! Yeah! Yeah! Yeah!" With every screaming word he feels his aching shoulders relax. There's more than one way to work and pray.

He prepares his phony William the Nice face for his first meeting with his Iowa probation officer, his twenty-six-year-old, blue-eyed, blond cousin, Michael Jonsma.

"You can call me Michael," says Michael.

"You'd better call me William," says Cosmos.

Michael nods and smiles. "I understand," he says.

As they chat about Cosmos's dad and the weather in Washington, Cosmos notices how his cousin is sizing him up, watching his hands, looking at the way he stands, and nodding his head when Cosmos talks. Cosmos sizes him up too: watching his shoulders, looking into his eyes, looking at his lips when he smiles. He has a pretty polished nice-guy way about him, but he also reminds Cosmos of his dad, Hans. A straight shooter, as Uncle Henry might say.

"There are temptations around here too," says Michael, "but I'm not worried about you. Uncle Henry and Aunt Minnie will keep you out of trouble. Just be careful when high school starts. There are a few bad apples, even in the Christian Academy. Just stay away from the bad apples at the Academy and you'll be all right. If you stay out of trouble, I'll stay out of your hair."

Cosmos senses that his cousin Mike is no phony, but he also knows he can't risk being himself in front of him. He keeps his mouth shut. He holds back an urge to ask a few sincere questions, like whether there are going to be any drug tests.

The next day is Sunday, and Cosmos knows this will be the true test of his William the Nice face. Church will be the real community that Uncle Henry talked about in front of the Commissioner in Port Swan. Today he will stand before the big-time judges and jury.

Cosmos wears a white shirt and narrow blue tie, only to see all the young people his age dressed in short sleeves and bright colors. He tries to remember his dad's advice: "Just do what the person next to you is doing, close your eyes during the congregational prayer, sing along with the hymns, have the Bible open to the table of contents so that when the minister says which book and verse he will be reading from you can quickly look there to see what page that book of the Bible is on. Don't fall asleep during the sermon. And just act natural."

Sure, Dad.

The church is immense, with rows of golden wooden benches that ripple on forever, and stained-glass windows glowing with their brilliant colors of shepherds and sheep and feasting disciples.

Cosmos tries to do the same thing that those around him are doing—though, when he looks out the corner of his eye to see what that is, the corner of his eye meets the corner of someone else's eye staring at him. They make him feel the way he did the first time he went to a formal dinner and didn't know which fork to use first. When some people take one of the books from the book rack on the seat in front of them, he does the same thing, only to find that he has taken the Bible when they are taking the hymnal and the hymnal when they are taking the Bible.

When the organist starts playing the prelude before church, he finds an odd kind of refuge. Any music, even if it is ponderous religious music, relaxes him. And he doesn't have to put on his Cosmos Coyote earphones for it.

The consistory enters, a long stream of stern men, who find their families in the pews. Are these "the elders" Uncle Henry talked about who will be visiting him if he gets in trouble? Then the minister, in a long dark robe, walks in like some prophet from the Old Testament, big sweeping steps that tell the world this guy has God on his side.

The sermon is the easy part. All he has to do is stare straight ahead and space out, which, he assumes, everybody else is doing too. Something about Jesus feeding the multitudes with five loaves of bread and two fish. Something about what is the real meaning of this story today, at a time of plenty? Cosmos assumes it will be a lesson about giving to the poor, but when he comes out of his daydream toward the end of the talk he hears that the sermon has not been about giving to the poor at all. "Today the government tries to act as if it is Christ by feeding the multitude with the five loaves and two fishes which are the taxpayer's money," says the minister. "Let Christ provide for those who have not prepared for the future. It is not scriptural for the government to pretend to do the Lord's work!" He shouts so loud that Cosmos has to believe the man really believes what he is saying. The minister ends on a softer note: "Let us follow the proper channels of benevolence with our special offering for the poor. As faithful disciples, let us honor the Lord's benevolence by giving to those who are less fortunate than we are, in His name. Amen."

When the collection plate comes around, Cosmos feels the way he did when he forgot his lunch money in second grade. Aunt Minnie, who is starting to remind him of his favorite baby-sitter when he was a child, comes to the rescue and hands him a dollar before the collection plate comes down their row.

After church, Cosmos heads for the back door that opens onto the parking lot. But the hallways are packed with people talking, and the talk he hears is anything but music to his ears. "Good sermon," he hears someone say. "Good point about the government trying to play God with its handouts," the voice goes on.

Cosmos pushes to make his way along, but bits of conversation that he wishes he were not hearing keep coming at him: "You hear about that gang from Sioux City that has been trying to sell drugs around here? We need more police." The person he is talking to responds with, "And tougher judges. Young people nowadays . . ."

Cosmos pushes on, trying to look over people's heads for the back door. "It wasn't on the church bulletin," comes an older woman's voice, "but the entire Women's Circle is arranging cars to go and march in front of the Planned Parenthood office in Sioux Falls."

Just as he reaches the back door, Cosmos hears someone say in a not-too-subtle whisper, "There he is."

Cosmos doesn't have to guess who they are talking about. When they get through blasting everyone else, he concludes, they'll probably change the topic to him. What do they know about me? he wonders. They probably think I'm a drug-dealing person on welfare whose girlfriend has had an abortion.

Cosmos hurries off toward Uncle Henry's car to wait for them. He stands next to it and watches people slowly emerge from the church building and break into little social cliques. The teenage boys huddle in one group and teenage girls in another. Some of the teenagers look his way, though none of them venture over to introduce themselves. Cosmos guesses that they know he is here as an alternative to juvenile detention. He looks at them again and sees that sharp glint of judgment in even the quick glances of the young people. They are my prison guards, he thinks.

But among the curious eyes spark those of one wholesome-looking blond girl his age in a modest blue dress. When their eyes meet, she smiles, a smile so instantaneous and so big and full that he cannot tell if it is a smile of mockery, admiration, judgment, or good-willed congeniality. It is a Christian smile, all right, but it is not the scary kind that looks like God Himself chiseled it in there as an advertisement for milk or deodorant or life eternal. His own face twitches in a pathetic gesture of a return smile, though he has no idea whether the girl in blue can interpret it as a friendly response. It doesn't seem to matter to her what his smile looks like: she walks toward him, a silver cross bouncing on her chest. Cosmos's back stiffens.

"Hi, I'm Cherlyn Van Dyke," she says. "You're William, aren't you?" She holds out her hand.

"Yes." He reaches to shake her hand. It's a firm and confident handshake. "Pleased to meet you."

The small talk that follows is awkward only from Cosmos's side. Cherlyn is like a hospitality hostess who shows no desire but the comfort of the person she is talking with. She tells him about the Academy, about which teachers to avoid, about the choir, about forensics, about roller-skating and hay rides, about bowling parties, about talent shows. "I know we're a farm community," she says, "but we do have a little bit of everything around here. I hope you find something you like."

This strangely friendly and compellingly lovely young woman is the only thing Cosmos can even imagine liking this Sunday. But no sooner has she walked away than he gets an odd feeling that something about her was too comfortable, too nice. Her beaming face and her beaming way of coming toward him made her seem like a salesperson so good at her trade that he didn't even notice what she was up to. She has something to sell bigger than Amway products, he has no doubt about that. It gives him the creeps. He feels the way he does when he has eaten some really unhealthy sweet food, then regrets it as soon as he starts to digest what he has taken in.

Uncle Henry and Aunt Minnie see Cherlyn saying goodbye to Cosmos as they approach the car. Their smiles suggest that they approve of the acquaintance. "That Cherlyn Van Dyke, she is a fine young woman," says Uncle Henry. "She'll be a senior at the Academy."

"Very nice girl," says Aunt Minnie. "A real leader. You can't go wrong by getting to know her."

Unfortunately, the after-church activities have just begun, since it is Uncle Henry and Aunt Minnie's practice to visit Grandpa Wilim in the nursing home. Cosmos hasn't seen his grandfather for three years and doesn't know what to expect.

The nursing home sits on the edge of town, a flat yellow brick structure with a large patio inside the horseshoe structure. Grandpa Wilim is in his eighties and makes Uncle Henry and Aunt Minnie look like youngsters. "He's not the same anymore," Aunt Minnie warns Cosmos. "Sometimes you'll see his good side, sometimes his bad—you never know."

When they get to the second-floor room where Grandpa Wilim lives, the bottom half of his door is closed. It is a Dutch door that can be locked near the floor on the outside. It is meant to be a mild form of restraint, a way of keeping him in his room but still giving him the freedom to look out into the hallway.

Minnie reaches down and unlatches the hallway lock to the Dutch door. Grandpa Wilim sits in his swivel chair watching a televangelist preaching in a sweet, assuring voice. Grandpa Wilim is still a big man and has his large farmer-hands folded over his stomach. He wears a green plaid shirt, dark-green wash pants, and a pair of well-worn leather slippers. For a moment he doesn't look up, but when he notices that Cosmos is with Aunt Minnie and Uncle Henry, he turns off the television with his remote, puts his hands on the armrests of his chair, and starts to get up.

"No, no, don't get up, Pa," says Uncle Henry. "Minnie has brought some cookies, and this is your grandson from

Washington. He went to church with us this morning, and he's living with us, you know. A good worker too, I'll tell you."

Grandpa Wilim may be old and he may have a few marbles loose upstairs, but he is still awesome. He has a full head of wild gray hair that Cosmos thinks probably looks the way his own hair will look if he lives to be this old. Gramps has only one eye, having lost the other in an accident years ago, when he was trimming an apple tree on the farm and got an eye poked out by a sharp branch. Cosmos remembers the glass eye, one that looked about the same color as his good eye, though it always pointed higher than the other eye. Gramps is not wearing his glass eye now, and the empty socket sucks the wrinkled eyelid into his forehead, making that part of his face look like it has been dead for months. As he fixes his good eye on Cosmos, his lips open slightly and Cosmos notices spittle crusted in the corners of his mouth. He seems simple, deranged, retarded. He looks like a has-been, a remnant of humanity. His zipper is half open and Cosmos spies a urine bag strapped to the inside of his calf, the bottom of which hangs out from under his pants. His nose looks as if it has grown longer, and the lines around his mouth are sharp and deep, though the rest of his face hardly has a wrinkle. The skin on his cheeks shines, as if it has been polished with a light coat of wax.

The good eye squints and hangs on to Cosmos, and

when Cosmos looks into it, it seems to grow larger and move toward the center of his head.

Gramps lifts a finger and shakes it at Cosmos. "You're the one who was in trouble, aren't you?"

The voice sounds even harsher and more threatening than the comments he heard at church. Here is the real voice of judgment. The one that doesn't beat around the bush. Here it is. Before Cosmos can muster a response, Aunt Minnie interrupts. "Oh, he's not in trouble," she says. "He's living with us. He's a good, hardworking boy—isn't he, Henry?"

"Good worker, good worker, that's the truth," says Uncle Henry.

"Best thing that could happen to a boy like you is to get you out of the city," says Gramps. "Cities will make a young boy like you rotten. You behaving yourself out here?"

Cosmos sees the old Bible open next to Gramps's bed. He wishes Gramps would turn the television back on. It would be good to hear a few of those "love" words from the televangelist about now. "Doing my best," says Cosmos, and reaches for one of the cookies Aunt Minnie has set out on the little round table next to Gramps's chair.

"You get yourself right with the Lord, that's your only chance," says Gramps. "Sit down."

Cosmos sits down.

"I can see you've been in trouble," says Gramps. "I can

see it. Older I get, clearer some things get. Don't need two good eyes to see a boy has been in trouble. You can't hide that sort of thing. The Lord puts the mark of Cain on all sinners. The ones who don't repent. You can't hide sin. It's like a stain that keeps working itself out. I've seen boys like you, they try to hide it. They think, Oh, I can do whatever I want to, nobody sees my sin. Yah."

"William is doing just fine," Aunt Minnie says. "Now, why don't you have one of these cookies. And tell us what you've been up to, then."

"Up to? Up to? Up to here is what I've been up to. Godless place, they treat you like a dog. I'm going home next week, you know. I've had it with this Godless place. I'm going home. I'll take care of myself. What did you do with the keys to my car?"

"They're taking good care of you here, Wilim," says Aunt Minnie. "And this is your home now. You're doing just fine here."

Gramps stares out the window as if he is listening to a voice coming from a distant place outside. Cosmos sees the change come over the old man's face.

"Cora's still at home. I can go there too," he says.

Silence hovers in the room as Aunt Minnie and Uncle Henry look at each other to see who is going to talk next.

"Cora is dead," says Uncle Henry. "She died years ago. You remember that."

"Yes, I remember that," says Gramps. He speaks sharply,

as if they have just insulted him. "You don't have to tell me that again. And tell me whose boy is this again."

"This is Hans's boy, William. They named him after you."

"I can see that," says Gramps. "You've been in trouble, haven't you, boy? I can see it. You can't hide that sort of thing. You've been in big trouble. Cities will rot a boy like you to the core."

"He's doing just fine," says Aunt Minnie.

Gramps grunts, folds his hands on his lap. He grunts again. "I've got to get out of this Godless place. They hide everything you need. I can't even find my car keys. You wouldn't do it to a dog, what they do to you here," he says. "I'm going home next week, you know."

Uncle Henry starts leaning toward the door. "We're going to have to go now," he says. "Why don't you let Minnie help you to bed. You can take a little nap."

"Put him to bed, put him to bed," says Gramps. "You're just like the rest of them. Always 'Put him to bed' in this Godless place." He reaches for the TV controls.

"I'm going to leave the rest of the cookies for you," says Aunt Minnie. "Now, say good-bye to your grandson and we'll come and see you again next week."

"Next week? Don't bother. I'll be home then," he says as the voice of the televangelist rises from the TV set. As Cosmos follows his aunt and uncle out, Gramps says, "You get right with the Lord. You get right with the Lord."

"Do my best," says Cosmos.

"And leave that door open," he says as Aunt Minnie closes it and bends to slide the lock into place.

As they walk down the hallway, Cosmos hears the voice of the televangelist, the sweet, assuring voice, saying, "And the loving arms of the Lord shall embrace His children."

* * *

Alone in his bedroom, Cosmos can no longer imagine any open spaces in Iowa. The place is booby-trapped at every turn with eyes that are watching and ears that are listening. And minds that are judging. He stretches his arms to relax and let Cosmos Coyote sneak out from his hiding place. He digs out his Salal journal and writes:

GIVE ME A FOXHOLE

I don't want to be here
this is not my song
I don't want to be here
the moon has got me wrong
I just play along
but it isn't very fun
when God has got a gun
and his troops are all around
and I'm the one they've found.
They have the advantage
with the Big One on their side.

Help me, keep me out of sight—No!

Give me a foxhole
Give me a foxhole
Give me a foxhole
for my soul.

I don't want to be here
this is not my song
I don't want to be here
the moon has got me wrong
where the eyes are all for ridding
me from any place I'm sitting
and I thought that they were kidding
me when they started their loud bidding
for my soul, they're spitting
at me and I'm a bird just flitting
out of sight. This is fitting—No!

Give me a foxhole
Give me a foxhole
Give me a foxhole
for my soul.

She's a real Jesus freak, man

FROM THE HOG YARDS to the hallways. In Dutch Center Christian Academy, which will be Cosmos's alternative sentence for the next nine months, some things seem familiar: the scrubbed-clean walls and freshly polished floors, the locker-slamming, the squeals and greetings of friends who haven't seen each other for a while, even the new clothes and shoes and the smells of clean bodies garnished with deodorants and hair sprays. This could be Port Swan or any other high school on the first day of classes, and for a few minutes Cosmos feels one with the crowd, getting bumped on the stairways and carried along by the stream of chattering students who, like ants on an ant hill, go every direction at once. Then a few eyes start catching him in quick flicks of attention, followed by longer stares. Some step aside and make a path for him, the stranger.

Cosmos tries to behave the way he would in an unfamiliar airport, minding his own business, reading the signs and directions, but all the while sizing up who and what is going on around him. He especially notices the boys' clothes. Aunt Minnie was right about the khaki pants and short-sleeved blue shirt he is wearing "fitting right in." A few surprises catch his eye: a couple of boys with earring studs, and more than a few in cowboy boots and tight jeans. Little slices of speech catch his ear too: "Rad, man," "Awesome, dude," "Chill, man," "That's mass trouble," "Bummer, man," "To the max, dude," "Gross, man"—a whole list of phrases he hasn't heard since grade school.

Through it all, Cosmos wears his William the Nice smile, ready to say, "Hi, you can call me Bill," to the first person who approaches him.

"Mr. De Haag," comes a voice from his left.

Cosmos turns to see a tall man with large wire-rimmed glasses wearing a brown tweed jacket. "I'm Harold Van Enk. I teach the sociology class you're taking first period."

"Hello," says Cosmos. "You can call me Bill."

Cosmos can see that Mr. Van Enk can see that he, Cosmos, knows that he, Cosmos, is different, but Cosmos can see that Mr. Van Enk can see that he, Cosmos, can see that he, Mr. Van Enk, is different too. Not only do his clothes look like something out of the sixties, but his hair is longer than anyone else's around here, and his manner is different. He has a wedding ring on his left hand, though he walks and moves his hands in a feminine way and his voice sounds more refined than any Iowa male voices Cosmos has heard so far. He almost sounds British. He doesn't fit the square that is the Academy. Misfit to misfit, he and Cosmos eye each other.

"I am aware that you are new at the Academy, Bill," says Mr. Van Enk. "Come by my office before classes start. I'll apprise you of what you missed by not being here your first three years."

That ten-minute conversation with Mr. Van Enk is serious from the moment Cosmos walks into his office. Mr. Van Enk opens up too quickly for comfort, admitting that he doesn't really belong at the Academy. But, he says, not to be here would be a betrayal of his parents, who, along with most of his relatives, live within ten miles of the Academy.

"I am rather like a Jew in Nazi territory," says Van Enk. He knuckles his Brillo-pad eyebrows. "But I know I should dismiss myself from this environment. If I do not leave on my own terms, I shall—to use the vernacular—fry on their terms."

Why is he telling me this? Cosmos wonders, but responds with, "You don't look like a Jew in the middle of Germans. You look like a Hollander in the middle of Hollanders. Just like me."

"Looks can, as we know, be deceiving," says Van Enk. "But listen. I know you must feel uncomfortable here too, and I want to be of as much assistance as I can, all right?"

"I figure if I watch what I say I won't get in trouble," says Cosmos. "It should be easy for you. As easy as it would be for a Holstein cow to hide in a barn of Holstein cows."

"That's good," says Van Enk. "With your wit you might

slip through for a year, Bill, but I wouldn't be too sure of that. Nobody on the faculty is supposed to know that you're here instead of in detention. But we all know it. Most students do too."

"I got my hair cut and everything," says Cosmos. "And the holes I had in my ears for my earrings, they're almost closed over. Nobody notices, I don't think, and, with me living with my uncle and aunt, other people will have to start thinking I'm pretty normal."

"That is where you are incorrect," says Van Enk. "This community can smell a misfit. They don't have to do anything, they don't have to say anything: all they have to do is wait. Just wait. Sooner or later, like a rotten egg, you will float to the surface."

"Then what?" says Cosmos. "They can't shoot me."

"That wouldn't be necessary," says Van Enk. "They'll send you clear messages that they know you are not one of them."

"I can handle that," says Cosmos. "So let them send their messages."

"You don't, shall we say, get it, do you, young man?" says Van Enk. "People around here can smile and cut you off at the same time. It's the isolation factor. They can make you feel empty, hollow, like a rotten egg. Like a shell full of air, you'll float up."

This guy is trying to be my friend? thinks Cosmos. He feels William the Nice slipping away and Cosmos Coyote rearing his head. But he holds back. He distrusts Van Enk more than the harsh voice of judgment that he heard from his grandfather Wilim. "Church has to be safe," says Cosmos in his most mild and controlled voice.

"Church is about as safe for you as a police station for Jack the Ripper," says Van Enk. "You in church, we might say, are like a fox in a chicken coop."

"Wouldn't I be more like a stained-glass smiley-face behind the pulpit?" says Cosmos, and smiles his first natural smile of the day. "No, I know. Me in church is like pee in the communion wine. No, it's like Monica Lewinsky in a nunnery. No, I got it. Me in church is like marijuana at a Dutch Reformed family reunion."

Van Enk does not smile. He stares at Cosmos in a deadpan academic way. "You don't fathom this, do you?" he says. "You really don't fathom this. They're just waiting for you to hang yourself. Already you're talking illegal drugs. I would wager they are taking bets on how soon you get arrested in Iowa."

Cosmos stares at Van Enk. What kind of jerk is this, he thinks, who dares to come in on him without taking time to get to know him? Cosmos can feel Cosmos Coyote getting ready to come out of his cage.

"I think you've got a victim thing going, that's what I think," says Cosmos, and now his own voice has the edge of a preacher, though the words are coming from the heart of Coyote. "I don't believe in being a victim. Point a gun at my head and I'm still free inside my own head. I'm free until somebody pulls the trigger, and even then I'm free to think whatever I want to before I pass out. Keep your head free and nobody can make you a victim. Nobody." His voice is almost shaking.

"Amazing," says Van Enk, and nods approvingly in a way that tells Cosmos Van Enk has been setting him up, egging him on until he got angry and blurted out his defense. "You're some young man," Van Enk goes on. "It's going to be refreshing having you around here this year. I feel as if I have an ally." Van Enk stands up and reaches across the desk to shake Cosmos's hand. "There's the bell. See you in class in a few minutes. And just remember, my door is always open. Come in for a chat any time."

"You set me up," says Cosmos. "You were hassling me just to see how I'd handle it." He doesn't take Van Enk's hand. "That sucks," says Cosmos, and starts for the door.

"I wanted to see if you could stand up for yourself around here. I think you will do just fine," says Van Enk.

"I will," says Cosmos.

Van Enk stands with his arms akimbo, like a proud coach who has taught him an important lesson about how to survive at the Academy, about how to survive in the entire community. The guy is twisted. Maybe this is what might have happened to his dad if he hadn't gotten out of the community when the getting was good.

But Van Enk is fabulous in the classroom. Cosmos sits

through his first lecture, spellbound. He is more interesting and dynamic than any teacher he ever had at Port Swan.

The first student Cosmos meets is a blond, greasy-haired thin boy dressed in tight jeans and cowboy boots and walking as if he has a balloon between his knees. This is the same person Cosmos saw rolling up into the school parking lot in a black Toyota pickup that had the rear window plastered with advertisements for motor oil and motorcycles. Cosmos couldn't believe his eyes when he first saw this character: hardly anything you'd expect to see at a *Christian* academy. But here he is, not exactly hiding who he is. It is also from the mouth of this renegade that Cosmos hears the first unsavory words in the halls: "Holy sheee-it!"

The speaker catches Cosmos's eye—and ear—and Cosmos, stopping in his tracks at the sound of an obscenity, catches his eye, and what Mr. Wild-Haired Foul-Mouth seems to notice most is Cosmos's smile. Misfit to misfit again, they connect. A few hours later, at lunch, Cosmos sees him coming and doesn't try to avoid him. "Over here," he says. "Elmer Vander Hevaalen." He holds out a hand that has a big ring with a skull and crossbones on it. "Yo. You just come 'ere to the big-mamma academy, right?"

"Right," says Cosmos. "My name is Bill." And they sit down for lunch.

In the next few minutes, Cosmos gets a quick taste of Elmer. In Port Swan or Seattle, Cosmos realizes, Elmer might be a skinhead. Here he's some kind of cowboy greaser. But when he talks, Cosmos's ears perk up. He wishes Spruce were here with his drums. Whatever this strange character is, he does have rhythm, and it pours out of his mouth in a flood of words that have more sound than sense. Across the cafeteria dining table, out of earshot of teachers and other students, Elmer's mouth lets loose: "Shivering shark meat, what is this shit they're serving the servants? Hey, look, beaver balls and biscuits. Shit, man, gimme some love meat, I'm on the trail of a fox named Goldilocks. Fork this fodder. I need me some food to put me in the mood, if you know what I'm saying, Jack. And I don't mean a short stack."

"Jeez, man," says Cosmos, "what are you—some kind of wannabe white-boy rapper?"

"Hey, call me the white-boy wrap-around rapper. Don't give me no flap. I'd like this flapper to wrap herself around me."

"Get real," says Cosmos. "You talking about a girl?"

"Talk about, walk about, gawk about! This babe is a babe!"

"Can you talk normal?" says Cosmos.

"Sure, man, just feeling my oats. Toasty-oats, preferably. Though I'd like to roll in the oats with Goldilocks."

Cosmos looks at him, puzzled. "You're outside my radar, man," he says. Cosmos sorts through the kinds of people he has met in his life. Elmer is not there. And Hans never warned him that, among the religious freaks, there'd be the fast-talking high-velocity likes of Elmer.

"I'm a Stealth bomber, man, I like being outa everybody's fuckin' radar. But you look like you've been on a few missions of your own, you know. Sure, I can talk like a fuckin' human being, but what's the fuckin' point, you know? Fuckin' boring."

"You just entered my radar," says Cosmos.

"So—you going to shoot me down? Throw your sloppy joe in my face?"

"Nope. But you can have my beaver balls and biscuits. You can have this tiger piss too."

Cosmos pushes the remains of his lunch toward Elmer, then turns his head at the sight of Cherlyn from church. She has just sat down at the next table. She folds her hands and prays before she takes the food off her lunch tray. Actually, all the students fold their hands and say grace except him and Elmer, but Cherlyn doesn't just say grace, she prays for a good minute or two—and her lips move as she prays.

"That's Cherlyn," says Elmer. "She's the smartest goody-goody in the whole friggin' school. Too bad her brain gets in the way of her body."

"I met her at church," says Cosmos. Cherlyn is not dressed in the same blue dress that she wore at church, but blue is her color and she does have on a one-piece blue flowered dress. She looks up and sees Cosmos staring at her. She gives him her sweet smile that shows a good set of white teeth, and when the mouth smiles, the whole face smiles.

"She's a real Jesus freak, man," Elmer whispers. "She can be a real pain in the ass. Brains and body and religion. Now, there's a combo for you."

Cosmos is not surprised about her religion, and he has just noticed her body. But brains? The conversation they had at church was not exactly a mind-bender, though Cosmos thought it might be a setup for something to follow. Cherlyn gets up and carries her lunch toward Elmer and Cosmos. "Mind if I sit?" she says.

"Be my guest," says Cosmos, and watches the way her hips swing to the side and her leg rises quickly as she steps modestly over the bench and seats herself across the table from him and Elmer. Her eyes are blue and bright, but when they focus on Cosmos the lids close into a near-squint. The eyes are calm and intense. It's almost a drugged look, but Cosmos is sure it isn't.

"Good to see you, William," she says. Her voice comes right out of her eyes, not with a squinting sound but with a round and soothing warmth. So much sincerity—so much sunshine!—in a simple statement.

"Good to see you again too," says Cosmos in the voice of William the Nice. He hasn't had the chance to look straight into her eyes at such close range before, and now he can't take his eyes off them. They really do look like the eyes of someone who is peacefully high. But it's not that slowed-down, watching-the-grass-breathe kind of high. Cherlyn's eyes are alive and upbeat while looking serene at the same time. Intense eyes with a hint of longing in them. But for what?

She does have charisma, a lot of it. He looks at her sweet face again, trying to see past the warmth to what is very likely her secret agenda.

Cherlyn unwraps her sandwich and takes a good bite. "I heard that you're a musician," she says. "Guitar?"

He is barely able to make out what she is saying, because, to Cosmos's surprise, she talks with food in her mouth. There is only one other woman in the world he has ever seen chewing and talking at the same time, and that was skinny Salal. But nothing else about Cherlyn is remotely like Salal.

"I play the guitar a little," he says.

Cherlyn swallows and takes a sip of milk. "Really?" she says in her sweet and earnest way. "I'm the student council president. Maybe we could get you to play for us in chapel sometime."

Cosmos was already introduced to school chapel at ten-fifteen. It's like a morning recess, except here, instead of giving the body some air and exercise, you're supposed to give the soul some air and exercise. Chapel happens every school day.

"I don't think that would be a good idea," says Cosmos.

He puts his hand to his cheek, and he knows that without wanting to he is grinning coyly at her. He glances up to see her reaction and again finds himself looking directly into her eyes.

She takes another bite of her sandwich and keeps looking at him. Cosmos sees in her eyes a sweet dreaminess, and a playful friendliness, like the eyes of harbor seals when they stick their heads up a few yards offshore and point their wet noses at you. Her eyes look so innocent and safe. Whatever danger may be lying behind her intentions, it feels good having her sit across the table from him.

Elmer has begun to squirm in Cherlyn's presence. Without finishing his food, he says in straight, boring English that he has to split. Cherlyn stays perched like a white dove across from Cosmos, talking to him in her soothing voice and encouraging him to talk about himself. But Cosmos's warning antennae are out, not because her company isn't sweet—97 percent honey—but the rest will probably be arsenic, and the arsenic will be God-talk. He's sure of it.

When he gets home that night, he sorts through the people he has met. All of these people seem off-key: Van Enk staying in a community where he doesn't belong; Elmer, who is just strange and friendly enough to trip Cosmos up and be his ticket back to Washington and Juvie. Like Uncle Henry says, one thing could lead to another.

And then there's Cherlyn. When he closes his eyes to

sleep, her face hovers in his mind. Behind the friendly dovelike smile, he imagines an albino vulture sizing up a man lost in the desert. It would be so easy to fall for her friendly invitations. She is like a tricky cop who knows how to get you to sign a summons without your realizing what you've gotten yourself into.

He puts on his headphones and cranks up an old Beck CD. Now, more than ever, he knows that his only protection is the privacy of his room and his music. And of his own mind.

Religion gives you the heebie-jeebies?

COSMOS WEARS HIS WILLIAM the Nice smile through the first days of school. William the Nice avoids the basketball players, who probably want to give him a shove on the stairway to see what he's made of; William the Nice says hello to the teachers in the hallways so they'll stop looking skeptically at him; William the Nice bows his head in chapel in case the principal is watching. William the Nice is the face in the crowd. William the Nice keeps his nose clean.

But Cosmos doesn't know which face to wear when Cherlyn approaches him in the cafeteria again. Cherlyn, with her wheat-blond hair cut like a shingle across her forehead—hair as sharp-edged as the chrome on a car grille above her high-beam eyes, and the rest of her hair like the wings of that big vulture he imagined her to be, hair that now lifts slightly off her shoulders as she turns toward him, and he feels like a rabbit, crouched under her gaze. But when she walks toward him, Cosmos sees that she is not dressed in her usual modest dress. Instead, she wears tight-fitting jeans and a blouse that may be buttoned high under her chin but shows the actual shape of the person underneath.

As she approaches, she does not try to flaunt herself. Herself doesn't need any flaunting. The fitted blouse shows the shape of her breasts, and the blue jeans have transformed her lower body into elegant legs that have both the shape and the muscles of a farm girl.

"Mind if I sit down?" she says, gesturing with her food tray toward the empty spot across from him at the table. Cosmos sees faces turn toward them as she approaches his table.

"I could use some company," says Cosmos. He tries to allow an honest Cosmos Coyote smile to break through the stubborn defense of his William the Nice lips as she places her tray down, then sits with her back to him before swinging her blue-jeaned legs across the bench and under the table. She looks up at him with her blue eyes, but a real smile won't come free on Cosmos's face.

She folds her hands and says her grace. As she prays, Cosmos notices freckles on her cheeks that he had not noticed before, then her dainty ears under her hair. She has on a pale and subtle pink lipstick. Her lips are small and pucker a bit when she is not smiling. Sweet lips. Even in her new body-revealing getup, she looks innocent and modest. Right now she doesn't in any way look like the white bird of prey he imagined. Cosmos squinches his face to try to get his lips to relax.

When she finishes and looks up, Cosmos smiles stiffly.

"What kind of music do you play?" she asks. "I'm the editor of *The Messenger*, and I wanted to talk to you about writing a music column."

"What?" says Cosmos.

She repeats the question and the request. "I thought, if you didn't want to play your guitar in chapel, maybe you'd write something about music."

Cosmos stammers for an answer, then says, "I'm not the best music critic, at least not writing about it. Maybe I'm not your man for the job." He has been working on his false smile so much that he still has trouble controlling his expression. He licks his lips.

She licks her lips too. She leans across the table and looks into his eyes. In spite of her beauty, he still waits for a judgmental mind behind that innocent face. But then she says, "I'm not the worst editor. If you know music, let me worry about the words. Give it a try. If it doesn't work out, no harm done."

She takes a big bite of food off her plate and chews hard. For someone with such small lips, she has no trouble handling a hefty mouthful of food.

"What sort of music are you into?" says Cosmos.

She swallows and says, "Oh, anything that's on. I listen to the public-radio classical station sometimes. I like folk rock and some of the new country-ballad things. I like Christian rock if it's not too rocky. Country is strong around here, and of course I listen to some of that. A little bit of everything, I guess. But I'm pretty open about music."

When she doesn't have food in her mouth when she talks, her speech is exact and cool. Her precise way of talking reminds Cosmos of the time he was interviewed by the Port Swan social worker who had taken him in for his first "diversion" interview.

"I have to tell you," says the honest voice of Cosmos Coyote, "I have a feeling you're not really here to talk music."

She looks at him quizzically. "What do you mean?"

"I have a feeling you're getting ready to talk religion to me, aren't you?"

"What on earth made you say that?" She leans across the table toward him, her eyes wide, as if she is surprised. Or insulted. "Do you think I'm the kind of person who would trick people into something?"

"I didn't mean that," says Cosmos, and wonders what kind of hole his quick tongue has dug him into. "It's just that I'm kind of uncomfortable with all the religious stuff around here. I guess I'm just not used to it."

"I don't talk religion much to anybody," she says. "I have trouble enough trying to live my faith. And you don't strike me as somebody who needs any special work. Didn't you go to church in Washington?"

"Nope," he says.

"And you got in trouble, right?"

"Not for not going to church," he says.

"I'm not a preacher," she says. "Two of my uncles are, but I'm not. If you want something more than what you've got, I'm sure you'll ask for it—and I'll send Uncle Reverend Ralph on to you."

"You're the friendliest person at this school," says Cosmos. "Maybe it's just that I'm not sure who and what I can trust. I'd like to know at least one person I can talk straight to."

"I'll try to talk straight with you, all right?" she says. "And I'm sorry other people aren't being friendlier. You don't look uncomfortable. You really look very comfortable. You look great, actually—I mean, very comfortable in that shirt. And I feel like you're somebody I've known for a long time. Aren't you comfortable with me?"

She actually acts a little bit nervous for a change. "Oh, I'm pretty comfortable. With you, sure. I mean, I appreciate that you're so nice to me and everything, but—"

"But what?"

"Maybe I'm not so comfortable. Maybe I feel I have to be on guard around here as the new kid. Maybe I'd like to quit feeling that I have to be a phony wherever I go. I'd like to be honest with somebody."

"You can be honest with me," she says. "I promise I won't preach at you, and I'll be honest with you too."

"So how did you know I was in trouble?"

"It's no secret. Our minister even told us—not the details, but he told us we should be supportive."

"So you are trying to rescue me."

"When I look at you, I don't see somebody who needs rescuing."

"What does that mean?"

She looks even more nervous now. "I'm digging myself in a hole," she says. "All right, I'll be honest. I kind of like you, and I admire the way you're holding up here. Your real name is Cosmos, right?"

"So?"

"I'm just trying to be honest. I don't want to pretend I don't know that. Would you rather be called Cosmos?"

"You called me William at church when I first met you."

"That's because I was told that's what you wanted to be called. I didn't want to make you uncomfortable."

"Just exactly how much *have* people been talking about me?" says Cosmos.

"I heard that you were in trouble in Washington and that you were coming here to get away from a bad situation. That's all. Nothing negative about you as a person. Nothing."

"I'll bet."

"I don't blame you for being skeptical. People around here do talk a lot, but I judge people from what I hear and see of them directly. I don't listen to rumors." She takes a bite of food and starts talking again. "I wouldn't put up with any bad talk unless you were right there to defend yourself."

Cosmos looks down at the table between them, then up at her, then down at the table. When he finally raises his eyes again, he says, "Hey, you can call me Cosmos if you want to. It's just that I'd rather you didn't call me that in front of other people who know me as Bill. They might think it's pretty weird and really start talking."

"Agreed. Some secrets aren't a bad thing. I'll call you Cosmos when other people aren't around. Cosmos."

"Good," says Cosmos. "Now I'll be honest with you. Everybody praying and reading the Bible all the time, you'd think the end of the world was coming. All this religious crap around here gives me the heebie-jeebies."

"Religion gives you the heebie-jeebies?"

"Yeah. Big-time."

"Not having religion would give me the heebie-jeebies."

"Are you going evangelical?"

"No," she says. "I'm being honest."

"I think a person needs to figure out for themselves what they want to believe, all right?"

"I agree. It's just that I feel God has a plan for me and I need to figure out how best to follow it."

"I can't get into that," says Cosmos. "That's too woo-woo for me."

Cherlyn laughs. "I'm not a witch." She raises her arms. "Wooooooo-woooooo."

"I'm glad you've got a sense of humor," says Cosmos. "I was afraid all you did was pray and study. And just what are you going to study when you get out of here?"

Suddenly her manner is more formal. "I want to go to college and major in political science or prelaw."

"You want to be a friggin' lawyer?"

"Excuse your French, I want to study law as preparation to be a political leader. Vice president, maybe president. Who knows? Senator at least. Maybe mayor or something first. I like history. I want to understand what leadership means. I've been studying the presidents."

"Of the United States?"

"Yes, of the United States," she says. "I'm studying Van Buren right now. He's from the Dutch Reformed tradition too, you know."

"Which one was Van Buren?" says Cosmos.

"The eighth one," says Cherlyn. "The one with the side-burns."

"Oh yeah, but he was nothing, right? I mean, who remembers Van Buren?"

"I do," she says. "I can trace my Dutch roots back six generations, just the way he could."

Saved by the bell.

"I'll tell you another time," she says. "See you in English."

When she gets up, many heads turn their way. Cosmos guesses that now more talk will be circulating about how

Cherlyn the Jesus messenger has gone to work on the delinquent from Washington. But the eyes that stay focused on Cherlyn are all male eyes. Cherlyn notices too. She picks up her books and holds them against her breasts as if she is trying to conceal them as she walks away. The male eyes follow her to the cafeteria exit. She can't conceal her tight jeans, but she takes big steps and disappears fast. Now the boys turn to each other, gloating and smirking. It's not hard for Cosmos to guess what they're talking about. He watches them for only a second, then gets up and makes his own quick exit.

* * *

In bed that night, Cosmos does his usual sorting through the day. Cherlyn fills the screen of his mind. Attracted to a girl who is into God up to her eyeballs. Wanting to follow God's plan for her life? Christian rock if it's not too rocky? How can I be attracted to a girl who is everything I'm not?

Cosmos puts his headphones on and listens to some rap, the crudest thing he can find in his stack, the one he hides on the bottom to make sure Aunt Minnie doesn't find it. Even with the heavy beat, even with the obscene words hitting his eardrums, he still finds himself imagining what kind of music Cherlyn is listening to. Probably the same Christian station Aunt Minnie has turned on downstairs.

He tries to get rid of any thoughts of Cherlyn by picturing Salal in his mind as the music pounds in his ears. Salal dancing in her snaky way, or Salal standing motionless in her chilly elegance, her arms crossed, and looking straight through him. He turns every bit of his head energy into not thinking about Cherlyn, but Salal blends and fades in his mind. Her long bony arms turn into strands of rubber. She becomes like a Salvador Dalí painting, her arms getting longer and drooping like the hands on a Dalí clock, her neck elongating like a stretched piece of taffy. And in the place of disintegrating Salal appears the sunshiny face of Cherlyn. Cherlyn. Trying not to think about her is like the game he plays where he's trying not to think about an itch he has on his nose when he's trying to fall asleep at night, and the harder he doesn't think about it, the more it itches.

Cosmos turns off the music and lies staring up in his bed. He picks a small spot on the ceiling and focuses on it. I'll hypnotize myself into a totally blank mind. But his mind is not blank. Her smile breaks through the dark screen on the inside of his eyelids. And then the eyes, looking at him deeply, serenely, their big blueness saying nothing more than, "I see you. I really see you." Am I imagining affection? he wonders. Or is she just on a mission to save my soul? But what about those tight blue jeans? She must have known exactly how dressing the way she did would affect him. She had to know, didn't she?

Give me a break, Lord

UNCLE HENRY WAKES COSMOS up early on Saturday morning. Some lethal disease hit the penful of forty-pound Yorkshire pigs and killed six of them before Uncle Henry had a chance to get the vet over with his syringes to stop the disease in its tracks.

Six white pigs get flung onto the manure spreader along with the brown filth from the pigpens. Cosmos recognizes some of the pigs. He fed one of them from his hand just yesterday. They were friendly little critters and acted like pets. Ten minutes later, he sees the dead pigs flying through the air like so many pieces of torn sheets as Uncle Henry drives the tractor with the manure spreader behind it, and the powerful churning spreader hurls its load of goodies into the air and onto the stubble fields left after the oats harvest. Flying dead pigs. Maybe farmers don't have time to think about dead animals, but to Cosmos it looks so easy, almost ruthless.

Corn-harvesting time is approaching, and when Uncle Henry gets back with the empty manure spreader, they'll fill the tractors with diesel fuel so they won't have to do it on Sunday, when all unnecessary work is supposed to be avoided. Aunt Minnie prepares to avoid unnecessary Sunday work too, by emptying the clothes hampers so she'll be ready for washing on Monday morning.

"Saturday is clean-up day," says Uncle Henry, as if Cosmos hasn't noticed. "This way we can rest and worship on the Lord's Day. You see."

By three o'clock, everything is as sparkling as things on the farm can get. With his hands still aching from the day's work, Cosmos picks up the old three-speed bike that Uncle Henry has fixed up and takes off down the gravel road to relax. He is in his second mile when he sees something along the edge of the cornfield. It's unbelievable, it's undeniable. It's marijuana. Huge six-foot plants beaming like palm trees, swaying like hula dancers. At first, he thinks he must be mistaken. He lays the bike down and walks into the ditch with its knee-high grass and up the bank to the edge of the cornfield. No doubt about it: a half-dozen marijuana plants five times taller than anything flourishing under grow-lamps in a Port Swan attic—and one of them is bent over a barbed-wire fence with its seedy top already dried in the sun. Was this some other person's preparation for harvesting? It doesn't matter. He jerks the seedy top off the dried plant and stuffs it into his shirt. Now, where, when, and how to smoke it. He doesn't have any matches, but he'll get around this problem as soon as he gets home. With Probation Officer Jonsma keeping his distance, life in

Iowa just might not be half as boring as he feared.

Cosmos finds some matches and an aluminum Coke can in the basement. He takes these into the grove, presses a little pea-sized indentation on the side of the can with a pebble, then punctures a tiny hole in it. He packs a good pinch of marijuana into the indentation and uses the opening of the pop can to inhale. He takes three deep hits and walks back out onto the yard. He gets on the bike and pedals slowly down the gravel road surrounded by corn and bean fields. He waits for the ripening world of Iowa to transform, to bend a little, to mellow out.

In a few minutes he definitely feels something, but it is not the kind of high he expects, not a mellowing slowdown of the world, not a heightening of colors and sounds and smells. Instead, it is a blurring and numbing. He feels dizzy, like he has just had some cheap, strong wine, and then the pain begins, a distinct ache that punches its way into his head directly above his eyebrows. Along with the headache, he feels nauseated. Iowa marijuana is not about to compete with corn as the state's leading cash crop.

"That is some bad shit," he says aloud and stops his bike. He sits down alongside the road and stares into the ditch and the bean field. Tastes and sounds are sharper now, but all the tastes and sounds he is aware of are from his own body. He can hear his heart beating in a lazy, loud thump, and he can taste the inside of his mouth—it's like mildew, or the kind of moldy taste a bad grape can leave.

Then he sees the carcasses of those pigs that got spread on the stubble field along with the manure. They lie out in the middle of the field like weathered little tombstones, and he feels in his gut there is something wrong. Sure, pigs are beasts. Sure, they're not human. Sure, the air smells like baked pig shit most of the time, but that doesn't mean folks should go treating pigs like manure to rot and to be pecked at by the crows.

He sits staring at the dead pigs out in the field. The longer and harder he looks, the worse he feels. Just yesterday the warm blood was flowing through their veins. Pigs outnumber people four to one in Iowa? So much for the rights of the majority. Pig heart valves are used in humans, he remembers. John Wayne, may he rest in peace, died with a pig valve in his heart. And insulin from pigs saves human lives. They are fellow creatures who shared the same planet, breathed the same air. Cosmos feels sad for them, then angry on behalf of those dead pigs lying out there half covered with manure. The anger gives way to embarrassment: what would Uncle Henry and Aunt Minnie think if they saw him feeling bad over a few stupid pigs? He looks around to see if anyone is watching him.

That night, at the supper table, he is especially quiet. He folds his hands for devotions, but he doesn't dare close his eyes, because his head still aches and he fears he might topple off his chair. He doesn't make eye contact with his uncle or aunt, because he is afraid that if he does he'll go on a rampage about people not having the decency to treat the pigs like fellow creatures when they're dead. At least Aunt Minnie has prepared chicken instead of ham for supper.

After Cosmos has taken only a few bites, Aunt Minnie asks if he's all right. When he says he is, she doesn't probe. After dinner he watches *Cops* on TV for a while, until Minnie walks in and says, "I don't like the way they talk on that show sometimes. And it's so depressing. So depressing. All those poor people who haven't found the Lord."

Cosmos has been sympathizing with the pathetic slobs who are being run down in ghetto alleys, not with the good-guy cops and their dogs and spotlights, but he holds his Coyote tongue.

Uncle Henry walks in. "We like to prepare ourselves for the Lord's Day on Saturday nights," he says. "I guess you might say it is the custom around here. You see."

"That's cool," says Cosmos. "I'll go upstairs and listen to some quiet music."

The phony face of William the Nice almost falls off as Cosmos heads for the stairs like a godly little saint who is getting ready for, as Uncle Henry says, the Lord's Day. When he enters his room, he finds that the hot and muggy weather has decided to spend the night there. So have all the smells of the neighborhood feedlots, which have gathered in his room like a congregation of stink bombs. No Saturday clean-up can touch that smell. It's no longer the dope that's getting into Cosmos's head, it's the real honest-to-God smell of Iowa on a simmering night. Cosmos goes to close his window, but when he does he just traps all the bad smells inside his room, traps the bad smells and doesn't let any circulating air into the stifling vacuum. He knows his uncle and aunt could afford to have air conditioning with air filters to make the evenings inside tolerable. This is one of their perversities. It probably has something to do with their religion: punish yourself enough while you're on earth and maybe God will go easy on you in eternity.

Cosmos lies down on his bed and thinks of the astronauts. Where does their bad air go? Does it stay inside their suits or is it vented into outer space? There is no outer space here. There isn't any space that isn't infested with bad air. It's as if he's in an outhouse that hasn't been aired out for five years. And the walls are closing in. And the temperature is rising. He gets up and opens his window again. This isn't that Iowa weed, he assures himself again. This is really the way this freaking state smells.

Cosmos's head swims. The smells come marching in like little inflated rubber figures in a toy factory coming alive at night and starting to dance, weak-kneed but graceful, silently across the plains, sleepers holding hands. The seething cattle manure struts and waves across the wilting cornstalks and the sour-mooded chicken droppings peck their way through loose feathers and are airborne.

Meanwhile, the pig muck that has been baking into a buff army-green bubbles a little and exhales itself into the humid air, where the tiny particles of warm mist sponge in the odors. The smells come together, in layers at first, each with its own density, a three-layered stench cake undulating and then slowly mixing—less like a cake than a latte, with the rich hog-manure smell on the bottom dark as French roast, the milder cattle stench in the middle like warm whole milk, and all of it topped with the foamy lemon-sharp smell of chicken crap, the three odors blending in the hot autumn heat into a modern barnyard tonic.

No babies will be born nine months from tonight in this community, Cosmos thinks. If there is an aphrodisiac, this smell must be the anti-aphrodisiac. Iowa birth control. If enough people are smelling what he is smelling, people from the Dutch Center church won't have to be marching in front of any Planned Parenthood clinics for a while.

Cosmos looks out into the muggy night, dark as the cargo hold of a ship. Maybe this is what the old cargo holds really smelled like. And isn't that what the Iowa farms are? A cargo hold for the world: corn, the biggest export crop of all. And beef. Pork. Chicken. Even turkeys. And how long will it be before Iowa soybeans will replace half the dead-animal products of the world? What would it be like to lie on your stomach next to a window in an Iowa farmhouse on a hot night smelling tofu instead of the fecal brew the different flavors of animal manure produce when fermenting together in the vat of a warm Iowa sky? What a relief that would be: soy smell in place of this super-hybrid animal-manure smell. Cosmos almost gags.

To blast away his bad attitude, Cosmos turns on the radio and finds a country-Western station. This one is the country-Western golden-oldies station—first a song by Waylon Jennings and then one by Willie Nelson. He hums along with Willie. This guy is not bad. Willie Nelson, if you're gonna be country, you're the way to be, he says to himself. He turns up the Willie Nelson song a little louder. Aunt Minnie does not turn on the Christian radio station to war with Willie.

By midnight, Cosmos still isn't asleep. His headache is gone, but his mind still aches. No music of any sort can save him from the hell that is Iowa. If I were locked up in a juvenile-detention center in Washington State right now, wouldn't I be feeling the cool sea breezes, clear and clean, blowing over me? he wonders.

* * *

Sunday morning, Cosmos wakes up with a headache. An Iowa-dope hangover? He comes in from morning chores and slumps down on a kitchen chair.

Aunt Minnie notices he is not well. "You need more rest," she says. "You worked hard yesterday, and I don't want to see you getting sick." She puts her hand on his forehead. "You don't have a fever."

"Maybe I shouldn't go to church," Cosmos suggests.

"That would be all right," says Aunt Minnie. "You can rest here and follow that part of the Commandment that tells us to rest on the Sabbath."

When he hears the car leave the farm, Cosmos goes to his room and hooks up his speakers. This will be one private little jam session without having to use the headphones.

Like me, Iowa is a battleground of contradictions, he thinks. One minute Iowa seems like a cesspool, and the next minute like a big scrub brush that is trying to clean him up. It's more than clean-up Saturday that's haunting him right now. It's how clean all the cars are. It's how clean-cut most of the students at the Academy are. It's the chapel and church and praying all the time. It's the straight rows of corn in all the fields. It's the church steeples sticking out all over Dutch Center like long barrels from a gun emplacement. It occurs to him that the cesspool part of Iowa might be the honest part, the part that stinks, the part that grows headache dope. The phony part is the clean, the straight and narrow side. This part is like a sterilizing solution. No, even harsher than that. He sees himself and every other free-spirited person who might be lurking in this community as people who are being dunked and preserved in embalming fluid. Stay here long enough and I'll be like a dead pig fetus preserved in a bottle of formaldehyde.

To keep from turning into a pickled pig fetus, Cosmos knows he has to keep working on his two faces, two voices, two totally different beings.

William the Nice will fit right in. William the Nice will watch his tongue. Right now, Cosmos decides to celebrate the privacy of being Cosmos Coyote while he has the chance. "Cosmos Coyote!" he declares aloud to the open windows. "You can come out of hiding!"

But already the hog-yard smells are waking up and prowling the air for a victim. It's almost enough to make the Coyote in Cosmos whimper and hide. The stench is in the clothes he wore to do chores as much as it is in the air. He sniffs his clothes. Now, like rich caramel-syrup smells from outside poured over the hot-fudge smells that are in his clothes, he's a veritable banana split of bad odors. Maybe I should think of the cesspool smells as the Coyote side of Iowa, the part that is telling the truth. Maybe this is what Sundays for him should really be for: a time to face the truth, and the truth doesn't smell very good. I've got to face the truth of this place or I'm going to go brain-dead.

He takes his clothes off and sits at his small desk to write his way through his aching body and throbbing head:

BRAIN DEAD

I'm lost in the cornfields
in the land of high yields
feeling kind of low
'cause I had a bad high now

feeling kind of slow now
this place is going to my head
and I'm going brain-dead.
Give me a break, Lord.

Cosmos tries finding a melody but runs into dead ends, runs into tunes that sound like tunes that have already been used. He tears the page from his journal and puts it in an envelope addressed to Rhody, so that he'll be the only one to read it. He takes the little raven totem that his dad gave him and rubs it with his thumb. Through his window he can see barn swallows sitting on the electric wires, their tan chests glowing in the sunlight, their little throats singing against the oppressive air.

Thanks—I needed that

MONDAY MORNING, COSMOS still feels like a moldy biscuit, but he gets up, helps Uncle Henry feed the cattle, and gets ready for school. It might be the Iowa diet, with no particular culprit making me feel down, he thinks. He hasn't seen a piece of fresh fruit for three weeks. It's not as if there's no fruit in the supermarkets, but the only use Aunt Minnie ever thinks of for apples is apple pie. Even the juices she buys are odd mixtures of sugar and chemicals with a little fruit for flavoring. And vegetables? Aunt Minnie thinks that all vegetables need cream the way bread needs butter. Then again, maybe his misery is a strain of Iowa flu that everybody else is immune to.

At breakfast, he says he is not hungry, but Aunt Minnie says he at least has to have some milk and cold cereal, even though she thinks eggs and bacon would give him more protein to get through the day. Cosmos catches the bus with his head almost clear and his stomach almost settled. My body might be declaring war on all the bad ingredients that have been poured into it, he thinks, and the smart part of my body is trying to get rid of them. That would make this miserable feeling a healthy feeling.

When he gets off the bus at school, he watches the herd of students ahead of him, pushing toward the front door. They remind him of the cattle he watched pushing and shoving to get at the feeders an hour ago. His whole body resists being part of that mass right now. Unless he could see Cherlyn among them. But he can't.

He considers skipping school for the day, just turning around and sneaking off downtown. No, he knows that is not an option. Merchants telephone the high school if they see students downtown. Elmer told him that. He decides instead that he'll avoid the rest of the students for as long as he can by entering the building through the back door. The longer walk around the gymnasium and past the band room that sits behind the gym will give him a few more minutes by himself.

He circles around behind the gym and follows a well-beaten path through the dense bushes that huddle against the building. He has gone about twenty feet when he hears voices, male student-age voices, talking just above a whisper. He doesn't want to walk in on something that is none of his business, something that might get him in trouble with whoever is there. He walks slowly, pushing the bushes back carefully with each step. They hear him at the exact moment he sees them and smells what they are doing. A huddling threesome are sitting on their haunches in the middle of a small cloud of marijuana smoke. They look up, but do not panic when they see him. They just look at him warily, the way they might study a stray dog to decide if it's dangerous.

"It's cool," says Cosmos.

"It's the dude from Washington," one of them says.

Cosmos doesn't know any of their names, but he's surprised at their appearance. Every one of them is neat and tidy, totally wholesome-looking. One of them he recognizes as a boy who sings in the junior choir. The other two are only vaguely familiar. They all look young, like freshmen. One has a small ceramic pipe and holds it toward Cosmos.

"No thanks," says Cosmos, remembering the misery that accompanied his last experience with Iowa marijuana.

They all hear it at the same time: heavy footsteps coming down the path through the bushes. As if on a practice drill, the three dive onto their stomachs and squirm away into a small space under the shrubbery that looks no bigger than space for a badger. They clearly have an escape-route plan and probably know exactly where they are squirming off to. Cosmos is left standing alone in the middle of the lingering smell of marijuana smoke. He's not about to dive on his stomach into the unknown, that mysterious dark opening under the shrubbery. Instead, he runs, pushing and shoving his way through the bushes until he breaks out into open air. He faces a long stretch of grass before he can reach the back door of the school and disappear inside.

Whoever is coming down the path will almost certainly see him before he can get there. His other option is to run to his right and hide behind the band building. He makes his choice quickly and bolts behind the band building, all the way around to the opposite side. Like playing hide-and-seek, he crouches and peeks around the corner of the building to see who will emerge from the bushes. Not one but two teachers step out onto the grass, and they have that quick and urgent look of hunting dogs on the scent of something. They smelled the marijuana, all right.

"I'll go back and check the bushes," says one, "you go that way," and he points toward the band building.

Cosmos's only option now is to run for the long line of school buses and hide behind them and wait for the danger to pass. He gets to the buses and positions himself so that he can see the band building through the windows of one of the buses, and waits as his heart pounds in his ears. His hands are shaking. It could so easily be all over for him in one stupid little incident on his way to school. Stupid, stupid, he thinks to himself. Detention back in Washington starts feeling like a much worse option than what he has been going through. Right now the idea of saying grace before every meal and smelling hog yards every night does not seem so bad. But the worst fear is that if he is caught for being on the scene of a cloud of marijuana smoke his friendship with Cherlyn will be over before he even gets to know who and what she really is.

As the bell for first period rings, both teachers appear next to the bushes. They talk for a few seconds and then start walking toward the back door of the school. They disappear inside, and in another minute the three boys appear from the bushes. They're going to get caught as soon as they walk in the back door, Cosmos thinks. But they don't go in the back door. They take a few steps, kneel down next to a basement window, lift off a frame of security bars as easily as if they were opening a door. One opens the small window, and again the three disappear, this time into the school. The last one in pulls the security-bar frame back into place and closes the window. They not only had an escape plan, they had a re-entry plan. Cosmos feels relief for them, but not for himself. In a few minutes, he hears the second bell ring. He is about to have his first tardy. No big deal, he figures. He'd rather be late for school than caught as a suspect for smoking marijuana.

"Sorry I'm late," he says as he walks into the front office.

The secretary looks up and recognizes him. "Oh, let's not worry about it this once, Bill," she says, and writes him a pass without asking any questions.

Van Enk calls on him in sociology class and he manages to give an answer that shows he has read the assignment.

At ten-fifteen, he files in with the rest of the students for the twenty-minute chapel service. Principal Marksema cuts the chapel service short for "an important announcement."

"As some of you already know," he begins, "we have had a rare and serious case of theft. The theft occurred during first-period gym class today. All items were taken from boys' clothes that were properly stored under lock and key in the storage baskets. The perpetrator, or perpetrators, picked the padlocks of four separate storage baskets. Among the items taken were a Swiss Army knife, two wallets with approximately ninety dollars in cash, one class ring, a silver money clip, and three wristwatches valued at two hundred and fifty dollars. The Dutch Center Police have not yet been called, because we prefer to handle a matter such as this ourselves. I am expecting the perpetrator or perpetrators to return the items, and to confess their misdeeds, before ten o'clock tonight. I will be in my office, and the perpetrator or perpetrators may telephone me there to discuss this matter privately. If a confession is not forthcoming, the Dutch Center Police will be called for a full investigation. Enough said. Let us pray together."

The bleachers are silent. A few students turn to the persons next to them, then quickly return to very stiff positions facing the principal on his little podium set up on the gym stage. Cosmos folds his hands and lowers his head with the others.

"Our Heavenly Father," the principal begins, "You know our needs and You know our weaknesses. We know that You reach out to those who have sinned, even as You reach out to those who have been sinned against. Move now, O Lord, the heart of him or of those who have sinned against Your Commandment, even as You have told us, 'Thou shalt not steal,' and move too the hearts of those who have been wronged so that at the appropriate time justice may be tempered with mercy. In His name, amen."

It doesn't take a rocket scientist to realize I could be in deep shit, Cosmos thinks as he walks out. First period? For the first fifteen minutes, I was unaccounted for.

As he walks down the hall, he can feel the heat of suspicion float his way, though he knows another suspect is probably Elmer. Or could it be the three boys who were smoking in the bushes? No, they probably made it to class on time and have nothing to explain. But how could a guilty person not respond to the principal's little speech and prayer? If these people are as good as they're supposed to be, he assures himself, they will confess and return the stolen items before ten o'clock tonight.

At noon, for the first time since school started, nobody approaches his table in the cafeteria—not Elmer, not Cherlyn, not anyone. His stomach has begun to settle, but he still can't imagine touching the miserable-looking cafeteria food in front of him. He takes a few sips of milk, one quick bite of the canned peaches that are passing for today's dessert, and heads up for Van Enk's office to give him a chance to be the support he promised he would be.

Van Enk is there, his own home-packed lunch spread out

across his desk. All vegetables. He is listening to classical music on his tape player and reading the local newspaper as he eats. "Please be seated," says Van Enk, and closes his office door.

"I didn't do it," says Cosmos.

"That's good," says Van Enk.

"I think everybody else thinks I did," says Cosmos. "Everybody's avoiding me like the plague."

"If you didn't do it, I hope you're not being set up," says Van Enk.

"Why would anyone set me up? That doesn't make sense."

"What I told you on the first day," says Van Enk. "If they have targeted you as a rotten egg, they'll do whatever it takes to prove themselves right."

"I can't believe how much you distrust these people," says Cosmos. "You distrust them more than I do."

"It's not a matter of distrusting them per se," he says. "It's a matter of knowing them too well. If you didn't do it, be advised not to leave your locker open or your coat hanging downstairs in the coatroom. Don't leave anything around where some unsavory individual could put the stolen goods into your possession."

"What?" says Cosmos. "I haven't done anything to anybody around here. What kind of jerks are you saying go to this place? This is supposed to be a Christian school."

"Correct," says Van Enk. "But you are not, shall we say,

one of us. And if you are different, you are going to be targeted. As I informed you."

"I don't believe you," says Cosmos. "And I'm not going to listen to any more of this crap. I thought you would give me some support." Cosmos gets up and walks toward the door.

"Mr. De Haag," Van Enk says, as Cosmos reaches the door. "It would be easier if I knew where you were the first fifteen minutes of class."

"Not stealing," says Cosmos, and walks out.

As much as he doesn't like what Van Enk has said to him, Cosmos walks straight for the coatroom and gets his coat. He checks the pockets to make sure no one has put stolen goods into them. As he walks out, he senses someone watching him. He whirls around, and finds that he is in fact right. Someone is watching him, and sneakily at that—sliding his cheek and one eye around a doorjamb to watch what's going on in the coatroom. It is the principal, Marksema. "So," says Cosmos, as he meets Marksema's eye straight on, "so," he says, and he is not using his William the Nice voice. He stomps up to the principal and holds out his coat. "Wanna search me? Here, take my coat, search it. Go ahead, search it!"

"Get control of yourself," Marksema says calmly. "That won't be necessary."

Cosmos stares at him and thinks maybe the principal has already searched the coat and now is just waiting to see if

Cosmos has come to hide some things in it. "If you're innocent," says Marksema, "you can start showing it by calming down."

"What does that mean—that I'm a suspect?" says Cosmos.

"Everyone is a suspect until this matter is cleared up," says Marksema. "Now, why don't you just go to your class?"

Cosmos goes to his book locker, looks through his books and papers—which look as if they've already been gone through—and stuffs his coat into the locker and locks it up. His stomach feels not so much upset for the rest of the afternoon as tense. Like there's a big knot right in his solar plexus. In class he pulls himself into his own space, locking his jaw as the teachers lecture and try to carry on discussions. He never makes eye contact with anyone for the rest of the day, and none of the teachers call on him. In English, he sits in the back of the room and stares at the back of Cherlyn's head for the entire hour.

But on his way to the bus after school, Cherlyn calls to him. He stops and turns around. She pulls up the straps on her backpack and comes bopping toward him. "Cosmos," she says. "I've got my dad's car. Let me drive you home."

He follows her off the sidewalk and onto the grass near the flagpole. "What's the matter?" says Cosmos. "You afraid they're going to beat me up on the bus for stealing all that shit out of the locker room?"

"You didn't steal that stuff, did you?" she says.

"No," he says. "But I noticed you made sure you weren't seen with me at lunch. Afraid I'm going to dirty your reputation?"

Now Cherlyn gives the shocked expression. "How could you ever think something like that?" she says. "As student council president, I had to meet with Marksema about this whole theft thing. I didn't even have lunch."

"Sorry," says Cosmos. "I get the feeling everybody thinks I did it."

"It never occurred to me that you did," she says. When he looks into her sincere eyes, Cosmos relaxes.

"I'm hungry," she says. "Ride with me and we'll stop somewhere for a bite."

Almost melting from the first friendly words he's heard all day, Cosmos goes with her to her car, a Ford Taurus that's probably a family spare.

"You do know I didn't do that, don't you?" says Cosmos.

"If you say you didn't, I believe you," says Cherlyn. "And I mean that."

They drive a few miles out of town to a flat-roofed place called the Tastee-Freez Truck Stop. They take a window booth, away from the truckers. Cherlyn orders a hamburger and fries. Cosmos's stomach still feels like a battleground of bad food and tense nerves. "Just water for me," he says. "So you really and truly believe me?" he asks.

"I really and truly believe you," she says. "I'm a believer

in more than one way, you know." She's smiling now.

"I believe you," says Cosmos, "and I don't believe much." He smiles for the first time today. He looks at Cherlyn. Her peaceful smile and her sweet face make all his muscles unclench themselves.

The hamburger comes and Cosmos watches her dig in. She's a real tiger when she's eating. After watching her eat a handful of fries and take a bite of her burger, Cosmos feels hungry too. She reads his mind. "Want a bite?" she says.

"Why not?"

He takes a bite next to hers and hands it back. "Look," she says. "You made a heart shape."

Cosmos blushes. He tries to let Cosmos Coyote give a real smile, but William the Nice gives a tight, nervous one. He looks at his watch, and when he does, so does she. He looks at her looking. "This *is* my watch," he says.

She reaches across the table and squeezes his forearm. "I know," she says.

When they finish and go back to the car, she sits behind the wheel looking at him. She leaves her seat belt loose and extends her hand to rest on his arm. "Everything and everyone around here is being so unfair to you," she says. "I really like you. I know you're a good person. I can just feel it."

She leans toward him just a little. He leans a little toward her from his side. She looks into his eyes and lifts her chin.

Her hand is still on his arm, and Cosmos can't tell if she is pulling him toward her or if he is leaning closer and closer toward her on his own. Their faces get closer, and then her hand leaves his arm and reaches up to his face. "I like your strong jaw," she says. Before he can respond, she kisses him, a solid kiss on the lips. Then she quickly settles back behind the wheel and puts on her seat belt.

Cosmos sits stunned for a few seconds, then reaches for his own seat belt. "Thanks," he says. "Thanks—I needed that. I can't tell you how much I needed that."

Hardly another word is said as she drives toward the farm of Cosmos's uncle Henry and aunt Minnie. Cosmos looks at her profile as she drives. The harder he looks, the more beautiful she appears. The perfect brow. The perfect chin. The perfect lips. And that glow she has. Occasionally, she turns toward him and smiles, but only a quick glance. She is a good driver. She keeps her eyes on the road and her hands on the steering wheel.

"I have another idea of how I could help you feel better," she says.

Oh boy. Cosmos looks at her. The possibilities are more than he can deal with, though not more than he can imagine. "How's that?" he says shyly.

"Could you list the names of the first ten presidents?"

"No," he says, "and I have to admit the question didn't make me feel much better. What you did before was a lot better remedy."

"Listen," she says. "I could teach you to recite the names of the first ten presidents in five minutes—before we get to your aunt and uncle's house. Just memorize these two sentences: Was Adam's son mad? Oh no, Adam's and Jack's son burned Harry's tie."

"'Was Adam's son mad? Oh no, Adam's and Jack's son burned Harry's tie'?" repeats Cosmos. "That's real cute. So what's the joke?"

"Not a joke," she says. "Every word stands for a president: *Was* equals Washington; *Adam's* equals John Adams; *son* equals Jefferson; *mad* equals Madison; *Oh no* equals Monroe; *Adam's* equals John Quincy Adams; *and Jack's son* equals Andrew Jackson; *burned* equals Van Buren; *Harry's* equals Harrison; *tie* equals Tyler."

"Cool," says Cosmos. "Once more."

Before they have gone a mile, Cosmos can recite the names of the first ten presidents.

"Your mind is quicker than mine," says Cherlyn. "That was fantastic."

"You're a fantastic teacher," he says.

"My parents are fantastic," she says. "I can't wait to have you meet them."

"Why on earth would your parents want to meet me?"

"They don't like to have me spend time with a boy unless they've met him," she says. "They're like that. Very protective. So I told them I'd invite you for supper, all right?"

Cosmos freezes, staring out the window. Then he says, "I don't know, I don't know. I just don't know about that."

"Think about it," she says. "I really like spending time with you, and I don't want to lie to them."

"I like spending time with you too," says Cosmos. "I just don't know. I don't want to disappoint you. I don't think I'd measure up to their expectations. And now, with people thinking I'm a thief, it's too much to think about."

"You measure up to my expectations," she says. "Even if you won't write a music column for me."

"Oh, that," he says.

They do not kiss before he gets out in front of the farm-house, but her big smile as he slides out of the car tells him she has no regrets about their kiss of a few minutes ago.

"I'll think about it," he says. "There's just been too much in one day, all right?"

"Take your time," she says.

Cosmos knows he's a few minutes late for evening chores and hurries to go upstairs and change into his work clothes. Aunt Minnie is busy in the kitchen. "Letter for you," she says, pointing at the table. It's a thick envelope with a return address from 1616 Quincy Street, Port Swan, Washington. On the back side is the dark-red imprint of someone's large lips. It's a letter from Salal. Aunt Minnie watches him pick it up. "Big lips," she says. "Is she a Negro?"

Alone in his room after supper, Cosmos tries to invite

Cosmos Coyote to his rescue, and he starts by trying to think about Salal. He picks up his journal, the one she gave him, and starts to write Salal a song. But he can still taste Cherlyn's lipstick. The words that come from his pencil are for Cherlyn: "All I want is your kiss." Nothing else occurs to him. He watches his hands write the same words over and over again down the center of the page. "All I want is your kiss." He giggles as he writes. "Some songs are like this," he says, and keeps writing.

When he lies down to sleep, he feels as if right now Cosmos Coyote and William the Nice are Siamese twins, attached at the hip, neither one clearly himself, neither one clearly free from the other. Maybe a few things in Iowa are getting easier, almost habitual: like folding his hands for devotions at home, or sitting politely through chapel at school. The marijuana scare and theft at school today could make school seem like nothing but poison if it weren't for Cherlyn. One hour with her cancels out all the bad feelings about school. One hour and one kiss.

He remembers Salal's letter and gets up to read it. Her handwriting on the envelope rises up like waving fir branches from the Northwest. Like sea spray and the taste of a cold beer. He stares at the envelope, but hesitates to open it. Behind the door of this envelope could be anything: a friendly face, a sneer, a nail in what is already the coffin of their relationship. He sniffs the envelope, holds it up to the light, and then rips it open with his thumbnail. It has a strand of Salal's long hair in it. It has two snapshots of Spruce and Rhody looking even stranger than when he left them. Their hair is longer and their clothes are sloppier, as if they're trying to relive the grunge scene. What Salal writes, which isn't much, she writes in four different-colored pens. "Cosmos, we love you. Cosmos, come home in one piece. Don't let the pigs eat you. We dream of you. Keep the music going. Rhody loves your new lyrics. So do I. That videotape from the Seattle concert—my music friends think if the right people see it the OughtaBs will be on the charts in a year. Love and blackberries, Salal."

Cosmos waits to see how he's going to feel about what he has just read. He doesn't feel anything—a big flat neutral. He tucks the letter in the back of his journal, then opens it to his last entry. He adds two more lines of the same words to the bottom of the page—"All I want is your kiss"—and goes to sleep.

I told you I didn't do it

"**I DON'T WANT TO** embarrass you in front of your parents," says Cosmos.

It's noon hour, and fallen leaves rustle around their feet as Cosmos and Cherlyn stroll through the city park across from the high school. Their arms almost, but don't quite, touch with each step. "You won't embarrass me," she says. "I saw the A you got on that Shakespeare quiz. You're a good student, and my parents like anybody who is an achiever."

"But you know I'm not into religion the way all of you are."

"You're a good person. What a person does tells me more than what a person says."

"What most of the kids at the Academy say I do is rip off stuff from locker rooms. You should have seen the way everybody looked at me after Marksema sounded off in chapel about the thefts. It was like their noses were magnets and my head was the North Pole. People talk talk talk around here, Cherlyn. How did your parents even know that you talk to me, for example?"

"My friend Margaret told them. And when they asked me about it, I didn't lie. I told them I liked you."

"You told them *that*?"

"I did," she says. "Because it's true."

"Humph," he says. "I kind of like you too. You're one of the few real people around here. But liking each other doesn't seem like something to tell other people. We're just getting to know each other."

"I trust my feelings," she says. "I believe what I feel, and I feel what I believe. So there." She touches him for the first time on this walk, a soft tap with her index finger on his ribs.

When they get back to school, they try to stay together through the shoulder-to-shoulder traffic in the hallways, but Cosmos gets edged out and behind. She waits for him at the top of a flight of stairs, then puts her hand on his forearm before they separate to go to their book lockers. Cosmos feels, then sees, the stares, males and females this time, and the stares do not look friendly. When he gets to his locker, something worse than stares waits for him. Taped to the steel door are two folded notes: "We know you did it, creepo," one note reads. "WE'LL GET YOU," says another.

He shoves the notes into his pocket and squirms his way to Van Enk's office. "So, Mr. Sociology, you were right," he says to Van Enk. "I'm the rotten egg and they're trying to make me float to the top. Have a look at these little gifts from the morons of suspicion."

Van Enk reads the notes, wrinkling his big nose a few times, nodding, and saying nothing. He looks at Cosmos calmly. "It certainly would appear they think you are the guilty one," he says. "Have the police talked to you?"

Cosmos does not see an ally in Van Enk's controlled manner. He just looks like a grown-up version of the morons of suspicion.

"Hell, no," says Cosmos. "Why should they? They wouldn't find anything. You know that."

Van Enk stands still, slouchy and cool. The sonofabitch doesn't believe me, Cosmos thinks. "You're one of them," says Cosmos, and turns to walk out of the room.

"Just a moment," says Van Enk, suddenly elastic in his gangly way, but Cosmos keeps going. He feels his farm-chore muscles tighten in his shirt. As he thumps down the steps, he bumps his shoulder against a senior boy.

"Hey," comes a voice from the bumped-against.

Cosmos whirls and faces him. "Got a problem, asshole?" he says.

The boy is bigger than Cosmos and hovers two steps above him with his own muscle-swollen shoulders. His shiny cowboy boots and tight Western jeans look like an advertisement in a cheap sales catalogue. "Whoa," he says, "somebody's in a bad mood," and turns to continue up the steps.

You're either a chicken shit or a good Christian, Cosmos

thinks, but his tight shoulders soften like Aunt Minnie's overcooked green beans at the sight of Cherlyn coming down the hallway with her arms full of books. If someone were to touch him now, he would not swing out, he'd melt.

From anger to sadness in a millisecond.

"What's up?" she says. "You look worried."

He heaves a relaxing sigh. "Look at this crap," he says. He hands her the notes.

"Oh no," she says as she reads. "Oh no." Then quickly she goes on, "Come with me." She leads him down the hallway to *The Messenger*'s office, lays the notes out on the desk, and studies them. She smoothes the paper down and looks even harder. She doesn't look angry. She looks fiercely analytical. "I don't recognize the writing, but you don't have to put up with this. You didn't do anything wrong, and there's no reason why you should take it even one minute longer." She purses her little lips. "Cosmos, I know you didn't steal anything in this school, but somebody did. Maybe even the people or person who wrote these cruel notes."

"So what else is new?" he says. "I can't quit school. That would send me straight back to Juvie. Staying in school, staying out of trouble—those are my rules. Not even Van Enk believes me about those stupid thefts. What do you think of Mr. Long-Legs, by the way?"

"Mr. Van Enk is a troubled man," says Cherlyn. "But I believe you." Cherlyn's face is still serious—and stiffening.

She closes her eyes. Tight. Her lips are moving again. She's praying. Cosmos waits. When she opens her eyes, he says, "Cherlyn, I really can't relate to that sort of thing. I don't know what kind of God you're praying to, but I'm sure he, she, or it has better things to do than figure out some jerk's handwriting, or even point a finger at the bastards who are trying to get my ass in trouble."

"I was just praying that the Lord would give me righteous thinking instead of anger," she says. "Anger leads in the wrong direction. But we're going to get those guys. We're going to get whoever stole those things from the locker room. If the police can't do it, we can."

"Yeah, sure," says Cosmos. "Give me one clue, one place to start."

Elmer walks by *The Messenger*'s door, sees them, stops and calls in, "Yo, Bill! Yo, Cher!" and then walks on.

"I don't think he did it," says Cosmos. "And if he did it, I don't think he'd let people go around pointing fingers, or whatever it is they're pointing, at me."

Cherlyn gets up and runs to the door. She comes back with Elmer. "Elmer," she says, "look at what somebody stuck on Cosmos's locker over noon hour."

Elmer looks at the notes, his eyes widening as he reads. If he's in any way guilty, he's a pretty polished faker, because he looks purely pissed. He knits his beetle-brow and blows through his tight lips. He looks like something halfway between silly and scary. "My cannonballs are startin' to roll on my deck, heck," he says. "Some slimy worm is whipping up my steam engine, know what I'm sayin'? We gotta get these weasely bastards."

"Nice talk," says Cherlyn, "but that's exactly what I had in mind. Justice." She leans toward Elmer. "Do you know who would know how to pick a lock? The thieves picked locks. We've got to start somewhere."

"Any hick can pick a lock," says Elmer. "Go for the pretty boys. Let's jostle some jocks. Strip 'em to their jockstraps, see what they're hidin'."

"Elmer," says Cherlyn. She is serious. She really wants to start her own detective squad. Cherlyn, who probably can't think an evil thought even if she concentrates, wants to outsmart a petty thief. Well, who knows? Why not? Cosmos figures. She seems to be thinking along the right lines.

The three of them huddle over the notes.

Cherlyn is the first to speak. "Let's be systematic," she says. "I'll go talk to Marksema and see if it would be all right to offer a reward of fifty dollars in *The Messenger*."

"Nah," says Elmer. "I say, let's spread the word that we know who the dudes are who did it, and if they don't fess up, we'll fetch the cops. Smoke the dickheads out."

"Elmer, please," says Cherlyn.

"Oh," says Elmer, "smoke the *bad boys* out. I know," he goes on. "Let's plant a Star Wars watch with a bomb that blows during chapel. Blam! Instead of arresting them, we can pray for their body parts."

"Elmer," says Cherlyn.

They play with ideas ranging from trickery to earnest questioning to a campaign of editorials in *The Messenger*. When the warning bell rings for afternoon classes, Cherlyn says she wants to stop in Marksema's office and talk to him.

But Marksema is waiting in the hallway. He wants to talk to Cosmos.

In his office, Marksema explains to Cosmos, half apologetically, that he is indeed a suspect in "the unfortunate robbery." He tells Cosmos that everyone in America, and especially at the Academy, is innocent until proven guilty. "I pray for you every day," says Marksema. "I know this must be a very trying time for you, whether you are innocent or guilty. I want you to know that what I said in chapel still holds true: a confession to the crime and the matter will stay in school."

"I didn't do it," says Cosmos. "And when I find out who did, you're going to be the first to know about it. All right?"

Marksema eyes him, a piercing squint, as if he is trying to see through Cosmos to the truth. "Taking matters into your own hands could just cause more trouble," he says.

"I won't be alone," says Cosmos.

"Cherlyn? Is Cherlyn going to help you?"

"She wants to find out who really did it, just like me."

"And Elmer? I saw him go into *The Messenger*'s office

with you. Elmer is not exactly the sort of person I would look to for help if you didn't do it."

"You're probably thinking that if I didn't do it Elmer must have, right?"

"I didn't say that," says Marksema. "But Elmer has his problems."

"Don't we all," says Cosmos.

"I hope you are not getting bitter," says Marksema. "I want you to have a good year here. And you still could have, even if you are guilty."

"I told you I didn't do it," says Cosmos. His shoulders are tightening again.

"Very well," says Marksema, "but there weren't very many students unaccounted for during first hour. I understand you were late for class."

"Fifteen minutes," says Cosmos.

"Why don't you tell me where you were for those fifteen minutes. That would be the simplest. Then I can scratch you off the list."

"I felt sick, so I took a walk. I lost track of time. I was right outside."

"Alone?"

"Alone," says Cosmos. "I needed some space. Like I said, I wasn't feeling well. Aunt Minnie will tell you that's true. I had to stay home from church Sunday."

"Where did you walk?" asks Marksema.

"Around the gym, then around the buses."

"Around the gym? Near the band building?"

"I guess," says Cosmos.

"Did you see anyone, or did anyone see you?"

Cosmos hesitates, then looks up and to the side, pretending to search his memory. In the next few seconds he tries to consider all the options. If he tells Marksema about the three boys in the bushes, he'll become a suspect for smoking marijuana, because the two teachers no doubt reported smelling marijuana in those bushes. Then, if he has to point out the three boys, they'll probably think Cosmos snitched on them, and if they think he snitched on them, they'll probably say he smoked too, and if they say that and his PO cousin Mike Jonsma hears about it, he'll want to give Cosmos a drug test, and if that happens, maybe traces of that bad dope he smoked last week will show up in his urine. Worst of all, if he starts talking, he'll end up being a snitch. One thing will lead to another.

"I didn't see anybody," says Cosmos. "I was alone. The other students were in school. Nobody saw me either."

Cosmos goes to his room as soon as he gets home that afternoon. If Cherlyn had been among the crowd of students going into school in the morning, he wouldn't have taken the walk that is making life too complicated for comfort. One glimpse of Cherlyn could have saved the day.

He decides to soothe himself with a little music before going out for evening chores. When he starts looking through his CD stack, he notices something is wrong. Nothing is exactly where he had it this morning. He goes to his clothes drawers. Someone has been in them too. He goes through his room like a detective on a crime scene, looking for clues. Someone has gone through all of his stuff. Someone has even gone through his bed. Someone has looked under the mattress. Someone has gone through the pockets of the clothes in his closet. Everything, but everything, has little telltale signs of a snoop.

He sits down on the side of his bed, and the truth collapses down on him. Somebody—maybe his probation officer, maybe Principal Marksema, maybe the police—has had Uncle Henry and Aunt Minnie go through all of his things looking for stolen property. That's what this is all about. They all think he is a thief. The thief! Everyone except Cherlyn. And maybe Elmer—if Elmer isn't the thief himself.

A burst of hatred, dismay, fear, sorrow, anger—the whole bucket of bad feelings anybody could have in one day—explodes inside him. Bastards! he shouts inside his head. Dirty, sneaking bastards! He walks over to his mirror and stares at himself. In the fury of his own face, he sees the biggest bastard of them all. Loser. Loser. Loser. The biggest loser of all. Juvenile delinquent. Smart-ass son who made his mother run off to Mexico. Pain-in-the-ass son who made his father scramble to keep him out of Juvie. Bad boyfriend who turned his lady into a lesbian. He imagines taking one of Uncle Henry's guns now and aiming it right at himself, right between the eyes. Why fight this shit? Why not just *not be* anymore? He doesn't feel like crying. He doesn't feel like anything. He assumed he'd come home, bring his mood back up with some music, and finish the day like William the Nice. Maybe lie down at night thinking of Cherlyn. Why bother? Why fucking bother! He gets up, and it's as if he dreams himself across the room. If he were to die, the only person who would give a shit is Cherlyn. She is the only person around here who believes him, the only one who seems to care at all. He thinks of sitting in a car, gassing himself while recording his last thoughts on a tape recorder. His last thoughts would be to Cherlyn. He would tell her how much he appreciates the way she believed him and cared about him. That would be peaceful. That would be a good end to all of this. Thinking of Cherlyn, he thinks less of himself. I am such a worthless piece of shit, no wonder they think I stole their stupid fucking whatever-the-hells. He doesn't feel like crying. He doesn't feel like yelling. He doesn't feel like anything. Why? Why bother? Why not just get out of this picture? Just fade out. Psst. He knows the medicine cabinet downstairs has a large bottle of aspirin. That would do it. Just take the whole stinking bottle and fade out. Just fade out. Turn the switch off.

When he walks downstairs, it's as if he is walking on air, as if he is a ghost already, something that nobody can hear or see. He opens the medicine cabinet. There it is. Almost a full bottle. He fills a glass of water, and it too is silent, ghostlike, as if all of nature is cooperating in making this easy. Easy. He stands looking at the bottle of aspirin, looking at the glass of water. Then a voice screams, "NO!" It is his own voice. "NO!" he yells again. He can hear Uncle Henry and Aunt Minnie clamoring around in the porch and kitchen. He can hear them talking. "No!" he yells again at the top of his voice. "NO FUCKING WAY, GOD-DAMN IT!"

Uncle Henry knocks on the bathroom door. "William!" he yells. "What's going on in there!"

Cosmos puts the aspirin back in the medicine cabinet. He flings open the bathroom door. "It isn't fucking William, it's Cosmos!" he yells. "You went through my stuff! You! You ever go through my stuff again, I'll knock your fucking block off, you understand me? What were you looking for? Stolen property! You think I stole those fucking assholes' goddamn fucking property, that what you fucking think! Huh? Huh? You think you got a god-damn thief living under your fucking roof! That what you think! Huh? Huh? I'm out of here! I'd rather live in fuck-ing butt-fucking detention in Washington than put up with this shit, you understand me!"

"Calm down," says Uncle Henry desperately. Aunt Minnie is in the doorway of the living room trembling behind her apron.

Cosmos can no longer talk. He pants uncontrollably. "We had to know," says Uncle Henry. "We had to know." He stands with his arms at his sides, keeping his distance from Cosmos. He stands. He waits. Cosmos still pants loudly, almost heaving, tears pushing through his eyelids. "We apologize. Now we know. You didn't steal anything. And now we will be your defenders. Nobody falsely accuses a De Haag. De Haags do not go down easy," he says. "If I ever hear anybody call you a thief, you won't have to do anything. I'll bust his f-f-fricking nose myself. That's a promise. Now no more bad talk. Let's act like a family. A De Haag family."

For the first time, his uncle Henry reminds him a little bit of the best side of his father. In a few seconds, Aunt Minnie approaches and starts crying. "We're so sorry," she says.

That's all it takes. Uncle Henry starts crying, and then Cosmos. Uncle Henry holds out his arms. Aunt Minnie holds out hers. The three of them wrap their arms around each other, all of them weeping onto each other's shoulders. So this is what it takes to get people around here to hug.

"We better stop," whimpers Aunt Minnie. "We all better pull ourselves together and get the chores done."

This is a new one: going out into the farmyard teary-eyed and sniffing. In Port Swan after a full-fledged uproar, no one ever did anything but sit and stew, sometimes for days. Especially when his mother, Melba, was still at home.

They would punish each other by refusing to do their usual jobs. They'd just turn into rocks. But here, when Cosmos comes downstairs in his work clothes still blowing his nose, he sees that Aunt Minnie has already gotten to work, furiously peeling potatoes. Uncle Henry has put his work shoes on and is heading out to work too. Why not? thinks Cosmos. Work seems like as good a thing to do right now as anything else. His arms feel limp from the emotional exhaustion as he picks up the big grain scoop and starts shoving cracked corn into the silo-shaped feeder bin. After a few difficult assaults into the mound of corn, the rhythm takes over, and the steady breathing of the steers next to him takes over, until his aching arms swing feed in a steady body-building, spirit-cleansing rhythm. The only thing that matters to the steers is that he not stop scooping, and the only thing that matters to his mind is what part of the grain mound he should attack next. This is one part of the Iowa formula that makes a kind of sense that he can feel in both body and spirit. Rescued from misery by work.

Suppertime is quiet and peaceful. Everyone's voice is gentle and polite. The vegetables are all generously overcooked, and as easy to eat as they will be to digest. Comfort food. Uncle Henry and Aunt Minnie both give him a pat on the back before he goes upstairs. He feels a love for his uncle and aunt that he did not have before, but his heart feels in shambles. A pile of rubble. So Uncle Henry and Aunt Minnie will be on his side, along with Cherlyn. But he knows he is still alone. He is alone and he doesn't belong here.

Here I go to earn my kiss

AT HOME, UNCLE HENRY and Aunt Minnie make life much easier after their big scene. They don't even ask him to go along with them to see Grandpa Wilim. "He's not very well," says Aunt Minnie. "I don't think you'd enjoy your time with him."

They're right about that, but there is no escaping bad company at the Academy. Cosmos Coyote comes out of hiding in the hallways and shoots sharp I-dare-you looks at any suspicious hawk eyes. When they're caught staring at him, they look away faster than a finger jerked from a blowtorch.

Principal Marksema apologizes to Uncle Henry and Aunt Minnie for being in on the search of his room, though he stops just short of apologizing to Cosmos. "I just wish we had a positive identification from somebody who saw you outside while the thefts were happening," he says. But he doesn't set the police on Cosmos. Probation Officer Mike mentions the incident, but assures Cosmos he takes him at his word.

Cosmos knows Cherlyn is at the heart of his survival.

She is the warmth he feels in his chest when he sees her in the hallways. She is the smile that curls easily across his face now when she joins him in the cafeteria. She listens, then reaches for his hand and almost gets teary-eyed when he tells her about his room being searched. "The world is so unfair to you," she says. "I'm on your side in all this, you know that, don't you?" she says.

Cosmos does, and says so.

Then, one day, she has on her tight jeans again, but she wears a knee-length coat in the hallways and between classes. It's only when she sits down with him for lunch that she takes the coat off. She not only has on the tight jeans, she also has on a form-fitting sweater. There she is. All of her. Cosmos no longer wonders if she is dressing just for him. He knows she is. Unfortunately, he can also tell from the looks on some of the senior boys' faces that they know it too, and they seem to have figured out that she wears those clothes for reasons other than awakening Cosmos's spiritual life.

"Look," says Cherlyn as she sits down, but when Cosmos opens his eyes wide to look at her, she holds up a copy of the next issue of *The Messenger*. "Marksema is letting me run this notice to catch the thieves."

Cherlyn does more than encourage Cosmos at school: she invites him to go with her to a band concert, and then to go bowling Saturday afternoon after he finishes his work on the farm. Cherlyn dresses modestly for this, in loose slacks and a loose sweatshirt, but other students are bowling too. The stares are getting longer and more persistent, especially when they laugh together, especially when they give each other little hugs if one of them gets a strike or a spare. Now the girls are staring as much as the boys. They don't look jealous so much as bewildered by the combination. They act as if they're seeing a chicken ride a bicycle or something.

When they're by themselves outside of school, Cherlyn is sweet but guarded. There is some hand-holding and a few moments that almost lead to a second kiss, but not quite. Cosmos knows she is holding back. Then she confesses why. "My parents are still asking when they can meet you," she says. "They say we shouldn't be dating until they have you over for supper. I tell them that we're not dating because we're not kissing, but that's not good enough for them anymore."

"That's weird," says Cosmos. "Your parents think kissing is bad?"

"They think kissing is the first step in a direction they don't want me to go."

"Ah, yes," says Cosmos, remembering again what Uncle Henry said to him about one thing leading to another, a kind of domino-effect breakdown of morals. "I don't think kissing is bad. The only bad kiss I know about is the one the preacher was talking about in church last week."

"Yes," says Cherlyn. "Judas' kiss of betrayal."

"I can't think that a kiss from you could ever be bad, angel lips. One good kiss would just lead to another good kiss."

"Stop it, you," she says sweetly. "Just come for supper."

"I'd like to kiss you right now."

"I'd like to kiss you too." She acts as if she has become self-conscious about her lips. She puts her hand to her mouth. "Just come for supper. Then I won't have to deceive my parents."

"This is blackmail and I love it," says Cosmos. "I think I love it. I love the part that makes me want to kiss you. I don't like the part that won't let me right now."

"I want you to see my home too," she says. "I want you to see the places on our farm where I played when I was little. I want you to see where I come from."

"Farms all look pretty much alike around here," says Cosmos. "Neat and tidy, with a smell of manure, disinfectants, and herbicides. I wish you could see where I come from too: clean sea air, hundred-and-fifty-foot fir trees, virgin red cedars. It's a land where things that grow can still grow in their natural way."

"Maybe someday I will," she says. "Lord willing and the crick don't rise."

"Lord willing and the crick don't rise?" says Cosmos.

"It's an expression my grandpa used to use. It's a folksy way of saying, 'If it be God's will.'"

* * *

"Oh, how nice!" says Aunt Minnie when she hears that Cosmos is going to meet Cherlyn's parents. "They are wonderful Christian people. And they've reared a fine daughter."

"Mrs. Van Dyke is a wonderful Christian anyhow," says Uncle Henry.

"Henry," says Minnie in a voice that sounds like a warning. "He is a good churchman."

Cosmos takes Uncle Henry's response to Cherlyn's father as a warning.

Cherlyn picks Cosmos up at two o'clock the next Saturday afternoon. The plan is to go on a little picnic along the river, then go to Cherlyn's parents' house at five-thirty for supper. She drives slowly west down the gravel roads, in the direction of South Dakota and the Big Sioux River, which separates it from Iowa. The fall air is cool, and the brown leaves from the box elder and ash trees have fallen. Much of the corn has been harvested, and the fields have changed from their dark-green summer colors into the brittle tans of fall.

As Cherlyn turns off down a small dirt road that winds between trees and around potholes, Cosmos watches little mind movies: his lips on her neck, in her hair, followed by long kisses. Little mind movies of his hand on her shoulder, on her waist, her back, his hand on her breasts. He watches her face now as she maneuvers down the winding path toward the river. Even as she drives, he can see the urge of a smile on her face. She seems familiar with this spot. She's obviously been here before, but with whom?

"You seem to know your way," says Cosmos.

"Oh yes," she says, "my Bible-study group came here on a retreat last May—before the mosquitoes came out. Now it should be late enough in the season that the mosquitoes are gone."

They pull up under a large tree, where there's an open spot and a picnic table perched on an embankment overlooking the river. It's a totally private spot, with only thickets and small trees on the other side of the river, making it impossible for anyone to see them from there. And if a car should come down the same path that they just came down, there would be plenty of time to get ready before anybody would see anything. This spot is as private as his and Salal's old love nest at Fort Wheeler.

Cosmos's mind movies stop as Cherlyn lays out a flowered plastic tablecloth on the picnic table. She's wearing a different, less tight-fitting pair of blue jeans and a blue buttoned shirt that is not tight but opens just far enough to be revealing when she leans over the table. Cosmos sits down and watches her spread out the lemonade and cookies. The brown river trickles innocently below them. His eyes move from the river, back to her, to the river, and back to her. One natural wonder competing with another. The dead leaves on the ground give a subtle rustle, like soft dinner music. Next to the car stands a big oak tree with its dead leaves still clinging and quivering in the breeze. Quivering as if excited about something they're not telling. The grass around the table is long but flattened down and covered with leaves, so that it sits there like an inviting bed just waiting for them to finish their lemonade and cookies.

"Our Bible group talked about being called to service when we were here last spring," says Cherlyn. "It was right here that the Lord told me I should become a leader."

"Cool," says Cosmos. "I wonder if Indians used to come to this place for a vision."

"Probably, don't you think?" she says. She looks toward the river. She turns back and takes a sip of her lemonade, staring into Cosmos's eyes over her glass as she does.

When she puts her glass down, her mouth opens just a bit. Cosmos can see her pink tongue inside the warm little room of her mouth. Her mouth looks as if it wants to kiss.

"I feel humbled by the call to be a leader," she says. "The path is not clear, but I'm working on it. I'm studying."

"I'd follow you even if you didn't study," says Cosmos, still staring at her lower lip.

"Seriously," says Cherlyn. "Should I not talk about it?"

"No, no," he says. "I'm sorry. Tell me. I really do want to hear about it. I don't have anything against visions. I believe strange things happen and we should listen to voices from the universe. I want to hear about your vision, I really do. So what kind of leader?"

"In my vision, I am the president of the United States—

or at least vice president. Or a senator."

"The vision wasn't clear about that?"

"Not entirely. Maybe it was senator first, then vice president, then president. It scares me. I don't feel I'm choosing this course. I feel I am called. When I read history, it all sticks in my mind. I understand it. I see patterns. In my vision I pick up where Martin Van Buren left off."

"Oh yeah," says Cosmos. "You were going to tell me more about this Van Buren cat."

"This Van Buren cat was the eighth president, right after Andrew Jackson. His first language was Dutch, but because he was born after the Declaration of Independence he's the first president to be born an American. I have a hunch I'm distantly related to Van Buren. Who knows? Maybe you are too."

"We're all related if you go back far enough," says Cosmos. "And I don't mean back to Adam and Eve."

"Didn't think you did," says Cherlyn. "Van Buren was Dutch Reformed. He was one of my people. Your people too, Coz."

"And the Dutch Reformed folks gave us apartheid in South Africa."

"Right," she says. "We all have something to be ashamed of. But Van Buren was a noble-hearted man, and he was anti-slavery way back in the 1840s," she says. "Late in his life he ran for re-election with a new anti-slavery party." She pulls up her shoulders and for a second reminds

Cosmos of a minister who is about to begin a sermon, or a teacher who is about to give a lecture. "Noble-hearted, but he had no charisma," she says. "He was good behind the scenes, a hand-shaker, so people called him the Little Magician, but he was a detail man who got all tied up in those details. It was like a shell, a shell of accuracy or something. He wanted to have all the details right, but he didn't know how to inspire people. Now, Andrew Jackson, he is another story. He was basically an evil man who could inspire people. Jackson was always upstaging Van Buren, even at Van Buren's inauguration in 1837."

"You actually know this stuff," says Cosmos.

"Am I boring you?" she says. She gets up and walks around the table. She puts her hands on his shoulders, then rubs the back of his neck gently. She is doing to him exactly what he wishes he were doing to her. The inside of his mouth dries out, and his tongue roams aimlessly around in his mouth, as if it has found a mind of its own and is either about to leave him speechless or to start speaking in tongues.

"Don't stop what you're doing," says Cosmos.

She goes on rubbing and starts talking again. "John Calvin and all the great reformers were hardworking men. Very hardworking, as were the founders of this country. Nobody worked harder than James Madison, for example. Martin Van Buren was a hardworking man too, he just didn't work hard enough at being a good presenter of his ideas. I think he was insecure about himself. He should have prayed for confidence. Then he would have had the style to persuade people openly. He should have had a little bit of Bill Clinton in him."

"You like Bill Clinton?" says Cosmos.

"My parents hate him, but he has charisma. It's just that he has a weakness for women."

"And that's bad?"

"Not at all," says Cherlyn. "I blame Monica. A woman should never tempt a weak man like that."

"What?" says Cosmos. "You blame Monica?"

"Totally," says Cherlyn. "If women are going to take power, they can't go playing on men's weaknesses and then expect the world to blame the man instead of the woman."

"She was only twenty-two!" says Cosmos. "He had all the power. He was wrong!"

"He was weak," says Cherlyn. "She knew it and went for that weakness. He misused weakness; she misused power. As a woman, I have to see her sin as the greater sin. If we want power, and I believe God does want women to lead the country back to God, then we can't blame men if we make them fall. Read the story of Lot's daughters in the Old Testament. No question about who is misusing power there. Same with Monica."

"I don't believe what you're saying," says Cosmos. "You're really surprising me."

"You know what I'd like to see?" says Cherlyn. "I'd like to see Chelsea get Monica in a mud-wrestling match and stuff her head three feet into the muck."

"Cherlyn!"

"Sorry," says Cherlyn. "I shouldn't have said that. I shouldn't even have thought that." She goes on rubbing Cosmos's neck. When he looks back at her, he sees her lips are moving. She is praying.

"I've been doing all the talking," she says. "What do you want from your life?"

Cosmos lets her continue rubbing his back and neck as he turns his head from side to side. "I want to be true to myself," he says. "That's all. I want to be one person, not faking it all the time. Not putting on faces to keep people from talking about me, saying I'm some kind of weirdo creep. If I'm a weirdo creep, then, fine, that's who I am."

"But you're not a weirdo creep."

"Thanks. But I'd like to quit being a phony just to get people to think I'm okay. I don't want to be their kind of okay. I want to be what I am, not fake it all the time. It's like you say you do, like live what you believe."

"It would be fun to hear you say what you believe instead of what you don't believe."

"What do I believe?" He pauses again, letting her continue the head massage. "I'll tell you what I believe. I don't believe in bullshit."

Her hands stop rubbing. "Translation?" she says.

"I can't pretend to know something I don't know, and I can't pretend to be somebody that I'm not."

"That makes sense," says Cherlyn. "Do you believe in God?"

Cosmos hesitates. It sounds like a trick question—but Cherlyn doesn't ask trick questions. "Sure," he says.

"And do you think God can be known?"

It sounds like another trick question. "Are you going evangelical?" he says.

"I'm trying to understand you," she says.

"I don't want to pretend to know what I don't know. The universe is filled with mystery. To me, believing in God means accepting the mystery of everything. I just want to be what I really am in the middle of all the mysteries of the universe. It's like harmony. Like being in sync."

"Like harmony. Like being in sync," Cherlyn repeats. "That makes sense to me too. That's actually what I pray for."

"But I don't pray, Cherlyn. I'd feel like a big phony if I did. When I see something beautiful, like this river, I feel, like, overwhelmed. I feel humbled. I feel thankful. But, you know, I couldn't pray that God protect this river from pesticides or something like that. Looking out for the planet is our job. And I think, if everybody respected nature and other creatures' natural way of being in the world, then everything would be in sync. There'd be peace. And I don't think I can be in harmony with anything if I'm pretending to be something that I'm not. When I feel guilty, it's because I've been a phony."

"So do you feel guilty around here?"

"Yes."

"Because you're being a phony?"

"Yes. I'm faking it, and I don't like it. I don't like being a two-faced phony trying to keep Aunt Minnie and Uncle Henry from seeing my CDs or the kind of music I listen to. And I hide my journal to make sure they don't see what I write. I fake it in church, where everybody, especially the minister, seems to believe everything that everybody outside the church is doing is evil. Then in school I have to fake it just as much. Trying to smile through chapel when somebody is up there nice-nicing along. It makes me sick. I'm a phony almost all the time. Except when I'm with you. I don't believe what you believe, but I know you're for real, so you make me not want to be a phony either. Most people who believe the way you do scare me. But you don't. I trust you."

Cherlyn had stopped rubbing for a minute while Cosmos talked. Now she starts rubbing his head again and doesn't say anything.

"Of course, there are lots of reasons to like you," Cosmos goes on. "An awful lot of reasons. But I really don't understand why you spend time with me. There are about fifty guys at school, when they see us together, they look at me as if they wish I'd fall off the planet. Or at least get sent back to Juvie in Washington."

"But they're not you," she says. "They may be fine for some other girl, but they're not you."

"But why do you like me? Why do you even spend time with me?" asks Cosmos.

Cherlyn takes her hands off his shoulders, sits down beside him, grabs him by the shoulders, and says, "Because you're not a phony either! Because you're a wonderful person! Because you're a good person! Because God loves you! No matter what you say, Cosmos William De Haag, I think you're saved."

"Don't remember being lost," says Cosmos.

"I believe God planned your being sent to Iowa."

"Now you *are* going evangelical on me, aren't you?"

She lets go of his shoulders and slides her arms around his neck. Suddenly her nose is touching his, and her lips are touching his, like whispers, like butterfly wings. Cosmos's lip starts to tremble, the way it sometimes does in the dentist's chair.

"I can't wait to kiss you," she says in a sweet whisper. "I can't wait. But I will. We both will, won't we?"

She pulls her face back, gets up quickly, and stands back, looking at him with the biggest of her smiles on her face.

"Oh, you cruel angel!" he moans. "You're driving me crazy!"

"Am I misusing my power?"

"Yes! Yes!" he wails. "And I am weak. Impeach me! Impeach me!"

When they both stop giggling, she says, "Come, let's walk along the river."

"Do you really like me?" she asks as they walk.

"I like you a lot," he says.

"Tell me why again," she says, teasing him.

He pauses, then answers seriously: "I like you because you are what you claim to be. One person. When you say something I know it's the real you, even if it is stuff I don't believe. I don't believe what you believe, but I believe you. You get the distinction."

"I get it."

"You're the least phony person I've ever met. You're the best thing in this whole friggin' state."

She squeezes his hand. "You're embarrassing me," she says. "I'm never living up to what I should be. I'm the biggest pretender of all. I pretend that I have everything I want, but I wish for more than I deserve. I try to please people I don't really like. Sometimes I have awful thoughts about my parents, especially my dad, but I always tell them how good they are to me. I know I'm dishonest with a lot of people, and I just do what they expect so they'll accept me. I'm always faking it. When I pray at night, that's what I pray about most. I pray to God that I can be the very kind of person you said you wanted to be.

Somebody whose life is true. Somebody whose life is like a song, a song of joy and thanksgiving."

"You sure you're not going evangelical on me?"

"I can't help it," she says. "If you feel that you're living in God's grace, that He is the source of all your peace, you really can't *not* talk about it. And I haven't been going evangelical on you all the time, have I?"

"No, you've been just fine," he says. "I can handle the way you believe in God. Most of the time." He stops and turns to her. "If I were God, I'd keep you in my grace pocket all the time."

Cherlyn giggles. "Stop it," she says. "You're making me want to kiss you again. Come on. You talk some more."

"The God I hear most people around here talking about is no sweet-talking grace-giver. He's a big boogeyman," says Cosmos. "A God who hates poor ghetto women who get pregnant and want an abortion. A God who hates gays. A God who likes to see people on their snowmobiles out shooting Bambi along the river. I can't believe the kind of mean-spirited crap the minister preaches about. Sometimes I can hardly keep my ass on the church pew, but I've got no choice, you know. All of this crap, and then a bunch of goody-goody rules on the side. Good Lord, you've still got rules about what you can and can't do on Sunday. That's like dinosaur religion. You're a history buff. Well, it's like people here got stuck in history sometime way back there and they said, 'This is how it's going to be, now and forever.' It's crazy. Do they have any idea what they look like to the rest of the world? I'll tell you what they look like. They look like right-wing dinosaurs, people who like to sit in their sanctimonious little community and congratulate themselves on how pure they are while the rest of the world is out there winging it as best they know how." He stops and looks at her. She has been squeezing his hand harder and harder the more worked up he was getting. "I'm sorry. Am I insulting you?" he asks.

"No, you're not insulting me," she says. "Maybe that's what bothers me. I agree with a lot of what you're saying. But I'll tell you exactly what I think. I think people here are scared that they might end up out there 'winging it,' like you say. They hear about all the crime and misery in the big world out there and they know that's not what they want."

"They're like canaries that don't dare to fly out of the cage because a big old cat might get them. Of course, they'd just shoot the cat."

"It's more like an alcoholic who doesn't go to bars because he knows the temptation may be too great," she says. "Not a fear of other people so much as a fear of your own weakness."

"So how do you feel about that?" says Cosmos. "You think everybody is damned to misery who doesn't huddle together in the security of the church? And see if you can answer me without quoting the Bible."

"You mean like 'Be ye *in* the world but not *of* the world'?"

"Yeah, like that," he says.

"All right, I'll tell you exactly what I think about going out into the big bad world. I learn fast and I'm ambitious," she says. "I know that's a dangerous combination. I'm never sure what is a blessing and what is a curse. I really do believe that whatever assets I have are God's gifts to me."

"Yes, you are well endowed," says Cosmos.

"Stop it," she says, but somehow they are now embracing. "No lips." They hold each other with their chins on each other's shoulders and listen to the river trickle by. She leads him to a log that lies along the riverbank, and they sit down.

"Seriously," she says, "I don't want learning to destroy my faith. I just don't want to give up what I have felt to be true and real. I want to serve humanity for God's glory, not my own. That's my worry: that I'll get so caught up in what I can learn and in what I can do that I'll forget the only reason for doing anything."

"You are something else," says Cosmos. "But you know, if there is a God, He's bound to be impressed by you. I am, and I'm not even God."

They sit quietly again, watching the river. Their silence gives nature confidence to show itself: a mother white-tailed deer with a colt-sized fawn step out of the trees to drink on the opposite side of the river, a brown thrasher sings and flushes from a small tree behind them, and a great horned owl swoops past them.

"Now, this is my idea of church," says Cosmos.

"You don't like churches very much, do you?"

"I don't like the us-against-them way of seeing things. I don't like the right-wing politics that echoes off the stained-glass windows. There are an awful lot of wacko religious nuts who come out of church wanting to kill faggots and Jews and are just all psyched up about doing in anybody who doesn't agree with their tight-ass ideas of right and wrong."

Cherlyn closes her eyes as if she is distressed by what he has just said. "I'm not lined up with those freaks," she says. "I go to church to find peace. I go to church to seek guidance in understanding other people and their needs, Coz. If God has called me to lead, then I need His guidance. Most leaders have no idea what little people want and need. I mean the little real people. The working people of this country. They just want to follow Jesus and not let the world get swallowed up by all the trash that comes from Washington and the media."

"Oh, please don't talk like those right-wingers, my Cherlyn, my dear Cherlyn."

She turns on the log and puts her hand to his face. "I'm sorry," she says. "I'm so sorry. I just want to live in love. I don't want to hurt anyone, especially you."

"No, I'm sorry," he says. "I trust you."

"It's just that I've been taught that people who don't put their faith first always end up doing the wrong thing, hurting themselves and other people. All people in this community really want is the security they find in the church and in what the church teaches. I want that too. It's just that I plan to go out into that big world," she says. "It scares me. I'll be honest with you: when I first met you and knew I was attracted to you, I thought, Is God testing me? Has He sent me someone who will challenge my faith?"

"I would never do that," says Cosmos. "I like you exactly the way you are."

"I know, I know, or at least I know that now," she says. "But don't you understand? You're the first person my age I've ever known who didn't grow up in the church and go to Christian schools."

"Wow. That's surreal," says Cosmos.

"But as I get to know you, my faith just gets stronger. I think you inspire me."

"Now, *that* I find hard to believe."

"This probably won't make sense to you, but you showed me that you could go to a place that is totally different from what you're used to and still keep what you believe."

"But I don't believe what you believe."

"Well, you say you don't, but I'm not even so sure about that. I don't think anybody can be as good as you are without God's grace. And I don't think I could love you the way I do if God didn't love you too."

"What?"

"I didn't mean that to come out like that."

"Cherlyn."

"Cosmos, I'm sorry. I know we're just friends, you haven't even met my parents, I didn't mean to use that word like that."

"Cherlyn."

"What?"

"I love you too."

They look at each other, stunned with what the conversation has led to. He does not reach to touch her and she does not reach to touch him. They keep looking into each other's eyes, longer and longer, deeper and deeper.

"I don't even know what this means," she says. "I haven't been here before."

"I haven't either," he says. "Not even close."

"Oh." She looks at her wrist. "Do you have a watch?"

He doesn't, but they know it is time to go. They walk back to the car briskly. Cherlyn checks the clock in the car. "My mom will have supper ready in less than an hour."

They have hardly touched their picnic snacks and pack them quickly. They walk to the edge of the embankment and take one last look at the river. She puts her arm around his waist and he puts his around her shoulder. "Right now Iowa is more beautiful than Port Swan," he says.

"We'd better go," says Cherlyn.

"Right," says Cosmos. "Here I go to earn my kiss."

When he puts his seat belt on, he starts to get nervous about meeting her parents. What if he disappoints them? What if they totally disapprove?

He tries not to think about it. He thinks only of the reward once supper is over. The kiss. "All I want is your kiss," he says.

My world starts in my heart

THE FARM WHERE CHERLYN lives with her parents takes the Dutch idea of neat and tidy to a new level: a straight and narrow black-topped driveway, which is outlined with poplar trees that are somehow all exactly the same height, leads to a yard area where the grass has the haircut of a golf-course green. The barns are painted tan and are uniformly designed with hip roofs. Perfectly aligned wooden fences, painted the same sandy color, connect the buildings. On the edge of a gentle hill, slightly higher than the other buildings, stands the gabled brick farmhouse with black roof and shutters, the whole structure surrounded by evenly spaced oak and pine trees and multitudes of fall flowers—dazzling, and as lush and delicate as the fringe on a doily.

"I hope you like our farm," says Cherlyn. Cosmos can tell by the way she is squinting her eyes that she is trying to change the subject in her mind from the two of them to the scene they are about to enter. "It's been featured on the covers of farm magazines twice," she adds.

The whole fussy layout does look like an advertisement for the good life in the country—which it probably would be if somebody else had the job of keeping it looking like this.

Cherlyn parks under a big-armed oak tree that is the centerpiece of a little cul-de-sac that circles around it, the smooth round edge of the circle set off with bricks that have a border of marigolds. The fall air has gotten cool. The leaves on the deciduous trees look tired or have already fallen and been raked up, but the flowers flourish, as if a dedicated plant nurse gives them physical therapy every day to keep them dancing in the breeze dressed in all their pretty colors. Cosmos opens the car door and breathes in the air of this place: he can't miss the smell of cow manure, but it's as if the sweet liqueur smell of the flowers has infused the animal odors. The smells blend and fight with each other at the same time. No, it's not a sweet liqueur smell. It's more like a cheap wine that has a lot of kick. A Boone's Farm smell.

"Here we are," says Cherlyn, bouncing out of the car and extending her arms open as if to say, "Behold, my world!"

Her cheerful voice tells Cosmos that, like him, she is trying to make the transition into this world. He tries to make it too, though he can feel the world where they have just been together throbbing in his chest. It's hard to look at her without showing his longing to be close to her.

"Cool place," says Cosmos, and walks around to her, not sure how to behave with her here, whether to act comfortable as an old boyfriend or timid as a stranger from the city.

"My mom loves flowers," says Cherlyn, and as if on cue her mother appears from the front door, dressed up—in a rose-colored pant suit. She looks healthy: sturdy but not fat, with a face that is rounder than Cherlyn's but with a smile that is as big. She walks toward them with a confident step, her well-coifed short hair bouncing over her ears, and holds out her hand. "You must be William De Haag," she says, pronouncing his last name correctly to rhyme with "bog." Cosmos is startled for a second, then realizes Cherlyn had done him a favor by not telling them his actual name. "I've known your uncle for years and remember your father as a teenager when I was a little girl," Cherlyn's mother goes on buoyantly.

"We saw a brown thrasher by the river—and a mother deer and fawn," Cherlyn interrupts cheerily.

"Why don't you bring the picnic leftovers inside," says her mother. Ah, here's the neat and tidy one who tends the flowers, Cosmos thinks. She goes on quickly: "Supper will be ready in fifteen minutes. Cherlyn, why don't you show William the music room." Turning to Cosmos and giving him her inviting smile, she says, "Cherlyn tells me you're quite the musician."

"Well," says Cosmos and smiles nervously.

"He plays the guitar and sings," says Cherlyn. "I'm

working on him to play in chapel."

Cosmos starts to feel like a lamb in a petting zoo with everybody trying to get their hands on him and nudge him first one way and then the other. "I don't know about that," says Cosmos. And here comes Cherlyn's father. He's dressed for supper too, though with a little less flashiness than Cherlyn's mother. Cosmos notices the perfect crease down the front of his dark-brown pants. He has Cherlyn's smaller lips and narrower face, or she has his, but he carries himself much more stiffly than Cherlyn's mother. It's his hair that spooks Cosmos: that dirty-blond, wavy hair combed back without a part, hair that doesn't have any looseness to it at all. Plastic hair. Hellfire-and-brimstone preacher hair.

"Mr. De Haag," he says, and there's a cool condescension to his voice. "It is good that you could be in our community for the year."

"I'm having a fine time," says Cosmos, and looks nervously to Cherlyn.

"He's living with his uncle Henry and aunt Minnie," says Cherlyn.

"Oh yes, Henry and Minnie," says her father. "Salt of the earth." His eyes do not leave Cosmos's face. Cosmos rubs his mouth to make sure there isn't food or some other of nature's residue on his lips. He nods his head as if agreeing with Cherlyn's father and looks back to Cherlyn for help.

Which she quickly gives him: "I'm going to show

William the music room," she says, "and then get ready for supper."

Cosmos feels new waves of panic. Everybody is going to "get ready" for supper, and he has nothing but his jeans and blue bumpy-threaded secondhand imported Ecuadorian peasant shirt.

He follows Cherlyn. Inside, the house is a nightmare of cleanliness—everything from the rust-colored tile floor in the kitchen with its subtle sheen, the immaculate counters, and the glowing mahogany table, to the wagon-wheel motif rolling around the room in the forms of plant holders and armrests for the padded chairs at the dining table. The huge living room has picture windows looking out toward the west and what will soon be a sunset over the fading golden fields. On the far end sits an extravagant entertainment center, complete with a centerpiece of a tractor-sized TV set encased by shelves of books—biographies of war heroes, history books, and a lower shelf of twentieth-century people like Ronald Reagan, his memoirs, then a guy named William Bennett, and, yes, a face-out book by Billy Graham with him smiling salvation all over the room. The pictures on the walls are larger than at Uncle Henry and Aunt Minnie's, with fancy ornate frames and scenes that do not show Iowa—more like scenes and people in Holland a long time ago.

The music room is like a den, with dark paneling. Family pictures hang on the walls, including Cherlyn as a toddler and little girl, and a parallel set that he assumes are her brother, though she hasn't talked about him. Cosmos walks past the piano to look at the portraits, most of them studio shots of her in cute frilly dresses holding different toys at different ages, all of them with her smiling. Pictures of the boy show less smiling, and when Cosmos notices the progression in the boy's age, he can see that he gets increasingly more sullen. He looks as if the world has given him all the sadness that Cherlyn didn't get. Only one picture shows them together and reveals the big age difference: her brother was a teenager when Cherlyn was about seven.

In the pictures of Cherlyn, she looks as if she had already found Jesus when she was three, beaming joy, beaming what only Cherlyn can beam. Even as he looks at the pictures of Cherlyn, it's as if someone is in the room reaching out a hand to save him from his uneasiness, an uneasiness that reminds him of how he feels when he knows he is about to be caught doing something he is not supposed to be doing. The friendly hand that reaches out to rescue him this time is the piano. It is a six-foot black grand, a Yamaha. The piano more than anything tells Cosmos that Cherlyn's family has money, and plenty of it. It also pulls at him like comforting arms. He isn't much of a pianist, but he eases down on the bench, puts his hands on the keys, and plays the two songs he learned in seventh grade, when his parents were still forcing him to take piano lessons. "Für

Elise" rolls easily from his unpracticed hands. The piano sounds are rich, like velvet, like chocolate mousse. He finishes and breaks into the second song he has memorized: "Chattanooga Shoe Shine Boy." No wonder religious people talk about choirs of angels. If there is a God, He has to be into music. If there is a God, He must be accompanying the choirs of angels on a Yamaha grand. Nobody could sound bad on this piano.

He feels Cherlyn's hands on his shoulders and is momentarily transported back into the wonderful feelings of being with her near the river. She sways with the beat.

"You're good," she says.

He finishes and lets his shoulders sag. "I'm not as good as this piano," he says. "Now, on the guitar, that's another story."

"You will play the guitar for me and sing sometime?"

"Sometime," he says.

Cherlyn leaves Cosmos alone in the music room while she goes off to get ready for supper. Cosmos tinkers around with a few chords. Then he softly plinks out possible melodies for the lyrics he has written in Iowa. In a few minutes Cherlyn comes back spruced up a bit, but to Cosmos it is obvious that she hasn't dressed up in a way that will make him look like a hobo at their supper table. Cosmos takes his turn in the bathroom. He sneaks a look in the medicine cabinet to see what secret life he might find, but it has only the predictable items of home medicines and cosmetics. Neatly and logically arranged by shelf, with cold medicines, Band-Aids, and thermometer on the top shelf, and working down to deodorants and mouthwash on the bottom. He sniffs the deodorant. It does not smell like Cherlyn.

Supper is T-bone steaks with baked potatoes, sour cream, and a big lettuce-and-vegetable salad. Cherlyn's father—and Cosmos realizes he doesn't know the first names of either of Cherlyn's parents—gestures to the place where Cosmos is to sit. Cosmos starts toward the chair, then stops and walks around to help Cherlyn with her chair. Cherlyn's stiff-faced father almost smiles approval.

Everyone sits down and Cherlyn's father says, "Let us ask the Lord's blessing."

Cosmos has gotten used to the prayers before every meal, but Cherlyn's father prays more earnestly, and with longer sentences. Cosmos can hardly follow the one that starts out, "Even when the tempests of this earthly life befall . . ." and ends up with something like ". . . now may it be Thy will to replenish in us that which we stand in need of." At least he doesn't follow Uncle Henry's practice of naming people at the table in his prayers. Cosmos feels relief at the "amen," which he has learned is the equivalent of "Now let's eat!"

Even if there is a bit more classiness here at Cherlyn's parents' house than there is at Uncle Henry and Aunt Minnie's, the clean-your-plate rules still apply. Cosmos follows the lead of Cherlyn's father, cutting and chewing, cutting and chewing, with very few pauses for small talk about weather and favorite subjects at school. Maybe it's because his stomach is tense already, but the last thing that Cosmos's stomach wants is an entire T-bone steak in it. He can feel his stomach tighten and fill with each bite. Five quick bites into the steak and he stops eating. "This is really good," he says, "but I don't think I can finish it all."

Cherlyn's mother looks hurt. Her father looks indignant, as if Cosmos could just as well have said, "I'm too good for your Iowa beef."

"I'm getting full too," says Cherlyn through her chewing, though she has managed to eat twice as much of her steak as Cosmos.

Cosmos and Cherlyn sit quietly as her parents finish their supper. She looks across at him, and when she runs her tongue along her lower lip, Cosmos feels himself becoming aroused, his erection forming so quickly that he has to shift in his chair. I wonder if it shows on my face? he wonders.

When he looks at Cherlyn, her eyes have widened and gotten more dazzlingly bright, a look that suggests to him, with his happy problem, that she knows exactly what is happening. Now she rubs her lips together and Cosmos's sweet pain grows more intense.

Cherlyn's mother breaks the uncomfortable silence. "We could give you a plastic container to take the rest of the steak home with you if you'd like," she offers to Cosmos.

"Sure, that would be great," says Cosmos.

"There's a plastic container right there on the counter behind you, maybe you can reach it," says Cherlyn's mother.

Cosmos looks around. There is indeed a plastic container on the counter behind him, but it is out of reach. He will have to stand up to get it, and to stand up right now with his arousal still in full bloom will be a spectacle that might not get him sent back to detention in Washington but just might cause him to be expelled forever from the company of Cherlyn's parents. The moment feels too much like too many moments Cosmos has had in his life, when every option seems as bad as the next. In a flash he considers saying that his leg is sleeping. In a flash he considers saying that he has changed his mind and doesn't want to take the leftover steak home. In a flash he considers flicking himself under the table in the hope that his problem, like an ill-mannered puppy, will immediately heel. Then he realizes that he still has his large napkin on his lap. Sheepishly, like Adam being expelled from the Garden of Eden, he stands up and uses the napkin to cover his embarrassment, holding it like a fig leaf over his privates.

Everyone watches him with slightly puzzled looks on their faces, but, Cosmos assumes, they probably just think I spilled something on my lap and am embarrassed about it.

Just as he settles safely back in his chair, Cherlyn's mother says, "I hope you have room for dessert. I have fresh apple pie with whipped cream."

"Would you like some pie, Cosmos?" says Cherlyn.

"Cosmos?" says Cherlyn's mother. "Cosmos?"

"It's a joke," says Cherlyn. "Isn't it, William? It's one of those names. Remember how you used to call me Angel Hair?"

"We dropped that when you were four," says Cherlyn's father.

"Oh, come on, Dad," says Cherlyn. "What's in a name?"

The question draws silence around the table. Everyone seems to be thinking about it, but no one has an answer. Cosmos glances at Cherlyn's parents as they finish the last bites of their steak. To Cosmos, they look as if they suspect some strange kind of cover-up, but they are polite, or stunned, or confused, or just plain stiff-lipped Dutch.

Cosmos eats the pie, slowly. Every bite of it. He figures it's the least he can do to get in sync with Cherlyn's family.

With supper finished, Cherlyn's father opens the Bible and reads a psalm. The whole ordeal is almost over. But not quite. When he closes the Bible, he turns to Cosmos and says, "Mr. De Haag, would you offer thanks?"

Cosmos knows what this means. Cherlyn's father has just asked him to say the closing prayer. All hands fold. All eyes close. So do Cosmos's.

A huge silence of about two seconds follows. Cosmos

straightens in his chair. "We thank you, God," he begins. Nothing else occurs to him. A huger silence of maybe three seconds follows. Lines from his own songs start flashing through his head. Then weird phrases like "Lazarus and the sheepherder's daughter" form themselves in a row of words that make a kind of sense. "It has been a good day" comes from his lips, "and we thank you, O God, for it. We thank you, O God," he says again, and waits for a fitting phrase to follow. "O God," he says again. A big two seconds elapse. "For it is good, O God," he says. "Jesus' sake, O God," he says. "Amen," he says.

When Cosmos stands up from the table this time, any hints of embarrassing protrusions have totally faded from his body. A few minutes later, he is outside with Cherlyn.

"That was really bad," he says.

"What was bad? You didn't like the food?" Cosmos looks at her. She looks genuinely worried. She doesn't know.

"The prayer," he says. "I've never done that before. I blew it. I looked stupid."

"Never prayed at a supper table?" She stares at him staring at her. "You don't think I tricked you? Please don't think that."

"No, no," he says, trying to free his voice from the tightness in his throat. "It's just so weird. Praying out loud like that in front of everybody. I know it's the custom and everything. And I can handle that. We used to do Indian chants in Port Swan, and I guess it's sort of like that. Tribes have rituals, I know that. Rituals are fine. I think it helps people get centered."

"I'm sorry," says Cherlyn. "I didn't mean to embarrass you. I never want to push you into anything you don't want to do. I just wanted you to see the world I go to when I go home. So often I imagine that you're here, seeing the world where I grew up. Sometimes I even talk to you. I just imagine that you're here and I'm showing you everything."

"You do that? You think about me when you're home? When I'm not around?"

"A lot," she says.

Cosmos is as comfortable, suddenly, as when he was alone with her by the river. An urge to cry moves up his loosened throat.

"You're too good for me, Cherlyn. I'm just not made for your world."

"Don't say that," she says. "My world starts in my heart. I think my heart was made for you. Or maybe you were made for it."

"I'm scared, I guess," says Cosmos. "I don't think I would be if we could live our whole lives inside our hearts. When I'm with you, I feel safe there. But the big old world outside the heart can get pretty messy. It always does for me, anyhow. You forget how much trouble I've been in."

"The world's unfair to you," she says. "I've told you that

before, and I believe it. But the big old world out here isn't all bad." He can see her making a transition again, shifting the scenery of the mind by shifting the attention of her eyes. She lifts up her arms toward the farmyard. "This is my world too," she says. "Come on, I want to show you our dairy herd. Beautiful Guernsey. We have three men over here at four o'clock every morning and four o'clock every afternoon milking them in the milking parlor. Now the cows are outside. They're so beautiful. You've got to see them."

Cosmos can already smell them, but doesn't say so.

Just as Cherlyn says, the cows are beautiful. All their heads turn as Cherlyn and Cosmos lean over the fence to look at them. And from among the cows walks a larger animal, the bull, colored like the herd but with the distinctly broad head and muscular shoulders. "That's Master Charlie."

Master Charlie walks toward them, awesomely large but mild-mannered in his approach. He's not charging. He just looks curious. Master Charlie comes up to the fence, then lifts his wet black nose toward Cherlyn. She holds out her hand and turns her palm to stroke his forehead. They know each other, it's clear. This is a side of honor-student Cherlyn that Cosmos has not seen before. She really is a farm girl. She really does know animals. In a few minutes Master Charlie turns and walks back toward his herd. As he does, Cosmos and Cherlyn get a clear view of the animal from behind, and from behind what is most obvious is the animal's sex, his huge dangling testicles, testicles larger than pears, testicles like eggplants, swaying as Master Charlie walks. Cherlyn leans against Cosmos's shoulder and takes his hand. "I love animals, don't you?" she says.

A light wind blows toward them, and they cannot smell the flowers that bloom near the house. They have only the smell of the large lot where the cows wander with their udders sucked dry and Master Charlie roams listlessly among his herd. As they turn toward each other, the sour fermenting smells of silage drift over from the silo, along with the odors of alfalfa in the bunkerlike feeding station, and the fresh and aging smells of cow dung, all the odors together making a nasal brew that is so complex that it is neither offensive nor pleasant.

"I'm getting to like animals a little bit," says Cosmos. Now that they're out of sight of the house, Cherlyn moves toward him with her arms up toward his neck. Cosmos knows that the delayed kiss is finally going to be delayed no longer. He embraces her around her waist, then lets his hands glide up her back, until, with his elbows on her ribs and his hands on her shoulder blades, he pulls her tight against himself, her arms around his neck, all of her pressed firmly against his body, and he feels the pressure of the stored beef in his stomach giving way to the pressure of his own arousal in his jeans, misplaced and trapped, straining but unable to rise, though when she stands on her tiptoes to kiss him lavishly on his lips and neck he can feel her pelvis rise up under his trapped sex, a pressure so painful and delicious that all the smells around them are like an aphrodisiac that makes his desire for her so intense that for a long moment he is as senseless as when he tried to think of the right words to offer in the closing prayer her father asked of him at supper.

When they break free and look around to see if they are being watched, they are both breathing in short, shallow breaths. She sighs and looks at him with such an intense and calm longing in her eyes that he feels forgiven for every way in which he may have failed her today.

This time Cosmos makes the transition: "Thanks for fudging a little bit about my name at the supper table," he says.

"I know. I try so hard to live in love, and sometimes living in love makes it so hard to be honest."

"What's with that picture of your brother?"

"That's Jake," she says. "He ran away from home after a big fight with my dad. That was five years ago. Dad thinks he's bad. He's living in San Francisco. I don't think he's bad. I just pray for him."

"I'm really sorry," says Cosmos. "I didn't think people

around here had sons who jumped ship like that. Of course, my dad did it, but that was a long time ago."

"I don't want to think about anybody but you right now, all right? Already I don't want next spring to come," she says. "I don't want you to leave."

"I don't dare to think of any time except right now," he says. "I don't want to hurt any more than I already do most of the time."

"Don't hurt, Cosmos," she says. "Please don't hurt."

They hold each other quietly now, breathing sadly on each other's shoulders. The light has begun to fade, and a hazy pink colors the clouds over their heads.

"I desire you so much, Cosmos, that I know it must be a sin. But how can love and the desire that comes with it— how can it be sin, when all I know of God is His love, and His love is not sin? His love is pure and holy. His love is what makes life worth living. I'm confused, Cosmos. I want to think my love for you is part of knowing God, not the beginning of my downfall. Like the earth, maybe I can seem to stand still while I'm actually spinning. Oh, Cosmos, be careful with me."

"You've handed a fragile egg to a blind man walking on a trapeze in a hundred-mile-an-hour wind," says Cosmos.

"I trust you."

"I trust you too," he says.

"We'll be all right, won't we, Cosmos?"

"We'll be all right."

They hold each other gently, warmly, as the farm breezes blow across their faces. He senses the moment when her body slowly moves back to the heartless world of time. "I'd better get you home," she says. "I have to be ready for bed before ten on Saturday nights so I can get up early to meet with my Bible group before church."

It all depends, you know?

"YOU SWEETHEART," SAYS Cherlyn when she meets him in the hallway before school on Monday. "That was so sweet."

"Thanks, but what are you talking about?"

"This," she says, and hands him a folded sheet of paper. It's a printed note that reads: "I come to school to see your bright face. I go to chapel to hear your sweet voice. Wherever you are the world is a more beautiful place. I pray to God that you will always brighten my life." It is signed, "Your greatest admirer."

"I just want to know how you slipped it into my locker without my seeing it."

"Cherlyn."

"What?"

"I didn't write this. I didn't put this in your locker."

"Oh no."

"It doesn't even sound like me. I wouldn't say some of these things."

Cherlyn blushes. Cosmos has seen her red-faced with

excitement before, but not this look. A look of blushing terror.

"I don't want a note like this from anyone but you," she says.

"You must know," says Cosmos. "You must know who would send this kind of note. He can't be a stranger. It must be somebody you know very well. People don't send notes like this if they don't think the other person will know who it is."

Cherlyn looks even more embarrassed and terrified. "Don't be angry," she pleads. "I would never hide something like that from you. I really don't know." She grabs the note and looks at it again. She tears it up and crumples the torn pieces in her fist. She goes to the large hallway wastebasket and throws the shredded note in. When she walks back to Cosmos, her eyes are wide and glassy.

"Let's go to *The Messenger*'s office," she says. She sits down at the editor's desk and puts her head in her hands. "This is awful. Why can't everything be beautiful the way it was Saturday?" She sniffs and puts a tissue to her nose.

Cosmos reviews in his mind all the male faces who have looked at them in a way that says they wish she was theirs and that he was at the bottom of the river. Too many faces come to mind for any one of them to stand out as the prime suspect. Whoever it is who sent the note, Cosmos thinks, it's somebody who doesn't think our relationship is real.

It's somebody who thinks Cherlyn is free for the taking. And what does that make him? The delinquent from Washington whom nobody has to take seriously.

"Please don't look so angry," she says and reaches to take his hand. When she touches his hand, it twitches away. "I love you."

"I love you too," he mumbles and takes her hand. "But it looks like I'm not the only one." He tries to smile. "I don't blame other guys for liking you. Who wouldn't? But only a jerk would give that to you when it's so obvious that I'm on the scene," he says.

"I know. But lots of guys don't like me. I scare them, for some reason or another. But that doesn't matter. I'm not interested in other guys."

"I believe you."

"Oh," Cherlyn sighs. "It's just that I was hoping we could start on a happy note." She inhales through a sniffle, then laughs. "Sorry, bad pun. It's just that I hoped we could be in a good mood before I tell you what I have to tell you."

"Now what?"

"I may as well get all the bad news out of the way. It's my parents. We're going to have to limit our time together to school hours," she says. "At least for a while."

"I knew it," says Cosmos. "I knew I blew it with them. I just knew it. Things were too good to be true." He stomps around the room. "I knew it, I knew it, I knew it."

"My mom likes you fine," says Cherlyn. "She thinks you're a very normal young man and that you look like the De Haags, and that is a good sign. But Dad, I'm so disappointed in him sometimes, but he's my father, you understand."

"I understand," says Cosmos. "He thought my prayer sucked, right?"

"It wasn't your prayer. My folks understand how nervous a person can get when they're put on the spot. It's just that my dad is so skeptical of human nature. He's really an old-fashioned Calvinist. He thinks all people are totally depraved but that God spares a few."

"Your father thinks we're all depraved? Like scum? That's crazy. So he was just trying to smoke me out by asking me to pray, right? Let me demonstrate how bad I am?"

"No, I don't want to think that is what he was doing. You'd have to know Calvinist doctrine to know where that total-depravity thing is coming from. When Daddy first found out that I was spending time with you, he thought I was trying to lead you to the Lord, so he approved. He thought I was trying to convert you. Now he thinks you're trying to subvert me."

"Subvert you?"

"Those were his words. Daddy is stiff-headed, but he'll soften. We just need to give him some time. I know what the real problem is. He's afraid what happened to my brother will happen to me. Jake went off to summer school in Iowa City for just two months and came back not wanting to go to church. They fought and fought, so Jake left. Now Daddy has totally given up on Jake. He thinks Jake, his own son, my brother, is, well, a bad apple."

"Don't you mean a 'rotten egg'?"

"I'm as disappointed as you are, but I want to look on the bright side. Maybe it's all right. Things were starting to go a little bit fast, don't you think?"

"When I'm near you, I forget about time and speed. The world stands still. Everything and nothing happens all at the same time."

"I know, I know," she says. "That's how it's been with me too. But things can only get better if we get to know each other a little bit more slowly at school."

The first bell rings.

"Speaking of time," says Cosmos, and they both head for the door. They touch hands and shape kisses on their lips as they part in the hallway.

* * *

Cosmos goes down to the locker room before classes start. His feet feel heavy. Everything feels heavy. He runs into Elmer.

"You look like a two-week-old pizza, man. What's going on?"

"Not now," says Cosmos. "I'm bummed."

"You're not bummed, you're in love, man. I got eyes.

And she's got eyes. And the eyes have it, man. It's love love love, and it's not all coming from above. Are you her turtle dove?"

"Either talk to me or let me alone, Elmer. Jeez." Cosmos walks up to the urinal. Elmer follows and stands behind him.

"Just trying to cheer you up, man. Hardly ever see you anymore, and when I do, your head's in the ozone and you look right past me. You have been, as Van Enk would say, 'shall we say,' preoccupied. Or is it stupefied? Just don't get like mummified."

"Knock it off," says Cosmos. "Can't you just for one minute be like nice?"

"Hey, I'm the men's-room pink of nice. Let's talk sugar and spice."

Cosmos goes to the sink to wash his hands. He doesn't look at Elmer. "It would be good to have a decent conversation with you sometime," says Cosmos. "When you're not performing. I've gotten, shall we say, very fond of Cherlyn. I don't like, so to speak, joking about it, all right?"

Elmer likes Cosmos's imitation of Van Enk and howls. "That's good, man, that's good." Then he says, "Okay, okay, no joking about love. I've heard that bum-drum with women myself, man, and it's hard to talk serious about it, you know. So have you got problems? She doing her God trip on you?"

"It's who she is. She doesn't lay it on me."

"With all due respect, man, I am a little bit surprised how thick you two are getting. I thought you'd go together like oil and water."

"Well, you were wrong. We go together the way oil and water don't."

"All right," says Elmer. "When I saw you two like melding, always sitting together, even in chapel, I thought, If that guy wants Cherlyn, he's going to need a halo and some angel wings."

"Cherlyn's beliefs are not the issue. It's her old man. He doesn't think I'm good enough for her."

"Oh, listen, man," says Elmer. "Her old man is a real prick. He's just a tight-ass prick. His own son told him to fuck off, and then split. If you want to have a thing with Cherlyn, stay away from that asshole."

"Right. It's not that easy. She won't defy him. He says we can't see each other outside of school, so that's the way it will be. But, hey, Elmer, thanks for listening. We almost had an actual conversation there."

They scramble up the stairs to get to their classes. Cherlyn is twenty yards down the hallway ahead of them.

"Hey, I think I get it now," says Elmer. "You'd like to get in those jeans, wouldn't you?"

"To tell you the truth, I'd like to *be* those jeans."

Elmer punches him on the arm. "Yes," he says. "Let's talk again, all right?"

"Fine with me," says Cosmos.

No sooner does Cherlyn disappear than Cosmos finds his mood slumping again. He can tell already that this is going to be one of those days: clouds followed by sunshine followed by clouds followed by sunshine. A yo-yo kind of day. His heart aches as he sits through Van Enk's class. His heart feels like it wants to go every direction at once.

But a little later, his heart goes in only one direction when he sees Cherlyn in the hallway before chapel. They sit together and hold hands between the seats. Sitting next to Cherlyn, having the smell of her shampoo touch his nostrils, hearing her lovely singing voice, listening to her breathe as one of the teachers gives a little sermonette—the very presence of her makes the burden of her father's orders get lighter. Sitting with Cherlyn anywhere holding hands is better than anything he once expected he could have during his detention year in Iowa. No matter what Elmer says about Cherlyn's father, in his own perverted way he's probably just trying to do what he thinks is best for her. It's not as if he has ordered Cherlyn totally out of Cosmos's life.

At lunch, he sits across from Cherlyn and they touch feet under the table. This is not like the privacy of being alone together along the river, but it is a lot better than nothing. After finishing saying her grace, Cherlyn says, "How are you feeling?"

"Right now I'm feeling great. Top of the world."

"Me too," she says. "Let's talk about the Shakespeare

we've been reading in English."

"All right, though, after this morning, maybe it would be fun to talk about something a little lighter."

"Like the weather?" she teases.

"I'd like to hear you talk some more about the presidents."

"I'll bet," she says.

"I would," he says.

"You're serious?"

"Yeah, I like it when you get excited talking about the presidents. I like to watch your lips when you're excited."

She smiles. "I think maybe this is going somewhere we shouldn't be going?"

"All right," he says. "Tell me how you're going to be a more charismatic president than Van Buren."

"Speaking of charisma," she says, "do you know which president at one time during his presidency had a disapproval rating of only three percent?"

"Not Martin Van Buren, I'll bet," he says.

"Gerald Ford."

"You're kidding. I've got one for you. Which president was born on the same date that I was?"

"I give up."

"Gerald Ford. July 14."

"Bastille Day," she says. "I'm going to put that in my birthday book. Now I've got a tough one. Who was the first and only president to marry a woman who was still married to another man?"

"Not Martin Van Buren, I'll bet," he says.

"Of course not," she says. "Andrew Jackson. And which president do you think was so scuzzy that at one time he made a living racing horses?"

"Not Martin Van Buren."

"Of course not," she says. "Andrew Jackson. And which president do you suppose once made an oath of allegiance to a foreign country, including a pledge to take up arms against its enemies?"

"Not Martin Van Buren."

"Of course not," she says. "Andrew Jackson. Which president had such a strong singing voice that he drowned out those around him in church?"

"Not Andrew Jackson."

"Of course not," she says. "Martin Van Buren."

They giggle. "This is fun," says Cosmos, "but not as much fun as sitting along the river having my back rubbed."

"I know," she says, and practically hugs him under the table with her feet. "I'll never be able to look at a river again without thinking of you."

The conversation is interrupted by Principal Marksema. He stands over them like a cloud without a silver lining. He needs to see Cosmos for a few minutes in his office.

There's been another theft, this time from one of the cars in the parking lot. It happened last Friday, during lunch hour. A jacket and three tape cassettes. Where was Cosmos during lunch hour?

"I called you in because somebody said they saw somebody who looked like you in the parking lot shortly after noon."

"I was with Cherlyn Van Dyke," he says. "Why don't we go right back to the cafeteria and you can ask her right now."

"Not necessary," says Marksema. "I figured maybe you were with her."

"I think somebody is trying to set me up to take the rap for this stuff."

"I've thought of that," says Marksema, "but the circumstances require that I talk to you. And I had to tell Probation Officer Jonsma."

"I understand," says Cosmos.

"Actually, he's coming right after school to meet with you. He said to tell you not to catch the bus. He'll drive you home."

Cosmos can't imagine there's anything he's done to get him in trouble with Cousin Mike, so he has no big worries. Still, he resents the fact that he is always the number-one suspect whenever anything happens. How can anything so pure and beautiful as Cherlyn exist in this uptight place where some faceless jerk can point a finger at him, where some other faceless jerk can try to move in on his and Cherlyn's relationship, and where people like Cherlyn's father can play God and decide who is good and who is bad? Cosmos's feelings do a nosedive. Where is Cosmos Coyote when he needs him, Cosmos Coyote, to stand up and give the finger to the whole stinking lot of them? To all of them except Cherlyn.

Cosmos knows Van Enk is the last person he should be talking to when he's feeling like this, but he still finds himself drawn toward Van Enk's office door as he heads for his afternoon classes. Cosmos has been getting all A's in Van Enk's class and hopes that this should make the guy warm up to him a little more. He stops outside the office and looks at all the rows of books he has. This man has books! Somebody who reads that much must have something going for him.

Van Enk sees him looking. "Mr. De Haag, come in," he says.

Cosmos tells Van Enk he was just looking at his books, and Van Enk says to look all he wants. Cosmos can borrow some if he'd like, as long as they aren't his valuable first editions, which he doesn't like to allow out of his office.

Cosmos walks in and looks at what is by far the biggest collection of books in any of the teachers' offices. There are two rows of psychology and sociology books, but the top row is a curious one: Gary Snyder, Terry Tempest Williams, Paul Gruchow, Scott Sanders, Rachel Carson, Barry Lopez, Edward Abbey, Annie Dillard, Gretel Ehrlich—quite a different assortment from the ones he saw at Cherlyn's parents' house or at Uncle Henry and Aunt Minnie's. And above these authors sits a framed plaque with the words

"THE EARTH, THAT'S NATURE'S MOTHER."

"Can I borrow some of those on the top shelf sometime?" he says.

"Those?" says Van Enk. "Any time. All those authors are people who, shall we say, love the planet and want to do something about preserving it."

"Cool," says Cosmos. He pulls down Edward Abbey. "How about this one?"

"Interesting choice," says Van Enk. "Birds of a feather."

"What does that mean?"

"It would seem that rebels find each other," says Van Enk.

Armed with what he assumes will be some interesting reading, Cosmos leaves Van Enk's office, and for once feels good about having been there. Maybe if I can stick to books and Cherlyn my life will be a lot better. Books, Cherlyn, and music.

After school, Cousin Mike drives Cosmos home. He knows about the suspicions Cosmos has been putting up with at school, he knows about the search of his room, he knows about the fight with Uncle Henry and Aunt Minnie, he knows about the budding romance between him and Cherlyn, he knows that Cosmos has been to her parents' house for supper.

"Is there anything you don't know about my life?" says Cosmos.

"I don't know if you're happy. How are you doing? Would you get on the first plane back to Washington tomorrow if you had the chance?"

"To go into Juvie? No way."

"No, would you go back to Washington tomorrow even if you didn't have to face detention?"

A few weeks ago, Cosmos would not have hesitated to shout back a loud "Yes!" But "yes" is not the first word that comes to his mind now. "It all depends, you know? Sometimes something happens that makes me feel terrific about Iowa. Other times, it's the total pits, you know? Sometimes I'm up, sometimes I'm down. Some days things happen that can put me in a different mood from one minute to the next. You know?"

"Where are you right now?"

"I don't know," says Cosmos. "I really don't know."

"If a certain young woman were in the car with us right now, would your answer be different?"

"Knock it off," says Cosmos, and his grin almost reaches both of his ears.

Bury my talent where?

SO NEAR AND YET SO FAR. That's how his relationship with Cherlyn seems to Cosmos over the weeks as the season starts to change and the brisk north winds from Canada start to suggest what a Midwest winter will be like. Not being able to see Cherlyn outside of school is like not being able to think up the last line for a song, that constant almost-but-not-quite feeling.

He meets Cherlyn at the same spot in the hallway every morning before classes. They wait outside the bathrooms for each other. Inside the restrictive cage that Cherlyn's father has placed around their friendship, they try to make the moments bigger, to make them fuller. They sit with each other in chapel and hold hands—if Cherlyn's friend Margaret is not there beside them, staring at them when they get too friendly. She is like Cherlyn's father's private eye.

"Margaret is like horseflies at a picnic," says Cosmos.

"She means well," says Cherlyn. "And she's so lonely. None of the guys shows an interest in her."

"Yeah, I wonder why not," says Cosmos sarcastically.

Even with Margaret's watchful eye, chapel opens the window for a new way of getting close. They find that their voices blend perfectly. In chapel, with Cosmos as tenor and Cherlyn as soprano, not even Margaret can see their hearts break through the barbed-wire cage. Were he here, not even Cherlyn's father would be able to see that the music of their voices only echoes the larger music they feel in their hearts as their voices harmonize and send back the song of their own love: "Beautiful Savior, king of creation, son of God, and son of man," pours from them in a harmony more glorious than the morning glory's opening in consort with the sunrise, rippling from row to row like a sweet rumor of sound, then bursting through in a crescendo, spreading like a wildfire of blissful music from row to reluctant row, igniting the listless vocal chords of all the students, until the whole assembly is singing beyond themselves, gloriously to the glory of God, gloriously to the glory of Cosmos and Cherlyn's love for each other. The beautiful music starts with them and returns in a feeling of intimacy that no rules can contain nor curious eyes discern.

"Don't you love chapel?" asks Cherlyn over lunch.

"I'm starting to," says Cosmos. "I like singing with you."

"We do go together like peaches and cream, don't we?" she asks. Before he can answer, she goes on, "And, Cosmos, you're such a talented singer, you're probably just as good on guitar. Why don't you sing in chapel as a special number some Friday? I'll bet you have a better voice than Van Buren had! If my dad heard that you sang a solo in chapel, he'd think differently of you. Especially since my brother was tone deaf and had no sense of rhythm at all. Jake hated music, maybe because Daddy wanted him to be good at it and he wasn't. If Daddy knew you were a good singer, he'd know for sure you're not just another version of Jake."

"So that really is what this is all about: I remind your dad of his own son. His reprobate son. His totally depraved son. His scumbag son."

"Jake is not a scumbag," says Cherlyn.

"I know," says Cosmos. "I'm sorry. But I don't think I could sing a solo in chapel just to prove to your dad that I'm not like Jake. Singing with you is great, but standing there in front of all the students and teachers singing in chapel like some recent convert dragged in from the accursed world of the damned—I don't think so. I'd try almost anything for you, but sing a solo in chapel? I couldn't fake that one."

That familiar flash of brightness comes into her eyes. "I've got an even better idea," she says. "The talent show! We have this big talent contest at the Academy—and my parents always come! You should stop burying your talent in the earth and do something at the talent contest."

"Bury my talent where?" he says.

"In the earth," she says. "That's in the Bible."

"Figures," says Cosmos. "You trying to convert me?"

"No," she says, "but you have so much light in you, why wouldn't you want to let it shine? You have such a good soul—not to mention voice," she says. Then she whispers across the table: "I wish you knew how much I'd like to kiss you right now."

"It's probably better that I don't," says Cosmos.

"The talent contest is only a few weeks away," she says. "You could practice. I really want to hear you perform. Please?"

"I'll see," he says.

She smiles her wonderful big smile. "I knew you'd let your light shine sooner or later."

That night, in his room, Cosmos decides he would only shock and hurt Cherlyn if he were to sing one of his regular songs. And he'd do more than shock Cherlyn's parents: he'd scare them so much that they'd build a wall of restrictions between him and Cherlyn. They'd put him in chains. They'd put her in chains. He considers writing a religious song just for Cherlyn's father, but Cosmos Coyote snarls in disapproval at the very thought. Writing and singing a religious song would be so phony that even William the Nice would blush.

Then he thinks of a happy compromise: he could write a kind of hokey country-Western song that wouldn't get him in trouble with anybody, one that would show Cherlyn that he can perform and that maybe would loosen her father's iron fist at the same time.

Cosmos works several nights on the lyrics. They are corny. They are fun. He uses his allotted Port Swan phone call to telephone Rhody. He reads Rhody the lyrics. "Give me some country-Western kind of music—you know, man, like bad silly country rock or swing or whatever the excuse-my-French they're calling it nowadays."

Rhody's voice is sweet. It not only carries with it the good sounds of the old world but spins up images in his mind of practicing with the OughtaBs. "Furioso," says Rhody. "That place is driving you totally nuts, I can tell, dude. I'll work on it and send you a tape of what the music might sound like. Don't let them make you go sane over there, man."

"Not a chance," says Cosmos.

Elmer comes up to Cosmos in school the next week and asks him if he's going to do anything for the talent show. "Not telling," says Cosmos. "A surprise. And you?"

"Oh yeah, oh yeah," says Elmer, "me and a couple guys, we got this bumpin' and bruisin' guts-and-bolts nuts-and-dolts little band going, you know? Call ourselves the Nitrates and we just want to poison a little soil, you know, make people's piss burn, you know—nothin' too stylish, nothin' too slick, but I'm the devil on the drums and I'll beat somethin' into their eardrums, I guarantee Marie."

"Cool," says Cosmos. "Could I listen to you maybe once?"

Elmer's little makeshift band has permission to use the

band room after school for twenty minutes twice a week to practice. That's all the practicing they'll be doing before the talent show. Cosmos goes down to listen to them. They're terrible. It's the only band he's ever listened to that's dependent on the drummer to give it any musicality at all. At least Elmer has a sense of rhythm. And they do have a decent sound system and use a tape recorder with sampler material to build a decent-sounding musical world around their own stuff.

"Listen," says Cosmos, "would you let me use your tape recorder and sound system and maybe you on drums for a number I want to do?"

The deal is on. Cosmos will be singing one song at the talent show. He tells Cherlyn, who doesn't hold back on her enthusiasm. "You darling, you darling," she says. Students stare at her as she gives Cosmos a hug in the hall-way. He can see in the eyes of the other students that most of them are still dumbfounded at the odd combination of Cherlyn and him as sweethearts. Like Cherlyn's father, they probably thought during the first few weeks that Cherlyn was out to save his soul, but seeing the sweetness, the clear indicators of romance, throws them for a loop. Their bewildered look suggests that they suspect either that Cherlyn is not as good as they thought she was or that Cosmos is not as bad. Sometimes the puzzled look turns to disgust. Cosmos watches for the look in the men's eyes that suggest jealousy, but, he figures, people who spend half their time talking behind other people's backs get pretty good at hiding what they're really thinking. Maybe everybody's got a little Cosmos Coyote hiding inside them, thinking his own nasty thoughts. Maybe somebody's Cosmos Coyote gave them the courage to write that sweet note to Cherlyn, but, try as he does, Cosmos still can't figure out who that secret admirer might be.

Back in Port Swan, Rhody must have gotten into the music for Cosmos's song. He sends a tape the next week. "Try this," he says, "and if it doesn't sound right, try sliding up to the key of D after the bridge." Rhody's tape has only piano and bass, but it gives Cosmos the idea.

Cosmos practices alone in his room. Rhody is a genius. The music has country rhythms, country sounds, along with a few twists and twirls, like musical puns. Cosmos makes a copy of Rhody's tape and asks Elmer to practice the drums with it. He'll do the melody on the guitar.

"How about the lyrics, man?" says Elmer.

"A surprise," says Cosmos. "Nobody is going to hear this song until the night I perform it."

The talent show is held on a Friday night. It's a chilly night with the first sprinkling of snow on the barren fields, and the first heavy coats and caps on people's bodies. The event is held in the gymnasium with chairs and bleachers set up to hold more than a thousand people—and more than a thousand people do come: not just all the students but most of the parents, and aunts, grandmoms, and granddads. A real community event. A crowd larger than any Cosmos has ever played for.

There are fourteen numbers on the program—everything from vocal solos, duets, and quartets to a short dramatic skit, a piano solo, a flute solo, and one stand-up comedy act. First prize will be a hundred dollars, second fifty, and third twenty-five, with three honorable mentions getting gift certificates to the Crown of Light bookstore. The gymnasium, in typical efficient Dutch style, is a combination of theater and gym, with a stage on one end. Cosmos waits backstage with the other performers as the auditorium fills up. He still doesn't recognize many people from the community, but he sees Uncle Henry and Aunt Minnie out there, along with all the teachers and their families, and near the front the warm face of Cherlyn's mother and the chiseled face of her father.

The event starts with opening remarks from Principal Marksema and, of course, an opening prayer. "God bless these talented young people, who, following the admonitions of Thy holy Word, have chosen not to bury their talents in the earth."

There it is again. If the earth got filled up with enough talent, maybe they wouldn't have to use so much artificial fertilizer, Cosmos thinks to himself.

The first number is a vocal solo. The singer is a young man, a baritone trying to be a tenor, whose voice quakes so pathetically that the pianist pounds the piano louder and louder, maybe to give him courage, maybe to cover him up. Everybody backstage looks nervous in response to the first bad showing. But then the stand-up comic comes on with a series of jokes about Iowa weather. "It was so dry and hot last summer that this one farmer fainted and it took a bucket of dust to wake him up. Then the wind got so strong that it blew the postholes right out of the ground, and chickens that had their backs to the wind laid the same egg twice." He's a senior boy who is going to go to Reformation College next year as a preseminary student. He has a good voice and the confidence of a polished speaker. He has the crowd in proverbial stitches. Five minutes of one-liners.

The other performers are more confident after the joke-book speaker gets offstage, and the next numbers go by without a quivering knee or a quivering voice. The Nitrates are third to last, with Cosmos's song following right on their heels. Elmer and the Nitrates' tape recorder and sound system will stay onstage when Cosmos comes up.

Cosmos does a final tuning while the Nitrates play their pathetic whatever-it-is—something like hard-rock country swing—number to a crowd that gives them polite applause. Cosmos doesn't feel nervous until he starts to walk out onstage, plugs in his guitar, does a quick test, and turns to face the audience. "I want to sing a little song I wrote, called 'Give Me a Word,'" he announces in a voice that doesn't sound like his own. He looks over rather than at the crowd, then down at his strings, and the music begins.

> *It seemed in my short sad life*
> *that love would never be mine.*
> *I had my horse, but I had no wife.*
> *All I really wanted was a rhyme.*
> *All I really wanted was a rhyme.*
> *All I really wanted was a rhyme.*
>
> *But try as I did every hour of the day*
> *something went wrong and I couldn't sing this song*
> *because my horse was a palomino,*
> *and nothing rhymes with palomino.*
> *There's just nothing that rhymes with palomino.*
> *There's just nothing that rhymes with palomino.*

Cosmos hears the first titter of laughter coming from the crowd, a female titter. He glances quickly across the audience and sees Cherlyn's sparkling face. She gets it. She knows Cosmos is being funny, and at least a few others are following what must have been her chuckle. He goes on, more confidently:

> *Oh, give me a word that sounds like,*
> *oh, give me a word that looks like,*

oh, give me a word that feels like
a ride on a good palomino.

I think the right word could have been my friend.
If lonely is what my life was meant to be,
just the right sound could have carried me to the end
without a lady friend to keep me company.
Without a lady friend to keep me company.

Now Cosmos hears a loud whisper from the first row, the kind of whisper that can only come from someone who doesn't realize that people onstage can hear sounds from the audience. A man's voice whispers, "He's good."

I rode east to west, doing my best,
searching my mind, I wanted to find
just one word that sounds like palomino,
when—hey!—I met this fine gal from Reno.
Yeah, I met this fine gal from Reno.

Someone in the audience yells, "Yeah!" Someone else whoops. The applause starts, and then some wild cheering. Should I stop while I'm ahead? he thinks for a second. He plays a few bars, following the tape-recorded music, then goes on, his voice louder at the encouragement from the crowd.

Yes! I met her at the Big Bell Casino,
and we spent all night drinking vino,
me and my fine gal from Reno.
Who needs a tired palomino!
Who needs a tired palomino?

Oh, I got me a word that sounds like,
oh, I got me a word that looks like,
oh, I got me a word that feels like
a ride on a good palomino.
Yeah, I got me a sweet gal from Reno.

The applause doesn't stop for a good minute. "Encore! Encore!" some of the crowd scream. But Cosmos doesn't have an encore—at least not one that won't get him in trouble with the school, and probably most of the people in the audience.

The winners are to be decided by three teachers who will try to judge the applause as each contestant walks across stage. It is clear from the applause that Cosmos is the winner, but when the judges make their announcement, they say that it is a tie between William De Haag and Marlys Vander Swiel. Marlys had sung a soprano solo: "How Great Thou Art."

No one boos, no one hisses. Cosmos grins. This is good. This is very, very good. He knows that he was best. He also knows that sharing the first prize will make him look better in everyone's eyes. It's a win-win, no doubt about it.

Cherlyn runs backstage and throws her arms around Cosmos. "I like the secrets you keep about yourself," she whispers to him. "You were fabulous, just fabulous."

But no adults come backstage to congratulate Cosmos. When the auditorium starts to clear out, Cosmos sees Uncle Henry and Aunt Minnie waiting for him. "See you tomorrow," Cherlyn says sweetly, and heads off to her parents as Cosmos heads off to join Aunt Minnie and Uncle Henry for the ride home.

Cosmos should have known from the polite way Aunt Minnie compliments him that there are some reservations in the air. Then Uncle Henry adds, "You have a fine De Haag voice."

* * *

It's not until the next day that Cosmos learns about the reservations, since it seems most of the adult audience share them. Cosmos finds out when he asks Cherlyn what her parents thought of his performance.

"Everybody thought you had a fabulous voice," says Cherlyn. "But my folks had some trouble with the words."

"Okay, tell me," says Cosmos. "What should I know?"

"It's this part of my people that I disagree with," says Cherlyn. "I think loving God is liberating. It sets you free to enjoy many different things. Including some satire. I thought your song was a great satire of country-Western.

Great. Fabulous. You were fabulous."

"But?" he says. "Tell me exactly what problem folks had with it."

"I'll tell you," she says. "But understand I don't share their objections, all right?"

"All right," says Cosmos. "Now tell me, all right?"

"Here's the list," she says. "Some people thought the reference to drinking wine was out of place at the Academy, especially for an audience of people who are too young to drink. Some people thought the reference to a casino was in bad taste. My dad even thought the 'ride on a good palomino' could be taken the wrong way."

"Jeez," says Cosmos.

"There's more," says Cherlyn. "Some people thought the ending was too suggestive, the part about spending 'all night' with this 'gal from Reno.'"

Cherlyn starts to giggle. So does Cosmos.

"Were you embarrassed that I was singing those words?" says Cosmos.

"Are you kidding?" says Cherlyn. "I thought it was great. The funniest song I've heard in ages. I loved it! I want to hear more of your songs."

"I think I'll quit while I'm ahead," he says.

"You're way ahead with me," she says. "But you want me to be honest one hundred percent, right?"

"Yes," he says, "I count on you for that."

"My dad is digging in his heels. Now he knows for sure

he doesn't want me to see you."

"So what really is his problem with me?" says Cosmos.

"He says he doesn't think you're a believer."

"Well, he's right about that."

"No, he's not," says Cherlyn. "You're one of God's people, I know it. I feel it in my heart. You can say you don't believe all you want to, but God has His own way with people. God can believe in you even if you don't believe in Him, or don't think you do. And God believes in you. You're one of His. I can feel it."

"That's good enough for me," says Cosmos. "If I'm one of God's people in your heart, it's fine with me."

"But my dad says I shouldn't see you any more than necessary," says Cherlyn.

"What on earth does that mean—'any more than necessary'?" says Cosmos.

"I guess it means 'when we can't avoid it,' like school business or whatever."

Cherlyn rarely looks tense. She looks tense now.

"So it's over?" says Cosmos. "Just like that, it's over?"

"It can't mean that," she says. "I think it means we have to be more careful. He can't banish you."

"Sounds to me like he's trying. So now we have to start hiding, not showing anybody how we feel?"

"I think so," she says. "I think it just means we're going to have to be a little bit more secretive." She watches him sink under the new, tighter restrictions. "Please don't look so sullen," she says. "Nothing can really separate us."

"Shouldn't love be lovely and free?" says Cosmos. "Shouldn't it be open?"

"Yes," says Cherlyn. "Like a light in a dark world."

"I feel like my love has been put in a cage. Put in a cage and bitten by a snake. What can love do when it is trapped?"

"Nobody can put a fence around love," she says. "Sometimes, when the stage gets small, the actors just have to be more inventive. All we really have to do is be a little bit more creative. A little bit more private."

"Wouldn't you have to lie to your dad?"

"Oh no," she says in defense. "I just won't tell him anything that would make him angry or hurt him. What would be the point?"

Where's the lie?

WHAT COSMOS AND CHERLYN hear at the heart of her father's rules is that they should be invisible in whatever they do. That seems to be her father's first and great commandment.

"'I don't want you to be seen with that De Haag boy. Period.' Those were his exact words," says Cherlyn. "And I don't want to disobey him."

"I understand," says Cosmos. "I'd never ask you to disobey your dad. But his orders do seem a little fuzzy, when you think about them. It sounds as if, maybe, if we're really really secret about things and nobody sees us, then it's all right? Is that what I'm hearing?"

"That's pretty much what I'm hearing," says Cherlyn. "But I think I listened to what he said closer than he listened to himself. Either way, I think he'll soften up with time."

Cherlyn and Cosmos hope that, just as the resolve of a government that has placed sanctions on a troublesome weaker country eventually weakens, so too will the resolve of Cherlyn's father begin to waver and fade after a few weeks of full compliance. Cherlyn goes the second mile. Not only is she not seen in public with Cosmos, but she toes the line with the rest of her father's orders too. If he tells her to be home at eleven, she's home at ten-thirty. If she goes to a debate tournament, she not only tells him the results, but shows him the judges' score card. She builds a bulwark of trustworthiness. It isn't long before her father isn't asking about Cosmos—or "that De Haag boy," as he says.

"I don't even talk about you at home," says Cherlyn. "I never say 'William,' and I certainly never say 'Cosmos.' In this community," she says, "silence is a good way to make something go away."

"I've been learning that too," says Cosmos. "If you don't talk about something, you can pretend it doesn't exist."

But in school their relationship does exist. In school he is not totally off-limits.

"I don't think Daddy worries about us together in school," says Cherlyn. "I think he figures that the Christian atmosphere here at school will protect me from whatever he thinks I need protecting from."

Cosmos and Cherlyn go on seeing each other as much as they did before her father's latest orders to be, as they understand it, "less visible." In the hallways, they brush their arms against each other's a little more gently, a little less obviously. To get close to her, Cosmos uses his hands less and his nose and eyes more. He sniffs her fragrance more often and more deeply. He doesn't let his eyes be distracted from her when she is near. And when they separate, he watches how her hips move as she walks, until she disappears down the hallway. If they have to be even less visible about their friendship, Cherlyn figures they'll need even more time together to make up for what they're losing by not being able to touch each other in view of anyone. She cuts her Student Council meetings short so that she can have the full noon hour with him. They sit at the table along the far wall, where there is less chance that anyone can see what their legs and feet are doing together under the table.

"I just like to watch you eat," she says. "I like the way you chew your food. I love the way your eyebrows make these little fluttering movements when you talk."

"I like the way your eyes smile when your lips smile," he says. "I like it when you rub your bottom lip against your upper lip. Like this. I like that when you do it."

"When I'm at home, nobody knows what I'm thinking," she says. "You're like a movie in my mind and only I can see it."

"I know about those mind movies," says Cosmos. "I watch ones of you all the time."

"Mom says I'm having mood swings," says Cherlyn. "She says I have dreamy eyes and don't hear half of what she says to me one minute and that I'm all sparkly and attentive the next."

"I think Uncle Henry and Aunt Minnie would be delighted if they knew I was thinking about you all the time," says Cosmos. "I think if you came over to their house they'd be very happy and would leave us alone wherever we were."

"I couldn't do that," says Cherlyn. "I'd have to lie to my dad."

"Just an idea," says Cosmos. "You know I'd never ask you to lie to your dad."

"You're the little jewel I keep hidden in the bottom of my purse, more valuable than anybody will ever know," says Cherlyn.

"I remember when I first saw you behind church, standing in the middle of all those people," says Cosmos. "You were the only one who looked my way. You were the rose in a field of oats."

"I'm going to make you the stowaway in the hold of my heart," says Cherlyn. "I'll feed you in the darkness of my dreams. What should I feed you?"

"Dungeness crab and lemon-meringue pie," he says. "You are the seagull in the blue sky of my mind. What should I feed you?"

"Hamburger and French fries." She giggles.

"With ketchup?" he says.

"With ketchup and a sauce of soft kisses."

"At night you can sleep in the nest of my heart," he says.

"But I'd be restless. I wouldn't be able to sleep. I'd flutter around all night thinking about you." She stares at him across the table. "I wish you knew how much I'd like to kiss you right now."

"The last time you said that I said I'd better not know. So this time, instead, let's both do our own mind movie of kissing each other. Right now," he says.

They stare at each other and their eyes glaze over with mutual desire.

"I ache everywhere with love for you," he says. "Your father's sanctions aren't working. If my heart has a border crossing, my feelings are like illegal aliens who aren't exposed by the searchlights."

"Daddy's rules aren't working on my heart either," she says. "My body obeys his commands. My mind does too, because I have truly tried to understand his fears. But my heart is like a night bird that no one sees."

"Sometimes I get scared," says Cosmos. "Not of your dad. Sometimes I'm afraid I'm not the right person. I'm not good enough for you. You are so pure it scares me."

"I'm not pure," she says. "I'm selfish and greedy and self-centered and a million other bad things. I don't really trust myself in anything. Except love. I feel my own life has been transformed by God's love, and I believe that any love I feel for you can only be a weak echo of God's love for me. How could I accept God's love without accepting my feeling of love for you? I won't lie to Daddy, but I won't deny my love for you either."

Cosmos does not have an answer. He sits in silence.

"Even with the new rules," she goes on, "the more I love you, the more love I feel I get back from you. Love really is like a mirror, isn't it? I can't believe that God's love is any different from ours, just bigger. A lot bigger, and purer. With God, the more faith I have, the more faith God gives back to me. I think I learned how to love you by loving God. I really do."

"Cherlyn," Cosmos says, and can say no more.

* * *

"We've been noticing that it's been quite a while since that Van Dyke girl has brought you home from school or picked you up to go to a basketball game or something," says Uncle Henry. He and Cosmos have finished the evening chores and are cleaning their boots off in the porch.

"I'll tell you the truth," says Cosmos. He hangs up his work jacket. "Her dad doesn't like me. He thinks I'm not good enough for her, so he's made this rule that she can't drive me anywhere. We are not to be seen together. Period."

"Huh," says Uncle Henry.

Cosmos can see that Uncle Henry wants to say more, but doesn't. "What do you think?" Cosmos asks.

"Well, you see," he says, "I have some problems with Cornelius. He's got plenty of money, but I don't think that gives him the right to judge others. 'Judge not that ye be not judged,' the Bible says, but I sometimes wonder how the Lord will judge him on Judgment Day."

"But he seems to be a good member of the church and everything, always parading up front and shaking hands with everybody after church."

"He gives the appearance of a good churchman," says Uncle Henry, "and he does have plenty of money, but he didn't much care who he had to run over to get it. Cornelius is the kind of fellow who can have one hand on the Bible while the other hand is in your back pocket."

It occurs to Cosmos that, if he put on his most hurt, William the Nice face, Uncle Henry just might take pity on him and talk to Cherlyn's mother, tell her that they are all wrong about Cosmos, that Cosmos is in fact a totally good De Haag boy who has his own way of worshipping God, and that, God knows, Jesus himself had different ways of serving the Lord, and that, God knows, Jesus himself had his arms open more to sinners than to the sanctimonious creeps who would try to keep young people from spending affectionate time together. If I knew the Bible a little better, Cosmos thinks, maybe I could make my own argument.

But he doesn't.

After supper, Aunt Minnie looks at Cosmos knowingly. She doesn't hide the fact that Uncle Henry has talked to her about Cherlyn and about Cherlyn's father's not allowing her to drive him anywhere anymore. "Is she not allowed to talk to you at school either?" she says and grins a little.

"Oh no," says Cosmos, and tries not to reveal too little or too much in his voice.

"Well, if she's not allowed to drive you anywhere anymore," says Minnie, "we'll be happy to drive you to school events that you'd like to go to, won't we, Henry?"

"Yes, we will," Uncle Henry says. "Any time. No trouble."

This will be a little bit awkward, Cosmos thinks, but it is a chink in the armor.

The next day, he tells Cherlyn about the option of just happening to be at the same basketball game Tuesday night, though neither of them is much interested in the team. "Yay! Yay! Hey! Hey! Academy Tulips save the day!" That sort of thing is neither Cherlyn's nor Cosmos's cup of tea.

"Are your uncle Henry and aunt Minnie going to the game, or are they just dropping you off?" Cherlyn asks in a way that sounds totally innocent.

"Aunt Minnie said she could just drop me off and that I could call her when the game was over and she'd pick me up," Cosmos answers in his most matter-of-fact tone.

"This is very good," says Cherlyn, and the innocent tone has left her voice. "Why don't you walk around to the west end of the parking lot and I'll wait for you in the car next to the Dumpster?"

"But wouldn't you have to lie to your dad?" he says.

"No," says Cherlyn. "I'll tell him that I'm giving Margaret a ride to the game. She really did ask me for a ride. Margaret will go to the game and we can have time together during the game. Then, afterward, you can call your aunt and I can give Margaret a ride home. Where's the lie?"

"I don't see any," says Cosmos.

On Tuesday night, Aunt Minnie drops Cosmos off at the gymnasium. The air is chilly and Cosmos pulls his jacket collar up against his cheeks, making it easy to disguise himself without looking like somebody who is trying to hide. He walks around the gymnasium, across the parking lot, toward the blue Ford idling innocently behind a large Dumpster. Cherlyn sees him coming through the rearview mirror and leans over to open his door.

When the door closes with Cosmos inside, the darkness opens them to each other. A wall crumbles between them. Too long separated by light, separated by exposure to the world. This is not love with the cover of darkness. This is love with the uncovering of darkness. The tantalizing sounds of sleek windbreakers sliding against the vinyl seats, the muffled clank of the seat-belt latch against the door, the sound of each turning on the car seat toward the other.

Then the beautiful sound of her voice. "It's been so long," says Cherlyn.

Cosmos leans through the bower of darkness into the

sweet scent of her—a bouquet of fragrances from her arms, her face, her neck—lavender, sweet lemon, sweet clover, and one unfamiliar scent, a bittersweet perfume, a fiercely fragrant aroma that comes at him like the sweetened breath of a lioness. Cosmos's shoulders rise as if he were going to spread his wings like a huge courting bird. Her arms slide around his neck and his own body squirms gracefully toward her. In their embrace her breasts press against his chest, and her lips, like a water lily rising through a sea of darkness, touch his. They are cool and soft, and the smell is of a just-budding rose.

"Cherlyn," he moans. She responds by pulling him more tightly toward herself, then takes his face in her hands and kisses him urgently, repeatedly, hungrily. In the darkness they kiss and sigh and kiss and gasp, their hands pressing each other's cheeks, their mouths open, their teeth clicking against each other's like small castanets, their tongues cavorting in an aural dance their Dutch Calvinist ancestors would never have been able to imagine on earth or in heaven. It is beautiful music. It is like that magic moment when music absorbs the world and makes everything outside itself cease to exist.

How long they kiss before taking a rest, they do not know. Perhaps the first quarter is over. Perhaps it is almost halftime. When they do pause, the inside of the car seems even darker, but the tiny light from the ignition glows like a single bright star, and it does cast enough light on their faces so that they can see the glow of each other's eyes. Cherlyn's lips look swollen from their incessant and bruising kisses. Cosmos puts his hand to his mouth, imagining that his lips must be swollen too. Then he notices that the windows are more than dark, they are covered with snow. "Look," he says. "We made the sky fall."

He tries to lean forward, but he is so aroused that he can hardly move.

She laughs at his comment, then looks toward him, and her eyes rest on his erection, upon which the tiny ignition light shines.

"If I were a man, I'd look exactly the way you do," she says. "Oh, Cosmos, aren't bodies beautiful?"

The turn in the conversation reminds Cosmos of nothing he has ever before experienced. Salal would never have said anything like that. Salal would have either grabbed it or ignored it, but she wouldn't have sat looking at it admiringly. For the first time in Iowa, Cosmos wishes he had a condom. It never occurred to him that he might need one out here. For a flash, he wonders if they even sell them in Iowa, at least in this part of Iowa.

"Nothing that I have is as beautiful as everything that you have," he says. He slides closer toward her. He takes her hand and places it on himself. "Is that all right?" he says.

"Yes," she says, and her hand tightens over his zipper. "Bodies are beautiful. I think God wants us to enjoy them.

There's nothing in the Bible that says we can't touch each other in a loving way. But even God's love has rules, and I think it is up to me to figure out what they are right now. I think everything can be beautiful as long as we don't take any clothes off, don't you think? Taking any clothes off would be tempting our bodies to do something we shouldn't do, but this?"

"Ah," says Cosmos as she squeezes him.

She takes her hand back and reaches to kiss him again. He puts his hand on her breast, inside her coat, over her blouse. "May I?" he says.

"Yes, I love the way you touch me," she says.

They go back to fondling and kissing until they hear nothing but the sounds of their own breathing. And then the car door opens, and with it the interior light. "Oh!" shouts a woman's voice. It is Cherlyn's friend Margaret. Hard-jawed, stern, and judgmental-looking Margaret. "Cherlyn!" she says, looking past Cosmos, who has quickly rearranged himself to look like an innocent passenger in a snow-covered car parked next to a Dumpster on a dark night. "I didn't see you at the game and got worried. Aren't you supposed to be staying away from him?"

She doesn't look at Cosmos. She looks at Cherlyn.

Cherlyn shows no signs of being flustered by the intrusion.

"I'm not breaking any rules, Margaret," she says.

"Did you see how much snow has fallen?" says

Margaret. "Most people left at halftime. I think we should go before the roads get bad too." For the first time she levels her eyes on Cosmos. "And I don't think your parents would be too happy to see you in a parked car with a thief."

Cosmos looks her straight in the face and doesn't say a word.

"Margaret, you are out of order," says Cherlyn. Cherlyn's voice is evenly controlled. Her debating experience is showing. Cosmos imagines her one day in a presidential debate, keeping her cool like this while her opponent makes a fool of herself.

"Wow, there is a lot of snow," says Cosmos matter-of-factly. "I'd better go call my aunt before the roads get too bad."

"Cosmos," says Cherlyn, and takes his hand. She looks worried about him. She looks as if she is afraid he has been hurt.

"Believe me, everything is fine." He leans over and gives her a kiss. "See you tomorrow."

He slides out of the car and holds the door for Margaret. "Careful," he says as she starts to get in. "Don't fall on your ass and break all the pretty little snowflakes."

Margaret slams the door and Cosmos walks away.

When he gets to the front of the gymnasium, he sees Aunt Minnie's car already parked out front. She sees him coming as Cherlyn with Margaret drives out of the parking lot. She opens the door, and he hops in.

She starts to drive away. They are directly behind Cherlyn and Margaret, creeping along down the snow-packed street. "When I saw the forecast, I thought I'd better come to get you," she says. "How was the game going?" She looks over at him, and when she catches his eye she winks.

"You'd better watch the road," says Cosmos. "It's looking pretty dangerous out there."

What's this crap?

"**D**ID MARGARET squeal on us?"

It is Cosmos's first question for Cherlyn the next day.

"Margaret and I had a good talk," says Cherlyn. "It was long overdue."

Not only did Cherlyn tell Margaret that she had no business talking about Cosmos the way she did, she told her that friendship meant not trying to hurt the person you call your friend. What's more, Cherlyn told her in no uncertain terms, she and Cosmos were not breaking her father's rule about being seen together. If she hadn't rudely opened the car door without warning, they would not have been seen together.

"Wow," says Cosmos. "You really let her have it. You're going to make some tough president."

"There's a really interesting ending to this story, Coz," says Cherlyn. "Margaret wrote that note you were so worried about."

"She what?"

"Yes. After I scolded her for being a bad friend and threatening to tell my dad about us, she broke down and started crying. She said, 'It's just not fair. You used to be my friend and I could talk to you any time. Now you're always with him.' Meaning you, my love. I felt really sorry for her and told her I still thought of her as my very dear friend and that I'd spend more time with her. She was terribly hurt that I didn't respond to the note. She figured that I'd know only she could have written it."

"Is she gay?" says Cosmos, remembering all too painfully how Bridgette moved in on his relationship with Salal.

"Is she what?" says Cherlyn.

"Is she a lesbian?"

"Oh no," says Cherlyn. "Nothing like that. She's just scared of being left out. She's not very popular. Scared and lonely, like so many people."

"Scared and lonely like me until I met you," says Cosmos.

"Actually, I'm relieved it was her, aren't you? I haven't dared to look another guy in the face since that note. I hardly dared to say hi to guys. I didn't like it one bit. I don't like being that way in the world, so full of suspicion all the time."

"I don't either," says Cosmos. "You know, nobody has been arrested yet for the thefts. The cops haven't talked to me, but I can tell most of the students think I'm the thief. So I just go along with everybody staring at me. Whatever trust I have for anybody, I have to thank you for. I wouldn't trust anybody around here any farther than I could throw them if I didn't have your trusting eyes to come back to."

"You're so kind. You're such a gentle spirit. When I pray, I thank God for putting you on this planet at the same time that I'm here."

"Luck of the draw," Cosmos teases. "When I look up at night, I count my lucky stars."

* * *

Cosmos awakens the next morning to see the entire landscape covered with snow. It is as if Iowa has been cleaned up; all the bad feelings about the place that haven't already been swept up by his love for Cherlyn are now swept under winter's white rug. The cold air has a cleansing effect too. Is this why people live here, he wonders—so that once a year everything you don't like about the world disappears, and in its place is a clean slate, for the eye, for the nose, for the mind? It even seems quieter. Peaceful.

On the clean winter slate of Cosmos's mind is written Cherlyn. But Christmas vacation begins soon, and he'll be flying home to Washington. Both he and Cherlyn know there will not be another chance like the one they had in the car during the basketball game. "It's a good thing," says Cherlyn. "We do need to slow down, don't you think?"

"Any kind of time is good time with you," says Cosmos. The only slowing down they do at the Academy is by lingering longer over the lunch table and lingering longer in the halls before each class. In chapel, they wait until Margaret is seated, then find a place of their own where they can hold hands without making her feel left out.

But the frustration of not being able to hold her in his arms and kiss her follows Cosmos home. Alone in his room, he feels his mood plunge. He looks at himself in the mirror and asks himself, "How did this happen? You're in love with an Iowa Jesus freak!"

He imagines hiding the truth from the OughtaBs, from his dad, but there will be questions about his life. How can he simply skip over her and pretend she doesn't exist? And if he does tell them about her, will they make so much fun of him that he'll feel more the outsider than he has felt here? Can he and his heart just rise up and transplant themselves back in Port Swan? What will happen to the disguises he has learned to wear to survive Iowa? Will William the Nice smile a false smile to his Port Swan friends, pretending he is not in love? Where will his real self be and what will it look like?

The day before he is to leave for the holidays, Cosmos sneaks around behind the school with Cherlyn as soon as school lets out. The snow is crusted and icy and their feet punch through it with each step, but they find a spot under the English-class window where they're practically hidden from view in all directions. Cherlyn takes off her mittens and holds Cosmos's face in her warm hands. They start kissing the way they did under the cover of darkness, stabbing each other with their tongues, devouring each other with their lips. Cosmos loses track of time, but Cherlyn finally pulls back. She looks up into Cosmos's eyes and he can see the tears coming. "I am going to miss you so much," she says. She reaches into her pocket and takes out a small wrapped package. "Open this in Washington, all right?" she says.

He takes the gift. "Christmas sneaked up on me," he says. "I'm sorry I haven't gotten anything for you yet. I'll get you something in Port Swan."

"You don't have to," she says. "Coming back in January will be all the gift I need." She steps back. "I have to go," she says. "Maybe I should leave first, so somebody besides Margaret doesn't see us and tell my dad. I still haven't lied to him, but if too many people see us, I will have."

"There's nothing sweet about parting," says Cosmos.

"And there's no sorrow knowing you still will be in my heart while you're gone."

"Go," he says. "Cherlyn," he calls when she is five steps away. She turns around to look back with her teary eyes. "I love you," he says.

"I love you too," she says. She blinks her eyes to stop the tears. She turns and starts trudging off through the deep snow.

"Read up on that Van Buren cat."

She turns back and is smiling. "I will," she says, and continues walking.

Cosmos waits for a minute, then follows the broken path she has made. When he gets out front of the Academy, he sees that Cherlyn has driven off and that all of the buses have too.

But Elmer hasn't. He is just getting into his black Toyota pickup when he sees Cosmos. "Yo!" he yells.

Cosmos walks toward him. Cosmos is stranded and doesn't have much choice. When Elmer offers him a ride home, he accepts.

Elmer guns the engine on the packed snow to make the rear end of the pickup arc around as he leaves the parking lot. Then he starts in. "I gotta tell you—what's your real name, Bill or Cosmos?"

"Call me Cosmos. Or Coz."

"I gotta tell you, Coz, you are one hell of a musician. That crazy number you did at the talent show? Ride on a good palomino? I about died, man. Nobody around here can touch you, man. You're a poet and you know it, don't blow it, just show it, dude."

"Thanks. Now, are we going to talk, or is this going to be a little circus of quick licks?"

"No, let's talk. You and me, we're different, man. You and me, we're the black sheep in this shit hole of a school, know what I'm saying?"

"Maybe so," says Cosmos, "but me, I'm trying to fit in. And things are pretty different since I got to know Cherlyn."

"Heard you had your ass in deep shit back in Washington, right?"

"Right," says Cosmos.

"Cherlyn know about that?"

"Not the details. It's never come up. She just accepts me for what I am. And even if I did tell her, it wasn't for any big shit. Graffiti, if you can believe that. Graffiti and a water gun somebody stuck in my hand and people thought it was real. I'll tell her sometime. That's what I like about her: she doesn't judge."

"Eeee-ow. You are one blown-away dude. So. No arrests for drugs?"

"Oh yeah, but that was earlier. They did a diversion thing, counseling and all that."

"Ever busted for booze?"

"Oh yeah, that too," says Cosmos. "I did community service that time, I believe."

"Like I said, man, you and me, we're the black sheep in this shit hole. Yours is a little different profile—shall we say—than Miss Van Dyke's."

"We shall say that."

The pickup bounces along, a less comfortable ride than the tractors Cosmos has been driving at Uncle Henry's. "You ever been arrested?" says Cosmos.

"Been hassled plenty," says Elmer. "But I know the cops around here, and my dad knows the dad of this one dick, just a young fuck, you know. So this one young-fuck dick, he graduated from the public high school here, and he talks to his old man about how he thinks I'm doing drugs, you know, and his old man talks to my old man, and I get the third degree from my old man, you know. Like that. I almost got busted in Sioux Shit City. Cops there are tough-asses. See a pickup with a farm kid in it and they start following you around, just waiting for a chance to bust your ass. Problem is, city cops sometimes quit and want to go to a small town. So they come around here with all their tough-ass big-city shit looking to slap somebody around. You gotta watch out for these big-city cops who drop out and come to the small towns. Fucking Rambos, they get bored and start fucking with you."

"You're sure not going to get a speeding ticket," says Cosmos. "You're going forty and there's about ten cars piled up behind you."

"Fuck," says Elmer, and steps on the gas. "I gotta get off the highway." He signals and turns off on the first gravel-road intersection he comes to.

"I thought I was going seventy," he says.

"You're stoned," says Cosmos. "What the hell are you on?"

"Want some?" says Elmer. He pulls over, sidling up against the plowed snow along the road.

"I haven't been doing any drugs," says Cosmos. "I still don't know if drug-testing is going to be part of my program here. I suppose Mike Jonsma could do it any time if he felt like it. I did smoke some weed I saw growing along the road by my Uncle Henry's house. Bad shit, I'll tell you."

"Oh, that's skag, dude," says Elmer. "Nobody but grade-school kids smoke that shit."

"Gave me a two-day headache."

"It's better if you let it get good and dry," says Elmer. "But not much better. You could better smoke dried cow shit, know what I'm sayin'?"

Elmer reaches down under his dash and pulls out his box of goodies, a tiny plastic fish-tackle box with separate compartments. Elmer has at least four options, two different-colored pills, a tiny bag of mostly marijuana heads, a chunk of opium or hash, and some white powder.

"Core," says Cosmos.

"Here's the real stuff," says Elmer, pulling out the tiny bag of white powder.

"I don't do anything white," says Cosmos.

"Yeah, well, you'd need more time for this stuff than we've got right now anyhow. You have to do chores when you get home, right?"

"Right," says Cosmos. "If I'm smart, I won't do anything tonight. Where do you get all this shit?"

"Not hard," says Elmer. "Sioux City. Sioux Falls. And

places in between. Know what I'm sayin'?"

"Where do you get the bread to buy this stuff?"

"I can pay for everything by selling half of what I get. I could get more, but, you know, why be greedy? Pass it around, you know."

"You're a dealer!" says Cosmos. "You're a dealer right out here in the cornfields of Iowa!"

"Nah, just friends. Not going to do anything stupid."

"There's a car coming," says Cosmos.

Elmer sees it too, a big red pickup coming in their direction from the front.

"He's got room to get by," says Elmer.

"What if he stops and you got all this shit on the front seat here?"

"You're a worrier," says Elmer. "Why the hell would he stop anyhow?"

The pickup slows down, and just as it appears that it is going to pass on by, the driver puts on the brakes and pulls to a stop right next to the driver's-side window. The driver of the red pickup is a big fellow about forty with a green Felco feed cap on.

Cosmos grabs the tackle box full of dope and slips it under the seat on his side.

"You boys got a problem?" says the guy in the big pickup.

"Nah," says Elmer. "No problem."

The driver keeps looking at them. He doesn't drive

away. His pickup is much higher than Elmer's and he's sitting high and close enough to look down into Elmer's little Toyota.

"I keep finding beer cans on this road," says the driver. Cosmos looks across at him. He's a mean one. He's got the eyes of a hellfire-and-brimstone preacher and the muscles of Arnold Schwarzenegger.

"No beer here," says Elmer. "We were just about to take off. My friend here had to whiz."

"I saw you pull over," says the big guy in the pickup. "Nobody got out to whiz. What are you kids up to in there?" He leans out the window to get a better look inside Elmer's pickup. "You'd better not have any alcohol or drugs in there," he says. And then, as if he is some kind of vigilante or something, he starts to get out of his pickup.

"I don't need your crap," says Elmer, and slams the Toyota into gear and guns it. The rear end of the light pickup slides to the right as he spins forward, then fishtails down the center of the road before leveling out down the straightaway.

Cosmos looks out the back window. The big farmer is looking back at them out of his rear window and he has his cell phone to his ear.

"Damn cell phones are the tattletale's pacifier," says Cosmos.

"What?" says Elmer.

"He's got a phone," says Cosmos. "The sonofabitch is calling the cops. Holy shit, man, I don't need this kind of crap. And I haven't even touched anything."

"Calm down, dude," says Elmer. "That shithead probably couldn't find 911 with his dick. Even if he does, he'll probably get some town twenty miles away. Calm down, you're out in the boonies, dude."

"Right," says Cosmos, "which means he probably knows who we are."

"You worry too much, dude," says Elmer. "Screw 'em." He turns at the next intersection and parks the pickup again. "Gimme my dope," he says.

Cosmos reaches under the seat to retrieve Elmer's tackle box. But instead of the tackle box, his hand lands on something else. A whole nest of something elses. Cosmos scratches under the seat, and with his fingers he drags out a Swiss Army knife and two watches. "What's this crap?" he says, but he knows what it is. Elmer is the thief after all.

"You stole this shit! And you let them blame me!"

Elmer guns the pickup and takes off again, his eyes straight ahead.

"Hey!" yells Cosmos. "You've got some explaining to do! Stop this goddamn thing."

Elmer accelerates harder.

"Hey! Are you nuts? Pull over!"

Elmer slows down. "You're one to preach at me," he

says. "You and your record ten feet long."

"You almost made it a hundred feet long. Pull over, I'll walk home."

Elmer pulls over. "Don't get out, man, I've got a problem."

"Damn right you've got a problem."

"So what do you want me to do, pay you? I haven't got a cent. Not a goddamn cent. Like I said, I give most of my shit away, and I've been getting squeezed a few times."

"Pay me for what?" says Cosmos. "What are you talking about—pay me?"

"To keep your fucking mouth shut about this."

Cosmos stares at him. "You really don't know me, do you?"

"What you sayin'?" says Elmer.

"As pissed as I am right now, there is no way in hell I would rat on you or anybody else. That's not an option in my book. I don't squeal on anybody. Unless somebody's getting hurt. The way I'm feeling right now, you're the only one around here who's likely to get hurt."

"Hey, I wouldn't blame you," says Elmer. He looks straight at Cosmos. "Like I said, man, I got a problem."

"Yeah. So why were you making your problem my problem by pretending you wanted to help after Marksema made that announcement? The whole goddamn school stared at me."

"I didn't want to get my ass caught. I didn't want you to get your ass slammed either for what I did. So I figured if those assholes saw me trying to help you they'd figure neither one of us did it."

"You did the second theft too?"

"No, that was Brad. He did it to buy drugs. Not from me."

"I don't know Brad," says Cosmos.

"You don't want to either," says Elmer. "I'm really sorry, man, but, swear to God, if the police had started harassing your ass, I would have planted the shit in some dumb fuck's coat."

"You wouldn't have confessed if they had nailed me for it, that what you're telling me?" says Cosmos.

"Not unless I'd of had to. My dad would kill me. My dad would peel my ass like a potato. He's beat the hell out of me for a hell of a lot less. Shit you not. But if I'd of had to, sure, man. No fucking way would I let them pin it on you, if it came to that."

"It damn near did," says Cosmos.

"You're really not going to tell Marksema about this?"

"Never," says Cosmos. "Ratting on people is not my style. Now just drive me home. And let me off on the corner. I don't want my uncle and aunt seeing you bring me home."

"Don't blame you, man."

Elmer parks a good city block away from the driveway to Uncle Henry and Aunt Minnie's house. "Merry fucking

Christmas," he says as he gets out.

"Merry Christmas," says Elmer. "Hey, man." Cosmos stops and looks back before slamming the door. "Be my friend, man. I'll make it up to you."

Cosmos looks in and studies him. Elmer's fingers are twitching. "Sure. Sure," says Cosmos. "I'm not going to judge you."

I can't do this

RISING TO THIRTY-FIVE thousand feet on the 747 bound for Seattle, Cosmos remembers the last time he was on an airplane—that time heading toward the Midwest. At thirty-five thousand feet, the mind is free to rise with the plane, to soar, to contemplate, to take stock. How do you compare the love you once had with one woman with the love you now have for another? And if you loved the first woman and don't anymore, does that mean it wasn't really love in the first place? And if love for the first woman wasn't true love, then how can you know the love you have for the next woman is true? And if you love one woman who is totally different from the next woman, does that mean that you must have changed, that you're a different person with a different love inside you? How else could you love somebody new who is so different if you haven't changed yourself? Was his love for Salal Cosmos Coyote love and his love for Cherlyn William the Nice love?

"I doubt it," says Cosmos aloud.

"I beg your pardon," says the woman in the seat next to

him through the G-flat roar of the jet engines.

Cosmos doesn't answer, but he does change the topic of his mind. Elmer. Little sonofabitching doper thief. What a squirrelly, immoral little creep. But you can't hate him. Hating Elmer would be like hating a wart on somebody's nose: you may not like to look at it, but it is not exactly like pouring nitrates in the drinking water. Elmer is a loser. He needs protection. Blowing the whistle on him would be like drowning a rat. Blowing the whistle on him would be like pushing a blind kid off a swing. Except Elmer could hurt me, Cosmos thinks. I've known that from the first time I laid eyes on him. He's a tar baby. But I still wouldn't snitch on him. Snitching is for the scumbags of the world. If I believed in hell, the only people I'd put there are the snitches, the tattletales, all the squealers of the world, people who try to destroy people they think are worse or weaker than they are. Snitching on somebody is like rape: getting kicks out of hurting somebody who is weaker than you are.

"That's a fact," says Cosmos aloud.

"I beg your pardon?" the woman next to him says again. Cosmos looks over at her this time. She's about forty-five, blonde, and beautiful, and she looks a little bit the way his mother would look if she cared about her appearance.

"Sorry," says Cosmos. "I was just thinking that if somebody snitches on somebody else it's like rape."

The woman looks slightly alarmed as she tries to process

that remark. Then she turns away and lays her head back, as if she intends to take a nap.

Cosmos lays his head back too. Sleeping through Montana would be a good way to get ready for whatever is waiting for him in Port Swan.

He awakens to the announced descent into Seattle. Approaching Seattle by air, Cosmos feels the cool glow of green coming up at him. It's a rare clear December day and the mountains are out, rising above the forests like the crowns of kings. Except for Mount St. Helens's head, which looks a little bit like a cowboy hat that somebody stepped on. The white dome of Mount Rainier rises through the forests higher than eye level as they descend, then bend to the north before leaning back over the city. The Space Needle, and, yes, there are the ferry docks, with one small car-ferry leaving West Seattle for Vashon Island and another, larger one from downtown for Bainbridge Island. It must be warm down there, he thinks as he sees the flashing whitecaps in the afternoon sun and several white sails and a few fishing boats with their small wakes rippling behind them.

In the terminal he hears foreign voices. Japanese on the announcement speakers. And in the crowds of greeters and passengers, the twangy Mandarin Chinese. Spanish. Some kind of African. And surrounding the voices are the faces, so many shades of brown, so little blank blondness. How strange, he thinks, to feel such comfort being around people who don't look like me. In the sleek subway to the main terminal, he feels cushioned by the multicolored inhabitants and the multicolored speech. He feels warmed by them. Except for a few of the most beautiful moments he has had with Cherlyn, he feels, for the first time in three and a half months, safe.

* * *

Cosmos's dad is an explosion of sentiments. He hugs and chatters and smiles and bounces his big body around, as if he is the happiest man in the world. "You look great!" he says. "Just great."

When they get to the house in Port Swan, Hans says to check the answering machine, that there's a message for him. The first message brings the deep-throated, raspy, sweet voice of Salal. "Cosmos, I hear you're going to be in town over vacation. Please give me a call. I do so much want to see you."

The next message is from Rhody. "Get your ass over here, man, and let's jam!"

The last message is a woman's voice that sounds familiar but that he can't quite place. As he listens, his eyes catch a long curly red hair on the counter. The voice and hair connect—it's Noreen. "Give me a call when you're free, love."

Good God. His dad is getting it on with Probation Officer Noreen.

"That was Noreen," says Cosmos. "What's up?"

"Didn't want to tell you until we knew for sure the fire

wasn't going to go out," Hans says. He doesn't look embarrassed. He's beaming. "She might be the one," he says.

Cosmos almost laughs. This is what he misses most about Port Swan: a surprise around every corner. And you never know who's going to be sleeping with whom from one minute to the next. The place is a nest of incest. A bit of graffiti he read in a coffee-shop rest room a few years ago is starting to make sense now. It said, "People in Port Swan don't fall in love, they just stand in line."

"So," says Cosmos, and he can't hide his smile. "You and my probation officer. How about a conflict of interest when I get back?"

"Very good, son," says Hans, "but I thought about that. When you turn eighteen next summer, there will be no problem. At eighteen, you're out of her control."

"And you're in it," says Cosmos.

"Good one," says Hans. He gives Cosmos a little shove and they sit down for dinner. Cosmos understands the plan for the evening without being told: he is having dinner with Dad, then he will go play music with the OughtaBs while Daddy has a little quality time with Noreen. Good old topsy-turvy Port Swan. Noreen as a stepmom. That would be strange.

Dinner at Dad's is a ride on a vegetable bandwagon. He has gone bonkers on a health fad, weirder almost than he remembers about his mom's New Agey diets. Turnip soup with cornbread? Everything, including the handmade place mats, is yellow or orange. The only thing that departs from the color scheme is the greens, a strange salad of spinach and spicy little green things and bitter salad dressing. But all this orange—Dad has changed his diet to match Noreen's hair.

"What's with the food, Dad? No oysters? No butter?"

"I've gone vegan," he says. "Getting older, and time to keep the arteries clean. You look like you've been eating pretty well."

"I work. I eat. I sleep. You get what you pay for."

"You look great. I'd say about fifteen pounds, don't you think?"

Cosmos sits up, holds out his arms, and flexes his muscles.

"Yes!" says his dad. "You're looking like a De Haag."

Cosmos lays his fork down. "So you, on the other hand, you've lost some weight," he says to Hans. "That mean you have to be a missionary to everybody else?"

"All right, no more about weight," says his dad. "But, speaking of missionaries, how's the church thing going over there?"

"I go," says Cosmos. "They don't make me visit Gramps anymore. Which is fine with me. He's mean as a werewolf, you know. Your dad."

"I'm afraid Gramps is what he has always been, only more so," says Hans.

"Whatever that means," says Cosmos.

"It means he was part of the old order: Follow the rules. Toe the line yourself and punish the ones who step out of line."

"Judgmental," says Cosmos.

"Exactly," says Hans. "But you have to look at those first generations of settlers as people who had to agree on rules to keep the community together so they could survive."

Cosmos dips some cornbread in the yellow soup. "Everybody around there looks as if they've survived pretty well, so why don't they loosen up a little?"

"They still want to keep a distinct identity," says his dad. "They keep the rules. They keep the rituals. I've always seen that virtue in it. Ritual is not a bad thing. Habitual tending to the spirit is not a bad thing."

At times like this, Cosmos thinks his dad hasn't quite grown up yet. Defending the community he would never go back to even if they gave him a million dollars. His dad is on a nostalgia trip, talking nice about the repressive folks he left behind while going his own freewheeling way in Port Swan. Having an affair with Cosmos's probation officer? Can't blame him for that, though. Cosmos imagines Noreen without any clothes. Yes. She would look good. No wonder his dad is happy. But where does her authority go when she takes off her clothes in front of the big hairy form of his father?

Hans slurps some yellow soup. He breaks off a piece of

cornbread and dips it in the soup the way Cosmos did. The only sounds in the room are the sounds of two males slurping. Then the old refrigerator next to them rumbles and starts up. Through the sliding glass doors and waning afternoon light over the deck, Cosmos sees carloads of strangers with California license plates drive by looking at the large Victorian house next door. Port Swan is being overrun with tourists, even in early winter now. It's turning into Yuppieville and his dad doesn't even seem to notice.

"You wishing you had done detention over here instead of going to the farm? Sounds like Uncle Henry and Aunt Minnie treat you well."

"They're good people," says Cosmos. "If the whole community could be like them . . ."

"So are you feeling like you're just getting by, or are you liking it a little bit?"

"It's all right," says Cosmos. "But I'd probably be done with detention by now if I'd stayed here."

"So you wish you had?" says Hans. He gets up and starts moving dishes toward the sink.

"Sometimes," says Cosmos. "They're not all as judgmental as Gramps, but it feels like they watch you all the time. You know, if there really is a God, don't you think He put us on earth to live it up a little?"

Hans gives out an unnaturally loud laugh. "I like that," he says. He stands next to the sink and lifts his soup bowl to his lips for the last little sip. "You meet anybody interesting at all out there?"

Cosmos gets uncomfortable and Hans notices. "Aha," he says. "You've got the hots for some little Dutch Tulip Princess, haven't you? Come on, come on. Haven't you? Haven't you?"

"Knock it off, Dad."

"Oooooo," says Hans. "That serious?"

"I don't want to joke around about it, all right?"

"Wait a minute," says Hans. "The same one Aunt Minnie told me about? That Van Dyke girl?"

"Cherlyn. Yes. Cherlyn Van Dyke."

"Is she as religious as her folks? The Van Dykes I remember were pretty hard-ass religious. Old-fashioned Dutch Calvinists. Her grandfather wouldn't even allow a TV set in the house."

"Her dad's a hard-ass, all right," says Cosmos. He gets up from the table and goes to the refrigerator for the milk carton. "I guess you might call Cherlyn a born-again," he says. He sits back down at the table with his father. "I care about her, Dad. She's really wonderful, and she doesn't lay any trips on me. Never. I miss her right now."

The talk stops. Hans finishes his soup. Cosmos sips his milk. "The rest of the community you can have. Most of the other people know about the trouble I was in back here, and most of the other kids just cut me off."

"So you feel left out, that what you're saying?"

"I'm not one of them." Cosmos wipes his lip. The sounds of more cars driving by comes into the kitchen. "You knew what I was going to be in for out there. I think you like it. I think you think I'm getting what I deserve for complicating your life out here."

"Whoa, that was a mood shift. Do I detect some bitterness there?" says Hans. "You know why I encouraged you to go there. We both agreed you needed a change. We both agreed there is something good about getting in touch with your roots. It doesn't hurt to know where you came from. You'll come away from there with your feet on the ground. And looking like a De Haag."

"For better or worse," says Cosmos.

Cosmos watches his dad hurry with the dishes. He can tell it is time to split. He gives Rhody a call to see if the band is ready to set up, and he is off.

When Cosmos gets to Rhody's garage, the band is ready to go. Cosmos stands in the door and looks at them. Rhody hasn't changed, but Spruce has. He looks like a kid on the skids. Everything from his complexion to his fingernails has gone to hell. Pale and pimply face. Fingernails chewed off, broken off, or cemented to his fingers with grease and dirt. His hair looks as if it hasn't been washed or cut since August. More than a kid on the skids, Spruce looks like a kid in the pits. He has lost his bounce. For the first time in Cosmos's memory, Spruce looks all bounced out. But he hits the drums when Cosmos walks across the room. He gives Cosmos his smile and a drum roll. "Yo!" he says.

Rhody gives Cosmos a high-five and a walloping hug. "Love some of your songs, man. Been working on them. Wait till you hear what I think we can do with that 'Foxhole for My Soul'!"

In walks Salal. Cosmos forgot to return her phone call, but here she is. By herself. Without Bridgette. When Salal strides in, the bare cement floor becomes a stage and the bare lightbulb a spotlight. Salal looks at him, almost timidly, very much unlike her. She looks at him like a little girl afraid that some grown-up is going to reject her. A smorgasbord of mixed feelings churns in his stomach. It's not as if he makes a habit of holding grudges—or even allowing little weasel-twinges of resentment—but handling this situation is not very comfy. Cosmos can't tell what feeling he is feeling. It's as if he has left both Cosmos Coyote and William the Nice back in Dutch Center.

The temperature outside is Port Swan's usual mid-December forty-four degrees, but Salal is dressed as if the temperature were seventy-five: short-sleeved black blouse with her snake arm-bracelet snaking up her left arm above the elbow. She wears loose but glossy black pants, swooshy ones, that look as if they are an advertisement from *Glamour*. Her hair still glows its dyed black color, and her face hasn't changed: her big lips and dark but not glossy maroon lipstick, the same color as the lipstick that sealed her one note to Cosmos in Iowa. Looking at her, Cosmos feels the old lights of lust being turned on—at a low and cautious setting, but still turned on.

"Hi, Salal," he says.

She strides over, not at all like a little girl now, but like a model, long confident steps that make the sharp edges of her long body flow with her movements. She smiles as she walks toward him in a way that is warm but does not try to be sexy.

Cosmos embraces her carefully. He puts his cheek to hers but doesn't try to kiss any part of her. If it weren't for the scent of her that he catches now, sex would be way back in the caboose of his mind. But she has on the same perfume, or face lotion, or something that she had on the first time they had sex. It is a sharp, bittersweet, musky smell that sends little shock waves through him.

Cosmos pulls back as casually as he can. Music is made for times like this, when all the crazy energy of your body is pulling and pushing you in every direction at once. "Let's jam!" he says.

Rhody brings out the guitar that Cosmos can use while he is back in Port Swan. They tune up and get into it.

"Let's go," says Rhody. "Here's the melody line I thought we might try for 'Foxhole.'" Rhody starts in, though Spruce, from his perch behind the drums, shows about as much life as he is going to show tonight, outside his drumming—which is surprisingly hot.

About an hour into it, Salal digs out her chillum from her

big black purse and lights up.

Why not? Cosmos thinks when it is his turn. He is not going to have to pee in a bottle while he is here, and nobody has asked him to back in Iowa. He is three beers and about a half-dozen hits into the wind when the jamming session ends.

"I'm smashed," says Cosmos as he hands the guitar to Rhody to put away. "I'm not used to this shit."

"Tell us about Iowa, man," says Spruce. "Like, you been in the haymow with one of them farm girls?"

Cosmos glances at Salal. She doesn't smile.

Cosmos breaks the ice with a few Iowa jokes: Why do they have Astro-Turf in all the Iowa football fields? To keep the cheerleaders from grazing. What's the state bird of Iowa? The horsefly. What's the state tree? The telephone pole. What's an Iowa man's idea of foreplay? Brace yourself. How do you find Iowa? Go east until you smell it, then north until you step in it. Iowa, where the men are men and the sheep are nervous.

"What about the pigs, man?" howls Spruce. "Do Iowa men make the pigs nervous?"

Salal huffs her deep laugh. Everybody laughs. Everybody is stoned and drunk, probably the only condition under which his Iowa jokes could have been funny. Laughter that breeds laughter now, laughter that feeds on itself, laughter that grows out of laughter, until everyone has forgotten what they are laughing about, and that is really really funny and good for another two minutes of uncontrollable laughter. "Hwwhoo hwwhoo argh argh pmph pmph oh oh oh oh oh!"

Through it all, Spruce finally starts to bounce, Salal loses her dignity and starts looking wonderfully loose and sexy, Rhody dances to the jerky rhythms of laughter like an out-of-control ten-year-old, and Cosmos, giggling and swirling around the room, forgets what it is like to wonder what people might be thinking of him now. Cosmos feels generous and warm and nice, nicer than William the Nice on a hard church pew singing a hymn, warmer even than Cosmos Coyote staring into the eyes of Cherlyn. But Cherlyn isn't here to stare at now, and Salal is looking at him in a way that probably would make Bridgette throw him out the window and over the cliff into the chilly waters of Puget Sound. As the room continues to rock with chuckles, and all possibilities of what might or might not happen swirl indiscriminately through Cosmos's mind, his eyes slide toward run-down Spruce, who is really bouncing now, slide toward his smiling thin face and down his arm, where they catch sight of the red puncture marks. He is using needles.

It is the first and only really depressing moment of the night, and everyone is probably following Cosmos's lead as he starts to sadden down, moving more slowly, sagging away from the mood of laughter and into the tired slouch that says the party is over. Spruce is the first outside and says he is walking home, followed by Rhody, who says he will turn the light off and lock up, leaving Salal and Cosmos walking six feet apart across the grass toward the street, where Salal's wagon is parked. Salal walks toward her station wagon, Cosmos toward the sidewalk and in the direction of home.

"Let me give you a ride," says Salal.

Cosmos stops and looks in her direction through the darkness. "I think I can walk home," he says. "I'm not that ripped."

"Please," she says.

Salal wants to do more than give Cosmos a ride home. She wants to talk. She starts the car and turns on the heater. She reaches into the back seat and puts on a sweater. Cosmos reaches across the seat and helps adjust it on her shoulder, then settles back on his side of the car.

Salal wants to tell him what she has been up to. And she wants to tell him that she thinks the OughtaBs are going to make it big when he gets back. "You sounded better tonight than I've ever heard you," she says. She puts the car in gear and drives slowly down the dark streets of Port Swan, staying away from the main streets, where the cops would most likely be riding.

"Spruce's into the heavy stuff," says Cosmos. "I saw needle marks on his arm. The OughtaBs aren't going anywhere if he's going to drug himself down."

"He's just dabbling," she says. "Rhody and I are watching him close. We'll have him out of the fire before you get back, Coz. Don't worry."

"I am worried," says Cosmos. "If you don't pull him out of the fire soon, there's going to be nothing left but ashes."

"He's not down because he's shooting up," says Salal, "he's shooting up because he's down. He'll be all right."

As she idles slowly down the road, Salal does not drive toward Cosmos's dad's house. She drives toward the water, toward the docks, where sailboats and small fishing boats rock inside the horseshoe-shaped pier. She turns off the car, and they sit in the darkness looking at the small boats rock and listening to the waves tap the pier.

"I still care about you," she says finally. Flatly, in the direction of the windshield.

"I don't know what that means," says Cosmos.

"I'm not with Bridgette anymore," she says.

"Don't blame you," says Cosmos.

They sit for a few more minutes, then Cosmos hears the quick little sniffs that tell him Salal is crying, or on the verge of crying. He doesn't move.

"I should be more grown-up by now," says Salal. Her voice is pained, strained. "Bridgette was such a silly thing."

"What are you saying?" says Cosmos. He tries to keep his voice level. He has no desire to hurt Salal, but he has no desire to be hurt by her either.

"I'd like you to come home with me tonight," she says. She leans toward him to kiss him. She turns in her seat so that her chest slides easily against his. Her musky scent by itself Cosmos might be able to handle, but the combination of the touch of her lips, the softness of her breasts against his chest, the long sleekness of her hips and legs stretching away from him before his eyes—all of these, along with the sweet dizziness of alcohol and marijuana, make every pore in his body feel like a tiny moistened seed in a sun-blazed greenhouse. His breathing gets deeper and his arousal rushes through him, starting somewhere in the middle of his back and filling his whole groin. Salal puts her hand on his erection and starts moaning. After they are interrupted by one set of car lights, she sits up and starts the car. "My place," she says.

She drives slowly again, and again avoids the main drags. When she gets close to Main Street, she turns down the alley that leads to the back of Wendy's Wine Cellar and the rear entrance to her apartment. Cosmos is no longer aroused and feels a nervous tightness in his shoulders. The alcohol and marijuana have lost their place in his mind and he is acutely alert, like someone who is watching a sky in Iowa for a tornado.

"Salal," he says. "I really care about you. I want you to always be my friend. But I can't do this. I can't go in with you. I can't have sex with you."

Salal puts her hand on his arm. "Did I really hurt you that much? Oh, Cosmos."

"It's not that," he says.

Salal turns off the engine. They stare through the windshield.

"Are you in love with someone in Iowa?" says Salal.

Cosmos doesn't answer. "I think we should wait until I get back next summer and see how we feel. I think we should just be friends for a while, all right?"

Salal holds the steering wheel and sobs. "I deserve this," she says. "I have been so so stupid. I love you, Coz."

"I care about you too," he says, but doesn't try to touch her. "Let's walk," he says.

Out in the chilly winter air, Cosmos puts his windbreaker over Salal's sweater. To give her more warmth, he puts his shoulder behind and against hers as they walk. Salal walks Cosmos up the long grade all the way to his dad's house. The lights are on, but there is no car out front to suggest that Noreen is still there. Cosmos turns and holds Salal before he goes inside. "Don't forget I'll be back, all right?" he says.

Salal is composed now, smiling and nobly gracious. She kisses his nose and says, "All right."

He watches her stride away, an elegant figure, into the night. Cosmos straightens up and goes inside.

It is almost midnight, and Hans is painting a daisy on the kitchen-cabinet door. He is humming as he dabs the tiny brush into the orange heart of the daisy. "You look like one happy fellow," says Cosmos.

"I know," says Hans. "It's true. I keep waiting to wake up, it's like a dream. But it's true. You're absolutely right. I've never been so happy in my life." He puts the tiny paintbrush down and stands back to look at his progress. Then he turns to Cosmos. "You're not spending time with Salal, I take it."

"That's over. We're friends. It's all right. But what about you? It's Noreen, isn't it? You're ass-over-applecart in love, aren't you?"

Hans laughs big again. "You got that expression in Iowa, didn't you? I haven't heard 'ass over applecart' since I was a kid."

"I learned the expression from Cherlyn. That's about as dirty as she talks."

"Everything seems to come back to Cherlyn for you." He stares at Cosmos, as if waiting for his surface to shatter and reveal. It does. Cosmos grins.

"Yeah, Cherlyn," he says. "She's a trip."

"You're talking to me about being in love big-time, aren't you?"

"Afraid so. But her dad won't even let me see her outside of school."

"So how do you think this is all going to play out?"

"I don't know."

"Her dad is Cornelius Van Dyke, right? He was three

grades ahead of me. He was an asshole already when he was ten."

Cosmos starts to laugh and almost stumbles as he tries to sit down at the table.

"Are you drunk?" says Hans.

"A little," says Cosmos.

"And stoned?"

"A little."

"And in love."

"Quite a bit," says Cosmos.

Hans stands there, grinning and grinning. "Father and son both in love at the same time. What are the odds for that?"

"Let's see, about forty-five to seventeen?"

Hans guffaws.

"Dad, are you on something too?"

"Noreen and life, that's all. I am one happy has-been hippie. I am one happy craftsman maniac. I'm flying, son. I'm buzzing on the good stuff of life."

"Is Noreen the only reason you're so happy?" asks Cosmos.

"That's part of it," says Hans. Now he looks very serious. "I'm at peace with the world," he says. He moves back to his unfinished daisy.

"Does Mom not being around have anything to do with it?"

"Not really," he says. "She's doing well in Mexico. Not

even coming up for Christmas. She sent this for you. Sorry I didn't wrap it."

Cosmos looks at the small lidded container. Inside are a half-dozen tiny Mexican doll figures. "Cool," he says. He examines the tiny dolls, then puts them back in the container and sets it on the table. He then gets up and walks closer to where his father is working. "Can I ask you something?"

"Shoot."

"How can you be happy out here when you know your own dad is such a mean bastard back there?" Cosmos has no idea where that question came from. Out of the blue. Out of the orange. "I don't think I could be happy if I had a dad like that."

This startles Hans. He wipes his hands and walks up to Cosmos. He blinks his eyes fast. "I just had to let go," says Hans. "Sometimes the deck has to be cleared before you can see the horizon."

"It would be awful, having a dad like that. I want to know more," says Cosmos.

"I dunno," says Hans. "I'm getting tired, and you're having trouble standing up. Maybe we should wait."

"I don't ever want to have to run from my roots the way you did. I don't blame you. Believe me, Dad, I don't blame you. I just don't want to feel I have to run to be who I am, you know?"

"I'm proud of you, Coz. You're not a faker." Hans looks

around as if he is trying to find a way to change the subject. He takes a step toward Cosmos, as if he is about to give him a reassuring hug. He stops and puts out his large hand and taps Cosmos on the shoulder. "Now get to bed," he says. "We both need our rest."

"All right," says Cosmos and weaves his way toward his bedroom.

Is there a problem?

ALMOST THREE WEEKS OF the old scene in Port Swan: the cool but mild weather, the hanging out on the beach, the daily jamming sessions with the OughtaBs. Spruce comes back to life after that first night, starts showing some of the old liveliness, almost as if he needs Cosmos around to keep himself together. A few walks with Salal on the paths through the abandoned gun emplacements, always avoiding the love-nest bunker of their past. She is not with anyone, she tells Cosmos, either male or female. She needs to sort things out, she says. She loves him, she says. Always will. But it is good they are not going to bed together. Sex has always been tricky for her.

"Maybe it's time we cool our jets," says Salal. They laugh together, though he doesn't tell Salal that one reason he is laughing is that the most important woman in his life has been saying the same thing. Occasionally, he and Salal give each other little hugs. Like friends.

Never during the visit does Salal lose her dignity, never after that first night does she try to come on to Cosmos. She shows up at all the practice sessions in Rhody's garage, and applauds, encourages, even makes some very good suggestions. She and Cosmos do spend one long night talking at their favorite downtown espresso joint, the Deuce of Cups, but this is mostly to discuss Spruce and his drug problem. At least Salal is willing to call it a "problem" now, though they both know he has held himself in check the whole time Cosmos has been in town. She is also getting more insistent about the future of the OughtaBs. If they can stay together in spirit while Cosmos is gone, she says, no agent in his or her right mind will be able to ignore them for very long.

"You're almost 'very hot' already," she says. "When you're there, when you're very, very hot, we'll strike, and the stars will be the limit. The OughtaBs are going to fly, Coz, fly. I'm sure of it."

So it is Salal the friend and manager that Cosmos leaves behind when he boards the DC-10 from Seattle on January 3. The weather is a more typical Northwest winter day, a rumpled gray quilt of a sky, one layer upon another, with deceptive light underneath, the green hills rising up into them, the rain coming and going and coming and going. On I-5, the large trucks produce clouds of blinding steam from their tires.

As soon as the plane takes off, Cosmos starts reviewing his re-entry into the Iowa scene. After the craziness of the past few weeks, he can actually think a few good thoughts about where he is going. Some things in Iowa are more comforting and steady than topsy-turvy Port Swan. Rhody might be a steady one, but in a pretty jerky way. Spruce is slipping and sliding, to say the least. Salal, who is she anyhow? If Cherlyn were not in the picture, he can see how easily he could fall back into the craziness of trying to be her man. Hans, good old Dad, he is the bouncy one this vacation. Cosmos saw Noreen only once, on Christmas morning, and she was as crazily in love with his dad as he was with her. She didn't mention Cosmos's alternative sentence. She didn't talk about her probation work at all. When Cosmos came home after practicing with the OughtaBs, there were always signs of her around the house. Strands of red hair strewn everywhere. The smell of her. And on at least one occasion after she had been there to see Hans, Cosmos could swear he smelled the lingering odor of marijuana in the house. But since he was usually slightly stoned when he came home from practicing, it didn't register in his mind as anything very important either way.

Being back in Iowa will mean a more regular diet of things. Not so many surprises. Maybe not as exciting as Port Swan or Seattle, but at least he figures he can count on Iowa to be pretty much the same as when he left it.

When he lands in Minneapolis, he sees that the Midwest has filled up a little more with snow while he was gone, but the only big change is that now the snow looks dirtier. Uncle Henry and Aunt Minnie pick him up in Sioux Falls, and he is relieved at the familiar sight of their thick green winter coats. They look happy to see him. They almost hug him when they meet him, then, at the last second, they hold out their hands to shake his.

It is only when Cosmos gets back to school that he has to change his mind about how Iowa doesn't change. He gets the story already on the bus—Van Enk has been fired for having an affair with a teacher from the public middle school. The woman from the middle school is divorced, but she talked, not because she wanted to get Van Enk in trouble with his wife, but because she was so in love with Van Enk that she had to tell somebody. Maybe like Cherlyn's urge to show her faith by talking about it, Cosmos thinks. Rumors floated like feathers through the air, and soon board members at the Academy started doing some spying, some detective work. They got a picture of Van Enk and Ms. Vander Plaats checking into a motel in Sioux Falls on a Saturday afternoon. Van Enk is history at the Academy. He probably was history before he could even undress in that motel and didn't even know it.

Van Enk was one rotten egg that floated to the top and got busted.

But Cherlyn hasn't changed. Well, maybe the clothes, but not the person underneath them. She is wearing what looks like a new dress she got for Christmas, a tight green-and-red pattern, and she has green tights on. But she is still the same gorgeous Cherlyn. To Cosmos, she looks innocent as an apple in the garbage can of loud and shoving students. She weaves and twists through the crowd and giggles at the sight of Cosmos, her clean blond hair loose and dancing around her face. Other students watch the reunion and most of them look less concerned, or less interested, than they were when Cosmos first noticed their stares. They probably feel that Cherlyn is all right and that makes him all right and that makes everything all right. At least that is how Cosmos wants to imagine it in this happy moment. They embrace in the middle of the hallway. They hug so hard the bell rings for first-period class. Sometimes this school has just a touch of coolness about it: a person can get away with a few indiscretions as long as he bows his head in chapel and doesn't say any swear words loud enough for the principal or a teacher to hear him. All day long, Cosmos and Cherlyn converge at every opportunity they have: between classes, before, during, and after chapel. They go off into the corner for lunch, and after Cherlyn has folded her hands and said her prayer, their legs play with each other under the table.

"We're being awfully open," says Cosmos. "Aren't people going to tell your folks?"

"I can't think about that right now, can you?"

"No," he says.

They feed each other slices of orange. They share a milk. They lock fingers of one hand across the table and eat with the other. When they look into each other's eyes, they can't stop smiling, almost laughing with pleasure.

"I love the beautiful ink-pen you gave me," says Cosmos. "It makes writing feel like dancing."

Cherlyn beams.

"I have a Christmas present for you too," says Cosmos. "From Port Swan."

Cosmos knows what she is going to say, and says the words with her: "Oh, you shouldn't have."

She squeezes his hand as he gives it to her, wrapped in glistening red paper with tiny gold bells on it. Inside, she finds the gift, a small onyx-colored soapstone carving of an otter swimming on its back. The Northwest Indian artist who carved the otter knew the otter's joy with life. The animal looks as if it is smiling with its chin on its chest as it swims on its back. Cherlyn cups the carving in her hands. Her whole body responds in its giddy language of joy. She bubbles, her eyes wide as a child's getting her first teddy bear. "It is the most beautiful gift I have ever gotten from anyone," she says.

"I got it because it reminded me of you," he says.

Their little party is interrupted by Principal Marksema, who comes over to their table and tells Cosmos that he has something in his office for him. When Cosmos goes up just before afternoon classes begin, Marksema hands him a box. "Mr. Van Enk wanted you to have these," he says.

There is a note inside that doesn't appear to have been opened by anyone. Cosmos reads, "Mr. De Haag, you admired these books and now they are yours. Sincerely, Mr. Van Enk."

The books are mostly nature and ecology books, not just the ones he had noticed before but also two pamphlets on the local county's soil-and-water management. One chapter heading reads "The Depletion of the Oglala Aquifer." Another reads, "Commercial Fertilizers and Our Rivers." The largest book in the box is the *Norton Anthology of Nature Writing*. Cosmos thumbs through the pamphlets that Van Enk seems to have spent the most time with. He has underlined sentences, whole paragraphs. In boring prose, one pamphlet says the county where they live will turn into a desert within decades if the aquifer depletion continues at the current rate. Other underlined passages warn about pesticides and herbicides getting into the food-and-water supply. If the information is accurate, it is horrifying. While the community fills its churches and the minds of its people every Sunday with what the ministers believe is the spiritual food they need to survive, the earth beneath them will die from poison and thirst. Too bad Van Enk wasn't as concerned with preserving himself as he seemed to be about preserving the environment.

"There's something else I need to talk to you about, Mr. De Haag," says Marksema. "Mr. Wounker, one of our board members, told us you and Elmer were parked suspiciously along a gravel road right before Christmas vacation. He says he thinks you were drinking or doing drugs."

"Neither one," says Cosmos.

"Very well," says Marksema. "You understand that when people see smoke they expect those of us in authority to investigate. To see if there's any fire."

"I understand," says Cosmos.

"Your probation officer needs to see you right after school. I said I'd arrange it."

"I have to do chores," says Cosmos.

"I've talked with your uncle Henry. It's all right. And Jonsma will give you a ride home after your meeting with him."

Cosmos assumes that meeting with Cousin Mike will be no big deal. He is one of the steady things in Iowa that is not likely to have changed. It will be fun to talk to him.

Cousin or not, Cosmos's probation officer doesn't waste any time: "I'm getting pressure to keep a sharper eye on you," he says to Cosmos. "No big deal, but we're going to have to start with a drug test."

"No problem," says Cosmos.

No problem indeed. Let's see. He smoked marijuana eight times in the last few weeks. It is time for a liquid diet, a very very wet liquid diet. A gallon a day minimum, he figures. All the home remedies for purging run through his head: goldenseal and coffee, gallons and gallons of liquids, juice, water. A drop of bleach in the urine when he pees in the bottle as a last resort, but one week of purging and he should be clean, he figures.

"So when do they want it?" says Cosmos, and he is already wondering how much money he has with him to start buying juices.

"Right away," says Jonsma. "I have the jar with me. We can just go down to the boys' room and get it over with."

"I think Uncle Henry needs me home early for chores," says Cosmos.

"We already called him," says Jonsma. "He said he didn't need you that much for chores tonight. Let's do it."

The moment of truth is upon him. There is no way he can test clean. A few excuses run through his mind: I don't have to pee. It would be too embarrassing to do it right here in school—everyone will talk. Cosmos knows his face is getting red. He knows he is fidgeting.

"Is there a problem?" says Cousin Mike in the voice of a real probation officer, which he just happens to be.

Is this what they mean by "frozen in silence"? Cosmos thinks as he freezes in silence.

Cousin Mike freezes in silence with him. All the students have left the building, and the place sounds and feels like a dull ache, like the inside of a beehive in cold weather.

"There's a problem," says Mike.

"Right," says Cosmos.

"How big?"

More aching silence.

"Were you smoking marijuana with your friends in Port Swan?"

"You got it," says Cosmos.

"Just marijuana?"

"Just marijuana."

"Are you dependent? Should I schedule you for drug counseling?"

Bad as that suggestion sounds, Cosmos hears only good news. "You mean you wouldn't send me back to Juvie in Washington?"

"You crazy? Of course not. Sounds to me like Washington's the worst place on earth for you to be right now."

Cosmos blinks his eyes hard. He looks at his cousin. Mike's face is calm, expressionless. His eyes have none of the judgmental hatred he expected to see.

"I've been really stupid," says Cosmos. "I'm sorry. It won't happen again. That's a promise."

"Are you sure you don't need counseling?"

"I'm sure," says Cosmos. "It won't happen again." He waits a few seconds. "Do I have to pee in the jar? You know it's going to be positive."

"How much did you smoke, how often, and when was the last time?"

"I think I smoked seven or eight times. The last time was four days ago, but that was a fatty."

"We'll wait a week," says Jonsma. "That should do it."

"You kidding?"

"No, I'm not kidding. I'll tell them that I was too busy to

get it this week. Which I am. I've got another appointment in ten minutes. Come here, kid."

Cosmos walks up to his cousin, who holds out his arms and takes Cosmos into them. He holds Cosmos in a big manly embrace. "I feel like a jerk. You trusted me," says Cosmos.

"I still do," says Mike. "And I forgive you, all right?"

"I'll be clean next week," says Cosmos.

"I know you will," says Mike. "Lots of water and coffee, but not too much the day before. We'll test you after school. First urine of the day would be a bad idea. Come on, I'll drop you off at Uncle Henry and Aunt Minnie's."

They ride without talking for a few minutes, then Cosmos says, "Tell me, why did they, whoever they are, decide I should be drug-tested?"

"It's about the thefts," he said. "You're still the number-one suspect, even if the police aren't talking to you. I told them I thought you had nothing to do with the thefts and they said we had to keep a closer eye on you, starting with a drug test. Then there's the little matter of the board member seeing you and Elmer parked along the road. He was really mad. He'd like to nail both of you. You and Elmer. I have to tell you, a lot of people would like to nail Elmer."

"Well, I didn't steal anything," says Cosmos, "and I wasn't doing anything illegal with Elmer. Anything that's in my pee got in there in Port Swan, not here."

"I believe you," says Jonsma. "I'd bet my reputation on your denial of the thefts too, but it's not that easy to tell them that De Haags never steal."

"We don't squeal on anybody either," says Cosmos.

"I'm not going to ask what you meant by that," says Jonsma.

"Thanks," says Cosmos.

That night, in his room, Cosmos expects to feel good, chipper even. Instead, he feels sad, almost depressed. It is as if his feelings are lined up inside himself, facing each other, and not agreeing. He feels grateful to Cousin Mike for being so understanding. He feels resentment that he should have to feel so bad about smoking some marijuana on vacation. A stupid, unjust system that put him up against the wall for such a stupid little thing. At least inside that stupid, unjust system there were a few people like his cousin Mike. Van Enk wasn't so lucky as to have a Mike Jonsma to forgive him. Word is that his wife has forgiven him and that they are sticking together, getting out of the community and going off to California to start a new life together. Good-bye, Van Enk, you poor bastard, floating off like a rotten egg. But I'm a rotten egg too, Cosmos realizes. One of these days, there isn't going to be somebody as kind as a Mike Jonsma to keep me from being busted like Van Enk. Being sent back to detention in Washington at this point doesn't sound like a total nightmare. Having to leave Cherlyn does.

We didn't really have sex, did we?

THE NEXT WEEK, COSMOS is clean as a bleached thermos bottle.

"Happy to help you out on this one," says Mike, "but I'll tell you straight—if you get into any other kind of trouble, I will have to send you back. This means drinking, this means getting into fights, this of course means drugs."

"Got it," says Cosmos.

During the next weeks, Cosmos and Cherlyn find ways to give themselves more time together. With Cherlyn's pressure on Marksema, Cosmos gets permission to spend his free period with her in *The Messenger*'s office. Cherlyn joins him and they are alone. They go off into the corner and open the large supply-cabinet door. Here they can kiss, but it is against school rules to lock or close the door, so they never know when someone might enter. Often during their kissing, Cosmos's hand roams toward her breasts, but Cherlyn gently stops him. "Not here," she says. "We'll have to wait."

And wait is what they do: wait for the bell; wait for chapel, where they can hold hands and harmonize like the vocal lovers they have become; wait for lunch, where they can embrace with their legs and feet under the table; wait for the quick glance in the hallway, the smile between classes, the sly embraces behind the closet door in *The Messenger*'s office. A long winter of waiting in the harsh winter arms of containment.

The weather has its own restricting ways, with its barrage of blizzards and storms, several of them so road-cloggingly severe that school is canceled. On these days, Cosmos waits in his room, and has to admit to his aching heart that the limited menu of affection with Cherlyn at school is better than staring out at the accumulating snowbanks, which no longer look like a welcome covering to the dull landscape of Iowa. The snowbanks become the earth's straitjacket, smothering the would-be life and affection that are waiting to bud underneath it.

In the cold confines of winter, he gets only one new song, a gentle little song that comes to him while the tune of "Amazing Grace" is running through his mind from a chapel when he and Cherlyn harmonized as never before. He dares to sing this song to the tune of "Amazing Grace" loud enough in his room for Aunt Minnie to hear it. "Amazing grace, how sweet the sound that saved a wretch like me," becomes

> *And if you live where winter comes*
> *you'll get to know your soul.*

You'll hear the voice inside you talk
while biting north winds blow.

You'll find that no one cares but you
when your world comes apart.
The lonely place where peace begins
lies within a frozen heart.

And in that lonely place begins
the budding hope of spring.
The warmth that comes when winter flees
will make your fresh soul sing.

The hope of spring greets Cosmos at school, where, through the long-winter doldrums, at least one glacier has already begun to thaw: the cold resolve of Cherlyn's father.

"I've started to hint," says Cherlyn, "and he knows you gave me the otter for Christmas. He didn't flinch. I dare to say your name in the house again. That's progress."

"So when do you think we could see each other outside of school?" says Cosmos.

"Here's my plan," says Cherlyn. "I've told him that you and I always sing together in chapel and that everybody around us tells me how beautifully we harmonize. He liked that."

"So what do you want me to do, come over on some Sunday morning after church and sing hymns with you around your wonderful piano? I'd do that, you know."

"I have an even better plan," says Cherlyn. "Pretty soon, when the roads are safe again, our church starts Young People's Society meetings."

"You mean your Bible-study group?" asks Cosmos.

"No, the Bible-study group has just a few young people who meet Sunday mornings. Margaret is part of it. The Young People's Society meeting is for all high-school- and college-age people in our church. The meetings are on Sunday night. I think he'd let me take you to a church event before he'd let me take you to a school event. He seems awfully leery about school events. I'm sure Margaret hasn't been talking to him, but somebody has."

"Surprise, surprise. No wonder you don't see any surveillance cameras around here—you don't need them with everybody keeping their eyes on everything everybody else is doing."

"I keep trying to figure out what is all right to hide from him and what isn't," she says. "I don't want to be two-faced. I don't want to lie. I do want to be honest, but I honestly want to see you alone."

* * *

Spring finally sweeps down, or up, or whatever it does when it takes over the Iowa landscape, the soil erupting, bubbling through the frost, old grass shaking its matted hair from the earth and rising up. The old stuff of the soil, all the floral packages opening at once, not smothering but eating up the droppings of winter. Even the dirty snow-banks that have been lying around like dead sheep along fences and against buildings have been drawn down into the soil to resurrect themselves in the green shoots.

It is a Sunday night, and Young People's Society has begun. Cherlyn was right about her father: he has given her permission to pick Cosmos up. She is not calling it a date. She is calling it "going together to a church event."

"I think he's softening up partly because he knows you'll be leaving in a few months," says Cherlyn.

"I don't want to talk about that," says Cosmos.

"I don't either," she says.

Cosmos and Cherlyn sit next to each other in the church-basement meeting room, harmonizing together through the songs and listening to the minister's sermonette for young people. At eight o'clock they are turned loose, most of them heading straight for the freedom their cars will give them—some in bands of boys, some in bands of girls, and many hand-holding couples. Where do they go? Cosmos has learned that few go to movies or other places of worldly entertainment. Though the rules of Sabbath Day observance—which in Cosmos's father's day meant staying away from all commercial establishments on Sunday—have grown lax, most young people still follow in the wake of those restrictive days by gathering in people's homes. Some go cruising, which means drinking beer and driving down gravel roads, where the highway patrol doesn't go.

And some, like Cherlyn and Cosmos, go off into the country in search of romantic private places.

Cherlyn and Cosmos have an agreement, drawn up quite simply by Cherlyn: they will enjoy the bodies that God gave them to enjoy, but they will not take any clothes off. They have already learned that progression in sexual games is a little bit like any sport—once you've reached a certain point, climbed a certain height, or run a certain distance, some surging ambition of the body or spirit wants to go a little farther. This is not so much because the last record that you set was not gratifying. It was gratifying. It was delicious. But it urged toward possibility rather than granting the satisfaction of completion.

When Cherlyn first said that there was nothing in the Bible that said they couldn't touch each other in a loving way, Cosmos imagined that there must be a million ways of getting to know each other's bodies lovingly without committing what Cherlyn would consider a sin. He calmed his fantasies down by studying the dictionary for exact definitions of human sexual contact. "The dictionary says that adultery doesn't mean two people making out under the stars on a beautiful spring evening," he says, wanting to give support to the rules she has laid out. "Adultery means when a married guy sleeps with somebody besides his wife, or a married woman sleeps with another man. And fornication doesn't mean you and I loving each other's bodies either. Fornication means we actually do it if we're not married."

Cosmos's eagerness to set clear petting rules puts Cherlyn a little bit on guard: "Let's just agree to keep our clothes on," she reminds him. "This way we can stay inside God's rules of love without looking in the dictionary for guidance."

Cosmos turns to her and nods. "I think the way you understand God's rules is just fine."

Cosmos fidgets nervously while Cherlyn drives. His hands feel big and cumbersome to him suddenly. Along with his lips, they are about the only parts of his body that hunger for her without the obstruction of clothing. Right now they feel so eager and awkward he almost wishes he had a face mask and gloves to keep them in check.

Cherlyn drives to an abandoned farm where the grass around the buildings has not been cut for several years. Although the grass is not yet fully flourishing, the sun for the past several days has been so intense that the sleepy grass is like a dry hay mattress springing to life. She drives past the dilapidated old house, past the crumbling red barn, and parks where the gravel path ends, near the grove and just outside the open gate to what was once a small pasture. She takes an old blanket from the trunk, one that has been part of the winter's emergency supplies, and they walk through the open cattle gate and behind a fence to the soft grass.

They lie on their backs staring up into the deep star-filled sky. A sliver of a crescent moon hangs like a cradle over the horizon. The air is warm but moist from the land's spring breath. Where they lie, there are no corn-drying silos in earshot and no feedlots in nose-shot. This is a truly abandoned farm, with rotting buildings where a family once lived, and rotting trees where squirrels and birds now live without the bother of humans. The south breeze brings nothing but the smell of the foliage around them, new grass, clover, and, yes, at the root of it, small sprigs of violets, a potpourri of plant life.

It starts with Cosmos putting his arm under Cherlyn's head as they stare heavenward.

"It's so beautiful," says Cosmos, "but there's more sparkle in your smile than in the stars. There's more light in your eyes than in the moon."

He feels his own poetic words relax him. They seem to have the same effect on her. She sighs and puts her head closer to his.

"Let's see who can spot a satellite first," he says.

"Or why don't we see who can spot a shooting star first?" says Cherlyn. "Something God, not man, created."

"This is so beautiful," says Cosmos and turns on his side toward her. He puts his lips to her cheek and rubs his lips gently against it.

"You have the sweetest lips," she says. "You are so tender and gentle."

"If I am tender and gentle, it's because what you are is

contagious. And you have the sweetest cheek."

She turns toward him, and as she does, he puts his hand on her breast.

She puts her hand to his cheek. "Let's go slowly," she whispers. "More like the moon than a shooting star."

He rubs the mounds of her blouse with his palm, then moves toward the top button of the V and slides his hand slowly under her bra. She lies still as he cups his hand over her breast, then draws his hand back slightly to touch her nipple.

"Wouldn't it be all right to take your bra off?" he says. "You could keep your blouse on, and you'd still be dressed. No skin would be exposed to the open air."

She doesn't answer, but her breathing has changed. "Doesn't this feel good?" he says, and continues to caress her breast gently.

"Yes," she says. "Almost too good."

"There would just be more room with your bra off," he says quietly, trying to keep his voice at a level pitch. "You'd still be dressed, really."

"I guess you're right," she says. "As long as I keep my blouse on. And let me take my bra off. I don't want to lose it out here. Let me take it off and put it in my coat pocket."

Cosmos watches her slip the straps over her shoulder and pull her arm through the bra strap without taking her blouse off. She gets both arms free, then moves the snaps around to the front, and the bra is off. She folds it neatly and tucks it into her coat pocket. "No more clothes off," she says. "Cosmos, we promised ourselves."

"All right, no more clothes off."

They lie back again, and Cosmos fondles her breasts under her blouse. "I want to kiss them," he whispers. "I've never wanted to kiss anything so much in my life. Let me kiss them."

She turns toward him, but when he puts his lips to her chest, he cannot move them past her buttons to kiss her breasts.

"Just the top button," says Cosmos. "If you just opened one button, I could kiss your lovely breasts."

"I don't want to break our promise," she says. "Cosmos?"

"All right," he says. "But I could raise your blouse without taking buttons loose. That would be all right. Your blouse would still be on."

He puts his hand on the bottom of her blouse and starts raising it across her stomach. She does not stop him.

He kisses her ribs, he kisses her stomach, and then her breasts, so much larger, so much firmer than Salal's. She reaches toward his chest as he kisses her. She pulls his shirt loose from his jeans and runs her hand over his stomach, over his chest. She runs her hand over his nipples.

"I want to kiss you too," she says. "It feels so good to be kissed there. I want to kiss you too. May I?"

A twinge in his own body surprises Cosmos. Is Cherlyn's

question innocent, or does this kind of desire come naturally to girls raised on a farm? Some kind of wild prairie thing? "You really want to?" he says.

"Yes, yes," she says. "I want to kiss you everywhere I can without taking any of your clothes off. You can slide your shirt up too."

Cosmos lies on his back and lets her slide his shirt up. She kisses his chest in much the same way that he kissed hers. Then she kisses his nipples the way he kissed hers. "Nice, nice," he says. "Cherlyn, that feels good. I've never felt anything like that before."

"I'm glad," she says. "I want this to be only ours." Her hair moves across his stomach as her lips explore his chest. Then her hip touches his erection. "Ah," he says again. "You're driving me half crazy, you know."

He reaches for her breasts and she turns from him, onto her back. She puts her arm on his shoulder and pulls him toward herself. They continue to kiss in their spring nest. Her mouth opens and their tongues touch.

"I'd like to read the book that taught you to kiss like that," she says.

"I learned it from you," he says. "I learned it from your lips."

"You're so much more experienced than I am," she says. "You know exactly what to do to make me feel good."

"No, I'm not," he says, then puts his parted lips to hers again. He moves his tongue over hers in small circles. Both breathe in shallow breaths as his exposed chest touches hers, gently, and their bodies begin to press against each other's and to move slowly in squirming pressure, until slowly he edges onto her, first letting one leg rest on top of hers, then nudging with his knee against hers until her knees part and gradually part farther and farther. All the while they both continue to kiss and squirm, with Cosmos easing up onto her in millimeters, so gradually but steadily that no one could have named the exact moment when they reach a fully sexual position, her legs spread as wide as her skirt will allow, then wider as she lifts her knees so that her skirt rises up toward her waist. Cosmos raises himself over her. Somehow his shirt buttons have come loose while they are petting so that it falls open and he hovers over her like a human tent. Her eyes are lit by starlight, gleaming in the grass below him.

"Is this all right?" he says.

"Yes," she says, "but you shouldn't have loosened all your shirt buttons. Just don't touch any belt buckles." She puts her hands on his waist, on the hard leather of his belt, then slides her hands up onto his rib cage, then onto his chest and under his arms, and pulls him toward her.

Fully erect inside his jeans, Cosmos wishes he had worn loose jeans like those he wore in Port Swan instead of these tighter things. But his momentary regret fades when he hears Cherlyn's breathing and sees the expression on her face. It isn't just the pressure of his erection that is giving her pleasure but also the hard ridge of denim, the double-folded fabric on the zipper of his jeans, which, like a long narrow finger, comes down on the most sensitive source of her pleasure. She moves against the denim ridge, rocks against it, then makes small circular movements which he can tell are taking her along the edge of ecstasy and pain. He lets her take control, following her hips and pelvis. As her breathing becomes panting and her movements grow faster and more intense, it occurs to Cosmos that it just might happen. Not in his most fact-defying fantasies has he imagined that a religious girl from a farm in Iowa could reach an orgasm under these circumstances. Until now he hasn't imagined that any girl like Cherlyn would be able to reach an orgasm under any circumstances. But it is happening. Like a person who is teetering high on a diving board looking down at the water thirty feet below, he can feel her body tense at that moment when she is leaping off into the explosive joy of her body. With the pain and pleasure of his own organ wedged inside the tight jeans, he joins her in the groaning roaring pleasure of the mutual plunge.

He holds himself over her, staring into her eyes, as they breathe together, slowly, and more slowly.

"Oh my," she sighs from under him. "Oh my."

"You came, didn't you?" he says earnestly, still hardly believing that this could have happened.

"I did something," she says. "Oh my, oh my. That was so

wonderful, and I feel so good because we didn't break our promises. We didn't really have sex, did we?"

"Of course not," says Cosmos.

She relaxes, with her hair spread out around her on the grass-cushioned blanket, her eyes and mouth wide open, as she stares up into the stars.

He puts his head under her chin, where her blouse has gathered like a large collar, then moves his lips down to kiss her breasts.

"I feel something moist," she says. "Did you ejaculate?"

"I would say so," he says. "Royally, I would say."

He rolls over on his back. "Feel this," he says. The semen has soaked through his jeans.

"We'd better be careful," she says. "If your seed soaks through my clothes the way it has soaked through yours, I could get pregnant, don't you think?"

"I don't think so," he says. "I don't think this one is in the book. If you do get pregnant, we'll have to call you Mary, because God knows you're still a virgin."

It sounds so clever as he is saying that, but as soon as the words pass his lips he knows he has said a bad thing.

"Oh!" she says. Her voice is not angry. It sounds more like somebody who has just been stabbed. Her body stiffens.

"Sorry," he says.

"Cosmos, Cosmos," she says, and sighs almost sadly. "What have we started?"

"I don't think we've done anything unnatural, do you?"

"No, no," she says. "But I hope God understands how much I love you. Even now I feel God's presence, and His presence is love."

He lies back down beside her and they both stare up into the starlit sky. In the far distance, a troubled steer lows its lonely cry into the darkness. In the far distance, a loud speeding car roars across the gravel roads. And then the distance closes in as the car comes closer, its headlights creating a glow behind a hill before it crests the hill at a fast speed, the sound of the gravel spitting and hissing against the fenders.

"That's the first car to go past here all night," says Cosmos. "This is a good spot."

But the car is not going past. First the deceleration, then the hard braking, and suddenly the headlights sweeping across the farmyard. The lights catch the glowing shape of Cherlyn's parents' car. With its headlights pointed at the car, the intruder comes to a stop.

"Is it the police?" whispers Cherlyn.

Car doors open, and the sounds of drunken teenagers clatter through the night air.

"It's a carload of drunks," says Cosmos. "Get down."

Laughter, loud drunken laughter, fills the night air.

"Hey, assholes!" someone shouts. "Wherever you are, you better put your pants on, the party's over!"

"Whose car izzat?" someone slurs.

"Ain't never seen it before. Fuckin' Taurus. Old-man fuckin' Taurus."

"Let's fuckin' break the fuckin' windows, what the fuck," someone else slurs. There comes the sound of an empty beer can hitting metal.

"Ain't fuckin' gunna break no fuckin' windows with no fuckin' luminumum can, fuckin' asshole."

"Awuminimum," says another. "You so fuckin' drunk you can't even fuckin' talk, fuckin' asshole."

"Shitface," comes the answer.

"Who shitface? You so fuckin' shitface you can't even hear when I say fuckin' aluminium, dumb fuck."

Cherlyn clutches Cosmos's arm. "They're bad, they're bad," she says. "Cosmos, they're bad and they're drunk."

"You can say that again. Oh shit," says Cosmos.

"You don't have to start talking like them," she says.

"What do you want to do? I can't afford to go getting into a fight with anybody."

Cherlyn struggles to get her clothes adjusted without raising her head above the clumps of grass that cling to the fence wire next to them. "My bra," she says. "What happened to my bra? It's not in my pocket." She scratches through the grass. "Cosmos, please find it. I can't let them or anybody see me without my bra."

Another car's lights create a halo on the crest of the same hill where the drunks came from. This car is going just as fast, almost becoming airborne as it crests the same hill. Its driver seems to notice the headlights at the abandoned farm and brakes hard, the back end whipping and skidding. It is not a car, it is a small pickup. It bounces across a few potholes and aims itself directly at the carload of drunks. A few of them flip their beer cans away from themselves and head for the open doors of their car. The two loudest and biggest ones stand their ground, facing the new headlights.

"Is that the cops?" says Cosmos. "I just don't want to see any cops. Not where there's drinking going on."

Still concealed by the fence and grass, Cosmos and Cherlyn peer out. "I know that pickup," says Cherlyn. "That's not the cops."

"I know that pickup too," says Cosmos. "That's Elmer."

All the drunks have gotten inside the car except the driver, who stands behind his open car door. Elmer is alone but shows no fear. He parks his pickup with his headlights shining into their rear window and jumps out. He starts walking toward the carload of drunks with his arms arched from his hips like a wrestler coming at somebody, or like a cowboy who is about to draw both six-guns.

"You fuckin' pussies," Elmer growls out. "You goddamn fuckin' pussies. Which one of you fuckin' pussies wants to step out here in the car light so I can see your fuckin' nose before I break it off your half-brain fuckin' head? C'mon, which one of you? C'mon, c'mon, pussies."

"Elmer's really pissed about something," says Cosmos.

"I've never heard so much filthy language in my life," whispers Cherlyn. "Oh God, help us." Cosmos hears her continue in a soft mumbling. She is praying.

The driver holds his ground behind his open door. He stands over six feet tall, a big burly kid in a leather jacket and a dark baseball cap. Elmer moves toward him. "All right, all right," says the driver, "I'll pay you tomorrow."

"Ain't gunna be no fuckin' tomorrow if you don't fuckin' pay me right fuckin' now, fuckin' pussy."

The driver lifts his hand toward Elmer. "Hold on, hold on," he says. Elmer stops and waits. The driver leans in the car and asks the people inside if they have some money. "I owe this guy," he says. "I need fifty."

The drunks inside the car scramble around, holding their wallets up to the light that shines through the back window. They hand the driver money. "Here," says the driver, and holds out a handful of bills toward Elmer. Elmer walks up and takes the money and goes into the headlights to count it.

"Now get the fuck out of here," says Elmer. He stands back and watches the carload of drunks turn around and leave.

Elmer looks at Cherlyn's parents' car, then in the direction of the pasture where Cosmos and Cherlyn are hiding.

"Good night, Cosmos. Good night, Cherlyn," he yells, then gets in his pickup and drives away.

What would Jesus do?

COSMOS HAS A LITTLE DREAD of the morning-after look he might get from Cherlyn, but when he first meets her in the hallway, her happy face relieves his fears. She is quick to touch his arm and to look into his eyes, but their warm touches and glances through the day are practically smothered by the rumor mill in the hallways. Everyone is talking about the thefts: one rumor says the thief has been caught, another that the thief has confessed and is already in jail, another that several people were caught, a whole theft-ring. By noon the rumors have settled on something that is probably close to the truth: an envelope with watches, a Swiss Army knife, and over a hundred dollars was put in the principal's mail slot before school.

In *The Messenger*'s office later that day, Cosmos turns the conversation to their evening under the stars. He asks her, "Any regrets?"

"Oh no," she says. "I do feel a little bit guilty for thinking of myself more than God on Sunday, but I don't think what we did is in itself wrong, do you?"

"Not if you don't have any regrets."

"Only thing that bothers me is Elmer," she says, "and those vile boys. But Elmer—it sounded as if he had been dealing drugs with those guys. That's what I thought."

"I think you're right about that," says Cosmos. He looks away.

"Is there something you're not telling me?" she says.

"I don't have trouble keeping secrets from other people around here," he says, "but I don't like keeping secrets from you. You're so open. I wish I could be too."

She sits at her desk and waits. "I'm not afraid of anything you might tell me," she says. "I'm not going to judge you."

Cosmos sits down. "All right. Let me start with a question."

"Shoot," she says.

"Do you think Jesus ever sinned?"

"Jesus was God," she says without hesitating. "Jesus was perfect. He couldn't sin."

"You actually believe that?"

"I do," she says.

"You think Jesus would have snitched on one of his disciples if, say, he saw one of those disciples stealing a piece of fruit from an open market, say?"

"Depends on whether the disciple was starving and didn't have any money, don't you think?"

"You're asking me?"

"There's the story of Jesus saving this sheep on the

Sabbath and breaking the rules to do it, remember?"

"Sorry, Cherlyn, that's not a story I have in my head to remember."

"So why are you asking about this?"

"I'm not sure. I was just thinking: how could anybody who didn't sin feel sorry for anybody who did? If Jesus had mercy for sinners, like I keep hearing the preacher say, I think Jesus must have 'been there, done that,' you know? How else would he be able to forgive if he didn't know what it was like to sin? I think that's just logic. You can't feel sorry for somebody who stubs their toe if you never stubbed your toe yourself."

"I believe Jesus is bigger than logic," says Cherlyn. "Jesus is God and God is love and God's love is bigger than anything I can understand."

Cosmos stares at the desk in front of him.

"Tell me what made you ask about snitching," says Cherlyn. "Somebody who is pretending to be good snitch on you for something?"

"No. Somebody who is pretending to be good is not snitching on somebody. That pretender is me. I'm not snitching on somebody, and I don't plan to. It's just that I don't like not telling you about it. If there's ever a time when we're going to be alone together again, I mean by ourselves at night, then I really don't want to keep any secrets from you."

"You don't have to tell me everything," says Cherlyn. "Some things are private. They're between you and God, or between you and your conscience."

"I smoked marijuana with my friends in Port Swan, for one thing," says Cosmos. "I don't like hiding that from you, and I know you probably think doing drugs is really wrong." He looks at her to see her reaction. She doesn't flinch. She gives no signals of disapproval. "I had to tell Jonsma, because he was going to give me a drug test. He gave me a week to clean up. I passed the drug test a week later. I'm clean."

"I would never smoke myself," she says, "but I don't have my eyes closed to the world. I know some drugs are worse than others. It's all the kids on meth nowadays that scares me. And my folks—they're both on drugs. My mom on Valium, my dad on antidepressants. It's just that the drugs they take are legal."

"Right," says Cosmos. "So you're not mad or disappointed with me?"

"Of course not. I can understand why you might smoke marijuana back with your old friends, people who do that sort of thing." She reaches over and puts her hand on his. "I'm not going to stop caring about you because you make mistakes," she says.

"There's something else."

Now Cherlyn does look worried. "Go ahead."

"Elmer is the thief," says Cosmos. "I accidentally found some of the stuff under the front seat of his pickup right before Christmas vacation. Watches. A wallet. Swiss Army knife."

"All the stuff that was returned today! Cosmos! This is great! Now everybody will finally know you're innocent! Of course, I already did."

"I know you did," says Cosmos. "But Marksema was standing by the front door when I walked into school. I figured out that he was checking to see if I was at school early enough to dump the goods. I wasn't. He didn't look surprised. I think he wanted to believe me all along too."

"So do you think Elmer will go to jail?"

"Elmer returned the goods and the money," says Cosmos, "but he didn't confess to taking them. I saw him in the hallway. He was smirking, a big smirk: maybe because he knew we were out in the pasture Sunday night, maybe because now he knows I won't have to worry anymore about being a suspect, maybe because he pulled a fast one on the whole system. I guess I don't blame him for feeling good about everything."

Cherlyn thinks for a moment. "Wait a minute," she says. "He let you be the prime suspect all these months? He even acted as if he was defending you against suspicion. That's really hypocritical. Marksema should know the whole truth."

"Should he?" says Cosmos. "I'm glad people don't know the whole truth about me. I'd be in detention in Washington right now if they did."

"So this is why you're asking me if Jesus would snitch?"

"Yeah," says Cosmos. "What would Jesus do?"

"He'd tell Elmer that returning the money and stolen property is only half of what he should do. He should confess. Clear the air once and for all, or else."

"Or else what? Jesus would snitch? I'm not going to snitch."

"Are you going to talk to Elmer about it?"

"Already did. I'm sure that's why he returned the goods. That's probably why he was collecting from those drunks too. They probably ripped him off, and he needed the money to pay back the school. I don't think Elmer is a big crook, but, wow, is he fearless. I thought that was awesome, the way he just intimidated that whole carful of guys. Awesome, but pretty crazy too. But I think he's more a drug distributor than a dealer, somebody who hands out drugs as a way of making friends. Like Margaret, he's a lonely one. He's desperate for friends. So he finds himself out of money and getting in trouble with the people who supply him, and he has to steal. That's how I put it all together. I've been thinking about Elmer a lot. He thinks that he is like me. That we're both black sheep. I think he's right about that. The big difference between him and me is that I have you."

Cosmos watches Cherlyn for her reaction. She has so much heart, she can feel sympathy for almost anybody—he knows that about her. But she also has such a quick mind that she can also figure out what rings true and what doesn't. Right now he can't tell whether she is thinking or feeling.

"I think you did what Jesus would have you do," she says.

"Didn't mean to," says Cosmos. "I just didn't want to get my own butt in trouble for what Elmer did."

"Jesus wouldn't have had to worry about getting his butt in trouble, because he was God. God knows we can't be perfect. So I think you did all that Jesus would expect a person to do. And if you feel all right about it, it's certainly good enough for little old sinful me."

"Thanks," says Cosmos. "Now, what say we go behind the closet door and not-quite-sin for a few minutes before the bell rings."

"Great idea."

* * *

The morning's April shower turns to freezing rain by the time school lets out. Cherlyn's father is gradually loosening the reins, and she is now allowed to drive Cosmos home after school, as long as she is home within an hour after school lets out. This gives them time to stop at the Tastee-Freez Truck Stop, where they went the first day she kissed him. They can sit in the corner booth where they sat the first time, share a Coke, and cuddle a bit. He'll still be home in time for chores.

They slip and slide down the icy sidewalk outside school. The trees glisten. Everything is glazed with ice and the world smells clean, as if what touches the nostrils is sent from the clean pine trees of Canada instead of the hog lots of Iowa.

"This is the wickedest ice storm I've seen in years," says Cherlyn as they slip and slide toward the parking lot. "I often wonder why beauty and danger always seem to come together."

Cosmos looks at her, puzzled but pleased. "That's how I always feel when I'm with you," he says.

They hold hands, half skating down the sidewalk.

"Except you're more beauty than danger," he says. He inhales and blows his steamy breath into the brisk air.

She gives him a smile that glistens like the trees. She slides her foot against his, as if she were trying to trip him. He plays along with her game by flailing his arms and spinning around on the ice.

"Oh, you're dangerous," he says, "so very very dayyyyyyngerous," and gives her a little shove back.

She clutches his arm and pulls herself close to him.

"Old Dutch trick," he says. "I knew I could get you to lean on me for protection against the wiles of Mother Nature."

"Oh, you're a real Hans Brinker, you are," she says, "but

you out there in soggy Washington probably never heard of Hans Brinker."

"Silver skates," he says.

"Oh, listen to the silver trees," she says. "They're talking to us." They stop and listen to the tree limbs click and tinkle against each other.

They stand looking at what the storm has done, and as they stare, the sun breaks through the clouds like a spotlight from behind a blue curtain, and the trees and bushes seem to shatter with light.

"It's so pretty it's like one of those religious paintings you see in Kmart," says Cosmos.

"Oh, Cosmos," says Cherlyn, "don't spoil it. It is kind of religious, don't you think?"

"You sweet-souled little angel," says Cosmos, and looks into her bright eyes. "You never stop."

"*It* never stops," says Cherlyn. "The heavens declare the glory of God."

"Give me a break," says Cosmos.

"Come on, we have some ice to clean off the windshield," she says, and tugs him toward the parking lot beyond the lineup of buses.

The nine yellow buses all have chains on the rear tires. Cosmos has not seen this kind of preparation before, not in Iowa, where everyone seems so fearless, so undaunted, by winter weather and the hazards it brings.

"It's not going to be much fun driving on this ice," says Cosmos.

"New tires," says Cherlyn, "and I'll go easy."

They take turns with the plastic ice-scraper cleaning the windows, then get in and buckle up, and Cherlyn eases the car out of the parking lot. The school buses take off just behind them, the chains on their large tires spitting ice.

Just ahead of them, Elmer's Toyota fishtails down the street.

"Showing off as usual," says Cherlyn. "He's going to kill himself showing off someday."

"He's still celebrating," says Cosmos. "He got a load off his mind today."

Elmer's Toyota keeps fishtailing down the road. Then he glides off onto a side street and does a complete spin in the middle of the street. It looks like a game to him, and he somehow keeps the vehicle under control, racing the engine, spinning the tires wildly, but never skidding out against the curb or parked cars.

"I'm glad you don't think he's all bad," says Cherlyn. "But he does scare me a little. I just don't want him to do anything that would hurt you."

"I don't think Elmer is likely to hurt anybody but himself," says Cosmos. "But I'll be careful."

Just out of town, the ice has been salted off the roads. Cherlyn accelerates up to a safe fifty miles an hour on the wet blacktop. Cosmos looks back and sees no sign of Elmer and his Toyota. About a half-mile away, he can see the yellow bus he usually rides. He turns to Cherlyn. "This is sweet," he says. "Can I turn on the radio?"

"Any station you want," she says.

"There isn't much choice, now, is there?" he teases.

He leans down for the radio dial and barely has the radio turned on when he hears a quick gasping "oh" from Cherlyn. He pulls his head back to see what she sees: a large black four-wheeler skidding on a long stretch of ice that has formed, or re-formed, in the sparkling shade of a large farm-grove along the road. Cherlyn touches the brake and her car slides too. As quickly, she releases the brake and turns toward the ditch. Cosmos puts his hands on the dash as the inevitable crash comes at them. For days he will remember the next two seconds, the car weaving, sliding, gliding, the image of Elmer's pickup shenanigans flashing through his mind. He'll remember the slow waltzing dance of the car as Cherlyn turns the steering wheel from side to side in deliberate but short movements, never putting her foot on the brake again, following the ice the way just that morning he watched a barn swallow coursing the unmarked path through air, not into the side of the barn that seemed to be its inevitable fate but, in a graceful weave, through an open window to its nest and waiting young, missing the wooden window frame by inches as Cherlyn now misses by inches the huge pickup that looks bigger than a barn, its high rear bumper gliding past the driver's side like a huge dagger at an angle that Cherlyn's car accommodates by angling away from the other vehicle at what should have been the moment of impact, and then the easy sideways glide on the icy shoulder of the road, the car coming to a stop the way a child's sled might come to a stop at the bottom of a hill.

The strange moment of silence in what should have been the moment of silence after the crash.

Cosmos holds his hands up and looks at them to see if they are really still there. Then he turns to Cherlyn. Her hands are still on the steering wheel, relaxed. Her eyes are closed. Her lips are moving.

There are moments of grace

TWO DAYS AFTER THE NEAR-crash, Cosmos and Cherlyn take a noon-hour walk in the park across from the Academy. Tiny leaves, soft as chiffon, have formed on some of the trees. The sky is blue, the air warm again. They walk along the curving asphalt path around the round flower-beds. Cherlyn wears one of her conservative blue dresses.

"Look," she says and points to the grass. "I've never found one before—right there, a four-leaf clover."

Cosmos bends down where she is pointing and starts looking. "No, farther to the left," she says. "A little farther. A little farther. There."

Finally, Cosmos sees it. He picks it off, a perfectly shaped four-leaf clover, and hands it to her. She holds it up to the sun. "It's one of God's little messages," she says. "Here, I want you to have it. Really. Please. I want to give it to you. For us."

Cosmos takes the four-leaf clover. "You really do believe in miracles, don't you?" he says.

"Yes, yes," she says. "There are moments of grace—when God touches us, opens our eyes."

"I believe that too," says Cosmos. "Moments of insight. Moments when things make sense."

"But I want to be there all the time," says Cherlyn. "I want to live in grace, live every moment with my eyes open to God's presence. I have felt this way ever since that night when God came into my heart."

"God beat me to your heart," he says, grinning.

She takes his wrist. Cosmos sees how serious her eyes are. "I can't joke about this," she says. "It's so important to me."

"Sorry," he says. "Tell me about that night. Was it with your Bible group down by the river, that time when you decided you wanted to become a political leader?"

"No, much earlier than that," she says. "I haven't told you about this. Do you really want to hear it?"

"Of course," he says. They sit down on a park bench and Cherlyn begins.

"This is just my story, you understand," she says. "Promise you won't get upset and say I'm trying to go evangelical on you."

"Agreed," says Cosmos. "I'm ready. All ears."

"All right," says Cherlyn. "Here goes. I was drifting along, being a good-enough Christian. Going to church. Attending catechism classes. Doing whatever I needed to do to be accepted by my dad and mom. Especially my dad. And by the church. I didn't know any other way. Then, after my sophomore year at the Academy, I went to this summer camp at Lake Okoboji. It was a church camp, but people there were different from the people around here. The leaders were so filled with joy that it sweetened the air. One night, around the campfire, we were singing the kinds of songs we all knew by heart, like 'Do, Lord, oh, do, Lord, oh, do remember me,' and 'I come to the garden alone,' and 'We are climbing Jacob's ladder," when out of nowhere this bird came flying high above the campfire, maybe an owl, but I couldn't tell. Seeing that four-leaf clover just appear out of nowhere brought it all back."

Cherlyn adjusts herself on the bench. She looks up at the blue sky, her eyes dreamy and peaceful, as if she is reliving the scene of that high-flying bird. "It circled above us in the darkness, and I could see light from the campfire hit the bottom of its wings when they flapped, and that light wasn't like real light, and the wings didn't look like they were made of feathers, more like they were made of silk or out of some outer-space metallic substance. Unreal wings. Unreal light. Then I had this powerful feeling. It was unreal too, like something that wasn't coming from earth, not from my body. It felt like nothing I had ever experienced before. I knew it was a sign that from now on my spirit would soar through the darkness of the world. I felt it so powerfully, like for a moment I wasn't even a human being. It was as if my own spirit had been pulled out of me, where it could totally be in God's hands. And then He put it back inside me, filled with this new knowledge. I felt as if I had been lifted so much higher than the things of this world that nothing would ever look the same again. I was transformed, Cosmos, and, believe me, I'm not preaching at you. I'm just telling you what happened to me. I had become a different person. I had been raised a Christian, but it was only at that moment I knew what God's love really meant. It was so much bigger than anything I had ever felt before that I knew my life would never be the same again. It was like an acorn had opened and for the first time in my life I knew who I really was. I knew what God had planned for me. Forever I would have this moment as a reference, like an eternal flame or something, a memory I would never be able to forget, of what it feels like to let God's love come alive inside you."

"That's awesome," says Cosmos. He looks at the four-leaf clover, then takes out his English text and carefully presses it between the pages. "I would never say that didn't happen to you," he says.

Cherlyn looks at Cosmos. He imitates her soft and peaceful smile. "You're always for real, aren't you?" he says.

"What happened that night is the most real thing that ever happened to me," she goes on. "Whenever I feel that light fading, I take a deep breath and ask God to refill me with His presence."

"I believe you, and I love you," says Cosmos. "I don't

want to make fun of you or anything, but I think people get stoned for the same reason. To get that feeling that everything is beautiful."

Cosmos regrets having made the comment immediately, but it doesn't disturb Cherlyn. "Sometimes true and false look alike on the surface, don't you think?" she says.

"Yes," he says. "I've thought about that a lot, actually. I have these two characters I hide behind. The real one is Cosmos Coyote and the phony one is William the Nice."

"That's funny," she says.

"But sometimes I get them mixed up—like now, and almost all the time when I'm with you, I feel really nice but I don't feel phony, and sometimes when I'm feeling really nasty, like a really nasty Coyote, I don't feel real, I just feel scared?"

"Ah," she says. "Like sometimes when you're trying to act like nasty old Andrew Jackson you're actually being a moral and good Martin Van Buren? But Van Buren's goodness didn't give him much confidence. One time he was so nervous about giving a political speech that he had to sit down without saying a word. He could have used a little of Jackson's feistiness right then."

"Now I'm really getting mixed up. You mean, when I'm trying to be an Andrew Jackson—that would be my Cosmos Coyote—I'm actually being a Martin Van Buren— that would be my William the Nice? But you just said Van Buren—your William the Nice—could use some of

Andrew Jackson's feistiness, you know, some of your Cosmos Coyote. Sounds to me like you're starting to think differently about Andrew Jackson. Nasty Andrew Jackson?"

"Sort of," she says. "You know, even though Andrew Jackson was an Indian-killer, he took this little Indian baby from a battlefield, a little orphan boy named Lyncoya— isn't that a lovely name, Lyncoya?—and he raised that child like it was his own. It's a beautiful and loving story. And he was awfully good to his wife—even though all the high-society types at the time made fun of her for being dumpy and out of fashion. I never get the feeling that Van Buren had much heart for his wife. She was weak and had tuberculosis, but he just kept getting her pregnant. Poor Hannah, she died in her thirties, and it's hard for me not to blame Van Buren for that. I think he was pretty selfish, and in some ways, Van Buren was the phony. Hitching himself up so tight in a corset that he looked like a woman. I guess he was always trying to look like your William the Nice, but, whatever fronts he put up, he never did develop much charisma."

"So do you love my Cosmos Coyote side or my William the Nice?" He kisses her cheek.

"I love them both," she says, and turns to kiss him sweetly back. "But I don't much get along with the William the Nice types either. I don't fit in with the regular church-folks, for example," says Cherlyn. "They're so stiff, so locked into traditions. God's love is something that keeps renewing itself with new light for new ages. They're always trying to put the new wine in old bottles." She sighs, as if she is recognizing the fact that she is as much out-of-touch with the people around her as Cosmos is. "That's why I joined the Children of Love, the CLs. We're that small group that meets before church, and we're probably the only people who understand each other. We've all been touched by God in a way that most people in the church don't understand. They don't understand any more than I expect you to understand. Maybe not as much as you understand."

"The only thing that's important to me about you, Cherlyn, is that the person you are one day is the same person you are the next day. It's great to know that you always are what you seem to be. That's more than I can say for most people around here. That's more than I can say for myself."

"After my vision of God's love when I was fifteen, I feel more different from the old-fashioned Dutch Calvinists of my church than I do from people who aren't sure what they believe. Strangers don't scare me, they make me curious. They make me want to show them the love God has given me. That's all I want to do. I don't think it's my business to decide what they should believe. 'His eye is on the sparrow, and I know He watches me,' the song says, but that must mean 'and you and you and you and everybody else too!'"

"If the God you believe in can put up with somebody like me, your God ain't half bad," says Cosmos.

"Do you think you could ever accept Jesus?" she says. "If you knew how much his love changes your life, how it makes you feel?"

His eyes do not leave hers. "Is this an altar call?"

"Not really," she says. "It really was just a question. But, Cosmos, be honest. We've always been honest with each other."

"Yes," he says. "I know. But being honest with you means telling you what I've told you before. I believe in God, but I don't believe anybody has a hot-line to the Truth—big 'T.' You asked me once if I thought God could be known? I feel close to God when I hear good music or when I see little kids playing and laughing on a school ground. I feel close to God when I feel my heart filling up with love for you. I feel close to God when I see you praying—because you are so beautiful, and because I know that's the real you. But I'd be faking it if I pretended to feel the same things that you do."

"We both know what love is," she says. "Our love is just a hint of God's love."

"But think of all the people your church sends to hell. Most of them. Don't you think there's something wrong with that? A person says, 'I accept Jesus,' and that sets them apart from the billions of people who don't say that?"

"But it does set them apart," says Cherlyn.

For the first time, Cosmos feels an invisible shield rise up between them. "Loving you is all the setting-apart I want," he says. "And as for God's love, you said His eye is on the sparrow. I think I'll have to take my place with the sparrows."

"I'm sorry," she says. "It's just that I love you so much, I want to give you everything that I have, and God's love is part of what I have."

"Your love is more than enough for me. My heart feels full of love. I ache with love for you, Cherlyn. If there is more love than this to be had in this lifetime, I don't know what I'd do with it."

Her eyes start to smile. "But human love is only part of it. I know there is more. When I don't try to control my life and just put it in His hands, that's when I feel His love most—when I just give myself up to Him."

"I don't think we have control of everything," says Cosmos, "but I still think it's up to me to make something of myself. Or not. I don't want to blame God if something goes wrong. If I can find some kind of harmony and pass that on into the world, then I'll feel that I've done something with my life. I just want to be honest—to be one person."

"Sometimes we seem so close. We want the same thing."

"Sometimes I watch my dad building things," says Cosmos. "He's a perfectionist, always needs to have it just right. Once he worked on this piece of wood for three weeks, making a blue heron. He was almost finished. Then he stood back and looked at what he had done, and he was almost crying. He thought he had the neck wrong. It wasn't perfect. That blue heron became firewood."

"Well, I'd never make firewood of you," says Cherlyn. "I don't expect you to be perfect. God doesn't either. And if you're good enough for my love, I know you're good enough for God's."

"I'm back to being one of those sparrows," says Cosmos.

Now she does smile. "Enough heavy talk for one noon hour," she says.

"I don't think we would have gotten into all this heavy stuff if it hadn't been for the other day, when we almost wiped out on the ice. Almost, but not quite—thanks to your driving skills."

"I know," she says. "We came so close to dying that I feel every moment with you from now on is all the more precious."

"Exactly," he says. "I didn't feel scared until the next day. Now it keeps replaying through my mind, and I wake up seeing that big truck in our laps. Last night, when I picked up my guitar, my fingers were shaking. Then I settled down, feeling thankful that you're such a fantastic driver. How did you learn to drive like that, farm girl?"

"Ice driving, yes," she says. "I learned to drive on ice and snow. They always say to pretend that you're driving a boat when you're on ice. But I've never driven a boat."

"Next time I'm driving a boat, I'll pretend that I'm driving on ice," says Cosmos. "You can handle a car on ice as well as Elmer. Maybe better."

She leans her head on his shoulder. Purple martins swoop over their heads like flashes of cobalt in the bright sunlight. "I don't know how to thank you," says Cosmos. "I really don't. You saved our lives."

"No, no," she says. "God was driving the car more than I was."

"I thought the streets of heaven were paved in gold, not ice."

"Cosmos."

"Sorry," he says.

"I think God was reminding us how close death is. It's always right there, like a door that could open at any moment. Even when you're young. It's always right there. Right there." She holds her hand in front of her, then turns it, like a door on a hinge. "A door that God can keep closed or He can open it. Right now I feel we are in this small room of the present. Of this earth. Of our lives. I think God was tapping me on the shoulder to remind me that it's arrogant of me to plan the future, because it really is not in my control. And my plans on earth are nothing compared to His greater plans, ones that I should try to follow more humbly. A reminder of that."

"I felt it was a reminder too," says Cosmos. "That life is short. I don't think I've ever felt so alive as I have these past few days, even if it means that my hands start shaking when I least expect it."

"Yes," she says. "I feel like my senses have been turned up on high. I want to smell, to hear, to touch, to taste everything." She puts her fingers to his cheek, then puts her fingers to her lips. She looks at him earnestly. "And I want you, Cosmos. I want you too much. Just when I'm feeling so wonderful, I feel like my whole being is split, part of it wanting to go straight to God, and part of it tingling with desire for you. I know you are flesh and blood, a creature of the earth, and I know my faith is not something that stops here with the moist spring dirt, or the new leaves, or even your skin. Though your skin is heavenly. You're the nicest creature I've ever found on this old planet. Like you, I love this old planet. I love the earth, and you more than anybody know that I love the flesh, but my faith is in heaven. I know our time here is so short. And then death. The beginning. What would you do if I died? Where do you think I would be?"

Cosmos doesn't answer as they walk back toward the school. Then a voice says from over their shoulders, "William." It's Cousin Mike.

"You can call me Cosmos in front of Cherlyn," he says.

Cousin Mike is not smiling. "I have some terrible news," says Mike. "It's your grandfather."

"Oh no," says Cherlyn. "My talking about death."

"Your grandpa Wilim is gone, Cosmos. How did you know, Cherlyn?"

"I just knew," says Cherlyn. "I just knew."

"**H**E WENT TO THE LORD** at high noon," says Uncle Henry to Cosmos and Cousin Mike. Uncle Henry stands with his back to the kitchen window and the afternoon sunlight behind him. Aunt Minnie and Mike stand beside him. They both have their hands folded, as if in reverence or acceptance.

Cosmos sits stiffly at the kitchen table. Whatever he is feeling, it is not shock. It doesn't feel like sorrow either. It may be guilt for feeling thankful that it is the judgmental old man and not Cherlyn who has died. Or could it be guilt about the unfinished business with Gramps, whose blood-lines lead to him? Not likely. Whatever had to be worked out with Gramps would be his dad's business. And Uncle Henry's business.

But a human being is dead. This has to mean something. Maybe now he can see what the community looks like when all the masks and phony faces fall away, when all the pretense and suspicion burn off like wax under the glare of the Big One: Death, the great revealer. Death, the lie detector. Death, the truth serum. Maybe now he'll be able to be who he really is among these people. Cosmos Coyote and William the Nice can be one person, the way they are when he is with Cherlyn.

Cosmos folds his hands in imitation of Uncle Henry and Aunt Minnie's stance. So does Cousin Mike. "Did he die in his sleep?" Cosmos asks.

"No," says Uncle Henry. "He fell."

"He fell down in the nursing home?" says Cosmos. "How did that kill him?"

Uncle Henry and Aunt Minnie, in unison, unfold their hands and sit down at the kitchen table. "It's not a nice story," says Uncle Henry. "He was trying to get out, you see."

"He what?" says Cosmos. What Uncle Henry says sounds more complicated than a curtain rising to show the world the way things are, clearly and honestly.

"They have dinner early, at eleven o'clock every morning," Uncle Henry goes on, "and he wanted to go for a walk right after dinner, but he hasn't been reliable lately. He doesn't come back when he says he's coming back. They have liability issues, you see, so they have to put him in his room until somebody is free to go with him on his walk. You see." He pauses. "All the nurses were busy helping people who are in wheelchairs get back to their rooms after dinner. When they told him he'd have to wait for his walk, he got mad and fought with them. He swung his cane at the nurses when they tried to take him by his arms.

They subdued him and put him in his room and locked the door so he couldn't leave. He did not like that one bit."

Now everyone is silent. In the background a hog lifts a feeder lid with its snout and lets it drop, a muffled thunk. Cosmos sees a flutter of starlings pass by outside the window. Light shines blue off the kitchen table.

Uncle Henry sits down. He puts his hands under his chin. The weight of his round face seems too much for him. A lump forms in Cosmos's throat. Uncle Henry looks like a real person with real feelings. Cosmos waits for him to tell more. The thickness grows in his own throat. He swallows and waits.

"They locked him in his room. He couldn't stand it." Uncle Henry puts one hand on the table top and rubs it slowly.

"But how did he fall?" says Cosmos.

Uncle Henry studies his own hands. "He opened the window and shoved the screen out. You have to take a safety latch off to get the window open that far. You see. He took the screws out with his fingernail clippers."

"He's on the second floor," says Cosmos. "Was he going to jump?"

"Oh no no no," says Uncle Henry, speaking quickly now. "He may have been getting a little senile, but he's not that foolish. I think he was just going to show them that they couldn't pen him up."

"He must have leaned out," says Aunt Minnie. "Somebody in the hall heard him yelling something."

"Yelling something?" says Cosmos.

"It sounded like 'Watch this' or 'What's this,'" says Uncle Henry. "He was just trying to get their attention. And then he fell."

"Is that what the nurses said?"

"They didn't have to say anything," says Aunt Minnie. "Of course he fell. He was leaning out the window and slipped. He landed on his head. His neck was broken. He was dead instantly. I guess you might say it was like dying in your sleep."

From this point on, no matter what Uncle Henry or Aunt Minnie says, Cosmos knows what has happened. His grandfather has committed suicide. Even now, Cosmos realizes, the charade will go on. Nobody is going to be real. The only people to show any honesty about this death are his grandfather and himself. At least they shared that much.

Cosmos looks over at Mike. His cousin gives no sign of believing or not believing the story he has just heard.

"They tried to pen him up and he couldn't take it," Uncle Henry adds, staring at the table and talking now as if he were talking only to himself. "De Haags don't like to be penned in, you know."

"I know," says Cosmos, and he puts his hand to his

mouth and starts to sob quietly. Aunt Minnie hands him a tissue.

* * *

It is like harvest time, the way the funeral machinery is put into motion for what needs doing. Most duties fall to Uncle Henry and Aunt Minnie, but all of the pieces of the machinery have been standing ready. The body will be prepared for viewing tomorrow morning. The funeral director, who is also the mortician, will print the funeral program for the church service. It is part of his package deal. He's like the general contractor for the after-death machine. Cosmos's grandfather's headstone is already in place at the cemetery, and he himself already purchased the casket—one to match his wife, who is buried a few feet from where he will lie. The mortician will take care of completing the dates, which now read:

MR. AND MRS. WILIM DE HAAG
They Have Gone Home to Their Father
CORA, B. 1917   WILIM, B. 1915
D. 1994   D.

"Is my dad coming?" Cosmos asks that evening. "I forgot to call him. Grandpa Wilim was his dad too."

"Hans is on his way," says Uncle Henry. "At least some good may come from the occasion. You must be looking forward to seeing your dad."

Cosmos hadn't thought about it. Even now, he thinks of Cherlyn more than anyone else. He would like to hear her voice, see her comforting eyes.

*　*　*

Cosmos cannot understand his father's weeping at Grandpa Wilim's funeral. Of course, Wilim was his father, and who wouldn't weep for his own father? Cosmos knows *he* would, but he likes Hans in a way Hans never liked his own father. It had always seemed to Cosmos that Grandpa Wilim had been dead in Hans's mind for years. The way Hans talked about his own father, it was as if they never had an honest conversation their whole life. They were never close. "Except for handshakes on special occasions, the only time my dad ever touched me," he once told Cosmos, "was once when he tripped on a wagon tongue and grabbed at my shoulder to keep from falling on his face. That's when I was fifteen."

Now he sits up front of the church in his big scraggly beard and scruffy tan sports coat looking like a drooping thistle in a clean cornfield of close family members, and he sobs as if he has just lost the most important person in his life. Cosmos has no tears for Grandpa Wilim, but his dad's weeping brings tears to his eyes. It occurs to Cosmos that maybe Hans isn't crying for the Wilim who was. Maybe he is crying for the Wilim who wasn't.

At the lowering-down at the cemetery after the church service, Cosmos holds his dad's shoulder as he weeps.

Then the return to the church basement for a big lunch prepared by the Women's Circle (ham sandwiches, Jell-O salad, cookies, cake with ice cream, and lemonade or coffee) and the handshaking and condolences from relatives Cosmos has never met or doesn't remember. Nobody, not even Hans, is crying after the lunch. Cosmos guesses that the food is their way of signaling that now it is time to leave the dead behind and go back to life as normal.

In the church reception hall after the funeral, Cousin Mike pulls Cosmos aside. "Maybe this isn't the time to tell you this," he says, "but I'm going to be seeing more of Elmer than of you from now on. He turned himself in to Marksema. I think Elmer spun out one too many times, if you know what I mean. He said he wants to straighten himself out. Elmer told me to tell you. I just didn't know if this was a good time."

"This is a good time," says Cosmos. "A very good time."

"I saw Cherlyn this morning," Mike adds. "She asked me to give you this card."

"Thanks. Thanks. Thanks for the news about Elmer, and thanks for this."

Cosmos slips the card in his pocket and walks over to his father. Hans puts his arm around him. "He didn't mean to be a bad man," says Hans. "He did the best he could do."

Cosmos doesn't answer.

Looking across the crowd gathered in the church reception hall, Cosmos sees not one suspicious glance, not one face of hypocrisy. Some farmers who Cosmos doesn't even realize know him or his dad walk up with their weathered faces and say, "I am so sorry. I am so sorry. May God grant you His peace." One holds out his hard-worked hands and takes Hans's and then Cosmos's hands tenderly in his. "He was an important man in the community, and he gave so much to the church," he says. "We all know how much he wanted the best for both of you. He always talked about you. He was proud of you both."

Neither Hans nor Cosmos responds, but the stream of people keeps coming toward them. The faces and hands of warmth that greet them in sympathy are a part of the community his father never told him about. In his own heart, Cosmos feels a sudden flood of emotion, a confusing but powerful feeling. Some of it is sorrow for what his father never had with his own father. Some of it is the confusion between his love for Cherlyn and his sympathy for his father. He knows that love and grief are not the same thing, but, weighing heavily in his chest, they feel like they come from the same deep source of accepting and caring for somebody and something other than himself.

Cosmos goes to the men's room and opens the note from Cherlyn. "I am thinking about you and praying for you, my love. Wherever you are when you read this, please know I am with you. All my love, Cherlyn."

* * *

When they get home to Uncle Henry and Aunt Minnie's house after the funeral, neighbors are busily doing the chores. This too must be part of the after-death machine: the ordinary tasks of the day are taken care of so that the immediate family members do not have to think about them. Cosmos sits with his dad in the living room, sipping tea. That night they have a quiet supper of soup and crackers.

"Can I get you anything else?" asks Aunt Minnie.

"I'm all right," says Cosmos.

"I'm all right," says Hans. "I just want to think about Dad for a while."

"Remember when we were kids?" says Uncle Henry. "He was always worried about being fair to everybody. That's a fact. He said that God was a just God, and he wanted to be as just with everybody as God was just with the world. You see. Of course, that meant rules."

"Didn't it, though?" says Hans, and for the first time today the two brothers chuckle.

"But fair rules—right, Hans? Pops was always fair, always fair."

"If spanking a kid for not putting enough water in the cattle tank is fair," says Hans.

"Oh, he could lose his temper if things weren't done right," says Uncle Henry.

"And he could be stubborn as a mule when he thought he was right," Hans goes on.

"He was always good to Cora, though," Aunt Minnie

interrupts. "He'd give her anything she needed."

"Sure," says Hans, "but he always told Mom what she did and didn't need! And he was such a tightwad that she usually wore clothes she sewed herself from leftover scraps. She made a blouse for herself out of feed sacks!"

"He just wanted to serve the Lord," says Aunt Minnie. She sounds irritated. Cosmos has never seen her look so disturbed, almost angry. "Don't forget that, Hans. And don't forget that following the rules meant providing for his children." She stomps out of the room while everyone sits tight-lipped in the wake of her scolding. She returns with a folder of papers. "Here, look at this," she says.

"I know what's in it," says Uncle Henry. "I don't think Hans does."

Hans unfolds the sheath of papers. It is Gramps's will.

Hans told Cosmos several years ago that his father had written him out of his will when he left home, so he figures that Aunt Minnie is punishing Hans now for the way he has been talking about Gramps. Hans studies the will, but he does not look punished. He does look stunned.

"Look at this, Cosmos," he says. "Here, read this. And then read this part over here."

Hans has just inherited two hundred thousand dollars after lawyers' fees.

Cosmos gasps.

"I got the hundred acres of the farm that I hadn't bought from him years ago," says Uncle Henry. "Valued at two thousand an acre. Fair is fair."

"I didn't know he had this kind of money," says Hans. "I had no idea."

"He didn't brag about it," says Aunt Minnie.

"Didn't spend it either," says Uncle Henry. "Nosirree. He didn't spend it."

* * *

The next day, an hour before Uncle Henry is going to drive Hans to his plane, Hans and Cosmos take a walk down the gravel road along the farm.

"I feel pretty weird about the money," says Hans.

"Do you feel guilty?" says Cosmos.

"No, no, not guilt," says Hans. "It's just that I know what money can do to people. My friend Sam inherited some money five years ago. He sold his bookstore in Port Swan and moved to Hawaii. High living for three years, and then he was broke."

"So he was back to where he started. What's wrong with that?"

"What's wrong with that is that he didn't like books anymore. No interest in books, and no interest in his old book-loving customers. Totally lost his sense of commu-nity. Totally lost his old values. All he wants now is to become even richer than he was when he inherited the money. He became a realtor in Seattle."

"I don't think you'd make a very good realtor, Dad."

Hans gives Cosmos a playful shove. "Smart-ass," he

says. "I'd make a damn good realtor if I felt like it."

"So what are you going to do with the money?"

"I'll help you with college when and if you need it," says Hans. "And I have this dream of starting a foundation at Fort Wheeler for the teaching and preservation of traditional wood crafts. I'd like to get a Makah cedar-canoe craftsman there. Maybe a Haida totem-pole artist. That would feel good."

"Cool," says Cosmos. "Maybe they could teach you how to carve a blue heron that doesn't have a neck as short as a turtle's."

Hans gives Cosmos another shove. "I see you haven't lost your mouth," he says, and the two continue their walk, mischievously kicking pebbles in each other's paths as they go.

I love your daughter

SO THIS IS WHAT SPRING in the Midwest is like. How different from Port Swan, where green is green is green is green, except for a few months of winter, when gray is gray is gray is gray. Cosmos can feel the quick-paced drama of it, the dark earth covered with scurrying actors—the corn shoots, the oats, the alfalfa, the roadside grasses and weeds, the trees suddenly full of leaves giving the distant horizon its tiny rounded domes in place of the skeletal branches of winter, the lilacs coming into full bloom in only a few days, the tulips blazing up on every street corner in Dutch Center, a reckless, wild abandon of nature erupting everywhere, and along with the exuberant colors a return of the exuberant smells from the cattle and feedlots, but somehow gentler and less oppressive than he remembers them. Good Lord, thinks Cosmos, am I just getting used to the smells, or are they really not as bad as they were in the fall?

With the changes in nature around them, Cosmos and Cherlyn know that they too will have to look at the big change that rushes toward them. Graduation. Suddenly all

those walls, all those classrooms that contained and controlled their lives, those walls that set boundaries and gave
directions, will fall away. And in their absence stands the
biggest question of all: now what?!

Alone in *The Messenger*'s office, they sit across from each
other over the "editor's desk." The last issue is being put to
bed. Cherlyn will have to clean up for next year's editor. A
stuffy sadness, so unlike the dancing green outside, hangs
between them as she packs her paper clips and pens.

Cherlyn has gotten scholarship offers to every college
where she applied, but she has put off the big announcement until now. She exhales a deep breath. "Cosmos," she
says. "I've made up my mind. I'm going to Sinai College."

Sinai is a small Christian College in Orangeville, only a
few miles from Dutch Center.

"Sinai?" he says, and cannot disguise his shock. "Sinai?"

As open as Cosmos and Cherlyn have been about their
feelings for each other, Cosmos suddenly realizes he has
avoided being clear about his own plans, and until now
delaying hasn't hurt very much. He has lived in a fuzzy
fantasy world in which he could have it all—putting off
college for a year while living with his dad, succeeding as
a musician with the OughtaBs, and still having the freedom to see Cherlyn, wherever she might be. But none of
his fantasies put Cherlyn so close to home. He thought she
was ready for the great adventure in the big world where
anything might happen outside the policing eyes of her

parents and the community.

"Cosmos, what's wrong?"

He shakes his head slowly. "Everything. Just everything."

After the silence and sighs of dismay, Cherlyn says, "This isn't easy for me either. But I prayed so hard about this. I am sure this is what God wants for us. Time apart will give us time for our love to deepen."

"I want to spend the rest of my life with you," he says directly.

"And I want to spend the rest of my life with you too, Cosmos. Don't you understand? We mustn't spoil it by rushing." She tugs him toward the cabinet door and pulls him behind it. She floods him with kisses.

"This is the kind of rush I want for the rest of my life," he says.

He is smiling again, and they pull apart when they hear footsteps in the hallway.

She sits down at her desk. "If I spend one year at Sinai, we'll have a year to know that everything is real. Then I can transfer. Anywhere. I even checked to see if you have a college in Port Swan. You don't."

"Ah," he says, smiling broadly now. "But did you check Seattle?"

"I did," she said. "Redemption University. But their fellowship money is low this year. Maybe next year?"

Somehow she has managed to make him feel all right

about next year. Cherlyn has a way of making the intolerable seem tolerable.

"Can you come visit me in Port Swan?"

"Maybe not. But my folks said it would be all right if you came to see me here. You could stay at our house."

"Stay at your house?"

"Sure," she says. "In the bedroom next to theirs."

"Maybe I could stay at Uncle Henry and Aunt Minnie's and we could meet in between."

"Maybe," says Cherlyn. "See? This isn't so hard to imagine."

When Cherlyn speaks sweetly, many things are easy to imagine, though some things are hard not to. As she goes back to cleaning her desk, one glance at her brow and her sweet cheeks with their freckles fills Cosmos with desire. Cosmos cannot resist fantasies of being alone with her in total privacy. At least once. Just one time all alone with her under the stars.

"Can't we be alone together just one more time before I leave?" he pleads. "Like last time? I think that could last me for a year."

"I know what will happen if we go out in some pasture again, Cosmos. I know what will happen. I love you too much."

"You said you thought God would understand our love." He stands in front of her desk, gesturing grandly. "You said yourself you don't think our flesh is evil. You said yourself that God wants us to enjoy our bodies."

"I know, I know," says Cherlyn. She looks up at him and smiles. "But I also know God has rules."

"We could keep our clothes on the way we did last time," he eagerly volunteers.

Cherlyn breaks the rules by getting up and closing *The Messenger*'s door. She returns to the "editor's desk" and folds her hands on top of it. "There has to be some way for everything to remain beautiful, not sinful. The beauty of the flesh. I hope I never lose the desire I felt that night, Cosmos. I hope I don't have to deny the truth of my flesh to be whole. But to be carnally minded is death."

"Are you quoting the Bible now?"

"Read it and find out," she teases him. "To be spiritually minded is life and peace."

"Whoa," says Cosmos. "Aren't you sliding back to the old-timers' rules? Toe the line? Why didn't God make us out of thin air if the flesh means nothing but trouble? That's what I'd like to know. This is where I have trouble with religion, Cherlyn. Not trouble with you, trouble with your religion."

He sits down.

"Are you angry?"

"Of course not," he says. "But I'm spiritually minded when I think of you. I've never loved anybody the way I love you."

"Nor have I ever loved anyone the way I love you, but I can't let my love for you fight with my love for God," she says. "I can't let your love for me fight with God's love for me either. I think God is testing our love. Let's let it grow naturally while we're not together. I'll write to you every day. We'll have more time to get to know each other at a spiritual level. I'll tell you everything."

"I can't believe how you can talk me into anything," he says. "Sure. I know I can wait. Not because I want to, but I know that what you and I have is the real thing, Cherlyn. Some people wait their whole lives for something like this and never find it."

"I know," she says. "It's too beautiful."

"Do you still think about me, like, physically, when I'm not around?"

"Too much of the time."

"What do you think about—kissing?" he asks.

"Yes. And a lot more. Too much more. I imagine touching you. I imagine the smell of you. I imagine the taste of you. All of it. I imagine being in bed with you. I imagine being naked with you, holding you all night. When I start to imagine making love with you, actually consummating with our clothes off, a voice from God comes into my mind."

Cosmos waits. "Your conscience?"

"You could call it that. Maybe I'm just remembering a passage from the Bible; the voice says, 'the trying of your faith worketh patience.' That's what we need, Cosmos. Patience."

"Argh," he says. "I feel like I'm wrestling with an angel."

* * *

Cherlyn is graduating at the top of the class and giving the valedictory. She builds her short talk around the words "certainty" and "uncertainty" and works out a paradox about how the only certainty we can ever have is in uncertain human faith in a God who is our only hope for certainty. There isn't one mean word in the whole speech. It's all love love love, trust trust trust. In short, it is about accepting the unknown without fear. "In our uncertain human way, we can only hope for the certainty of God, which is love," she concludes. It is vintage Cherlyn.

Afterward, Cherlyn's parents stand near her in the reception line, almost like bodyguards. But William the Nice is tired of himself, tired of bowing to other people's stares and intimidation. He walks straight up to Cherlyn's parents and, in a recklessly high-spirited Cosmos Coyote voice, he says, "What did you two do to deserve such a wonderful daughter!"

Cherlyn's mother laughs. Cherlyn's father doesn't. Cosmos holds out his hand to Cherlyn's father and says, "I love your daughter."

Mr. Van Dyke's face twinges and then gives way to a sad smile. "I know," he says, "and I suspect the feeling is mutual."

With that, Cosmos moves toward Cherlyn to give her a large and long embrace, and no one tries to stop him.

* * *

The day before Cosmos's departure, Cherlyn picks him up for an afternoon together. Instead of driving to the river, where he hopes she will go, she drives back to school. She parks next to the city park where she found the four-leaf clover and they start walking. Walking and talking.

"We can't let this time be sad," she says. "We can't be sad when we have our love."

"When I'm with you, everything seems to be all right. You can get me to accept anything, you know that, don't you? But when I'm alone, it seems crazy to separate for a year. I hate it."

"I believed what I said in the valedictory address," she says.

"Yeah, I know," he says. "Accepting uncertainty. I'm just afraid that after your year at Sinai College, you'll be afraid to leave this community," says Cosmos sincerely. "Even I have to admit that the fence does keep a lot of bad stuff out."

"I never thought I'd hear you say that," she says. "Like what bad stuff?"

"Well, there wasn't any violence at the Academy all year. I didn't see anybody point a gun at anybody else. I saw people pointing guns at other people three times in Seattle in one year. I haven't heard of any rapes all year. Not around Dutch Center. There are drugs, but there aren't pushers hanging out around convenience stores. And the grown-ups don't really seem to hate kids the way the authorities do other places. I haven't seen the cops going nuts trying to nail kids for everything. Elmer never even got a ticket for skidding around on the ice the way he does. Then there's somebody like my cousin Mike. He sure gave me the breaks. Even Marksema is a good guy. For a high-school principal, he's a pretty trusting fellow. Things like that."

"Do you think you could ever move out here?" she asks.

"If it was the only way I could be with you, maybe," he says. "But I admit this area doesn't seem quite as bad as it used to. The way people live out here makes more sense to me now. There really is a community. We don't have that in Seattle or Port Swan. Everybody does their own thing. Everybody minds their own business. There are plenty of good things about that, but I hope someday I can be part of a real community. You know what I'd do if I came out here?"

She looks at him smiling. "Besides that!" he says.

"What?"

"I'd pick up where Van Enk left off."

"Now that's not a good direction."

"No, I mean with the ecology stuff. If I were part of this community, I'd work to save the earth that sustains it."

"That's beautiful," says Cherlyn. "Sinai College has an Earth Stewardship program. 'Christians For The Environment' is one of the strongest groups on campus, I've heard."

"You're kidding," he says.

"Not kidding. Remember, God not only loves the sparrows, He loves the earth. He made it for us to care for."

"You sweet little sermonizer," he says. "Don't try talking me into something that would be even crazier than our being apart for a year. I really can't imagine living here for the rest of my life. It doesn't really suit me, you know?"

"I know," she says. "It isn't me either."

She reaches and strokes his hair, which is ruffling in the gentle breeze. "You look like a De Haag," she says. "You would fit in around here, you know."

"As long as I didn't open my mouth."

"What about your mom? Do you look like her? You never talk about her. Will you see her in Port Swan?"

"Mom doesn't live there anymore. She's on her own spiritual quest, I guess you could say. She's in Mexico, studying with some guru."

"Is she a believer?"

"Oh yeah, she believes a little bit of everything. I don't think she's big-time into any one thing. I guess she's one of the sparrows, like me."

"My sparrow," says Cherlyn, and leans on him. Then she

says, "Look!" and points at the trees. "The trees are feeling playful. They're shaking the sparrows off their branches and fanning the air to make a wind!"

"Huh?" says Cosmos.

Just then a strong breeze touches their faces. "See? I told you so. When I was a little girl, I thought the trees waved their branches and shook their leaves to make the wind."

Cosmos laughs. "I like that. Now I understand why you always get A's in science. But, hey, Miss Science, then what makes the wind off the water in Port Swan? There aren't any trees on the ocean."

"The waves, don't you think?" she says playfully.

"Of course! Of course!" says Cosmos. "Why didn't I think of that?! You're absolutely right: whenever there are big waves there's always a big wind! Of course the waves are causing the wind!"

They stand and giggle together. "The world is beautiful and magical through your eyes," he says. "If you can believe in that kind of magic, who knows what the future may hold." Before she can respond, he holds up a finger and says, "I know, I know: 'the heavens declare the glory of God and the firmament His handiwork.'"

"Hey, you've learned something."

"I haf bin in-doc-trinated," he says in a mock-Dutch accent.

"And you haf bin my guru," she responds in the same accent.

"What?" he says. "I didn't do anything for you. In fact, I'm still scared that I'll mess you up, wipe out your wonderful purity."

"Pure I am not," says Cherlyn, "but you've made me look at myself in a way that no one has ever demanded of me. I thought love of God and love for you could be the same thing. They can't. My love for you must follow my love for God, not the other way around. Without you I would never have learned that."

"How did that go?" says Cosmos. "Patience worketh understanding?"

"What I always say—you're a quicker learner than I am."

"Let's sit," he says. "I have something for you." They sit down on their bench and Cosmos takes out his gift. He has framed the four-leaf clover she found. Pressed it and framed it under glass. "For you," he says.

She holds it, staring at it in wonder, then sniffs and wipes her eyes. "This is ours, isn't it? It's our future." She closes her eyes, and Cosmos knows she is praying that the four-leaf clover will be something more than good luck.

* * *

At the airport, Cherlyn and Cosmos stand with their arms wrapped around each other in the waiting area. Before Cosmos's row number is called, he hands Cherlyn a final good-bye gift. "What is it?" she says, looking at the small object in her hand.

"It's a raven," he says. "My dad carved it and gave it to

me before I came out here. Raven is the Trickster of the Northwest, just as Coyote is the Trickster of the Plains. Tricksters know how to survive the tough times."

"I love it," she says, and takes it to her lips. "I love it. And I know what you mean by Trickster ways. When you're in your Trickster outfit, you're just being honest."

"Exactly," says Cosmos. "And playful."

"And sometimes a little bit naughty?"

"Yes."

"I love it, I love it," says Cherlyn.

Cosmos has a send-off party of four: Cherlyn, Cousin Mike, and Uncle Henry and Aunt Minnie. When Cosmos has to board, they all step forward for a handshake. Cherlyn steps back for their final well-wishing, then steps forward for a last embrace and kiss.

"Remember, we're not going to let this be sad," she says. Her bright smile fills the waiting area.

"It is not sad," he says. "But when will I see you again?"

"Well, there's a three-week mission program at Redemption University in Seattle this summer," she says, and grins. "I think it starts on July fourteenth."

"Gerald Ford's birthday!" says Cosmos, smiling, and gets on the plane.